PRAISE FOR CINDY

P9-CJF-172

"Don't miss the Laurel McKay books. Like me, you'll be 'dying' to read the next one."

–Brenda Novak, USA Today Bestselling Author

"*Dying for a Donut* is a riveting story with snappy dialog, a stellar plot, entertaining characters, and a first-rate mystery. It doesn't get any better than that! Cindy Sample writes a wonderful murder mystery!

– Heather Haven, IPPY Award-Winning Author

"Cindy Sample has cooked up another delicious mystery starring Laurel McKay, soccer mom extraordinaire. *Dying for a Donut* offers romance, intrigue and fun set in California's scenic Gold Country. If you're hungry for a 5-star cozy mystery, you'll be glad *Dying for a Donut* heads the menu."

– Mary Beth Magee, National Reviewer, Examiner.com

"Quirky narrative peppered with quips. An intoxicating recipe for fun... *Dying for a Daiquiri* is a must read for the romantic mystery reader and contemporary romance reader!"

– Connie Payne, Once upon a Romance Reviews

Cindy Sample's writing is positively fun, imaginative and all around tantalizing."

– Romance Junkies

"Cindy Sample knows how to weave a story that satisfies and excites. Time literally flew by as I turned the pages... simultaneously harrowing, exciting, tender, and uplifting, a true who-done-it combined with a romance that will warm the heart and sheets."

– Long and Short Reviews

"Sample's sleuth is an endearing character readers will adore."
— *RT Book Reviews*

"Cindy Sample has mastered the art of REAL dialogue.
The characters are wacky and believable. Any woman who
constantly finds herself in awkward situations will love this
book. This is a story that will make you wonder "who did it"
and make you laugh out loud. Of course, the romance
simply is divine!"
— *BookReviewsRus*

"All of the elements of an excellent cozy mystery. Interesting
characters, plot and setting. Fast paced writing. I struggled to
figure out what it was that stood out that made me really enjoy
the book and I decided it was the tone. *Dying for a Dance* is a
feel-good book, it makes you smile."
— *Examiner.com*

"I have rarely been more cheered up by spending time
with a book. *Dying for a Dance* is the perfect antidote
to a bout of the winter blues."
— *Kings River Life Magazine*

"*Dying for a Date* is packed with zany characters, humorous
situations, and laugh-out-loud narrative. Consider reading
this book in one sitting, because once you start, you
will be reluctant to put it aside."
— *Midwest Book Review*

Other Books in the Laurel McKay series

Dying for a Date (Vol. 1)
Dying for a Dance (Vol. 2)
Dying for a Daiquiri (Vol. 3)
Dying for a Dude (Vol. 4)

American River College Library
4700 College Oak Drive
Sacramento, CA 95841

DYING FOR A DONUT

A LAUREL MCKAY MYSTERY

CINDY SAMPLE

DYING FOR A DONUT
By Cindy Sample

Copyright 2015 by Cindy Sample

Cover Art by Karen Phillips

1st Digital & Trade Paperback Edition, 2015

All Rights reserved. Without limiting the rights under copyright reserved above, no part of this publication may be reproduced, stored in or introduced into a retrieval system, or transmitted, in any form, or by any means (electronic, mechanical, photocopying, recording, or otherwise) without the prior written permission of both the copyright owner and the above publisher of this book.

This book is a work of fiction. Names, characters, places, and incidents are the product of the author's imagination or are used fictitiously. Any resemblance to actual events, locales or persons, living or dead is coincidental. The author acknowledges the trademarked status and trademark owners of various products referenced in this work of fiction, which have been used without permission. The publication/use of these trademarks is not authorized, associated with, or sponsored by the trademark owners.

Visit us at http://www.cindysamplebooks.com

ISBN: 1518633749
ISBN: 13-978-1518633744

DEDICATION

This book is dedicated to my wonderful children, Dawn and Jeff, and to Harriet Bergstrand, my mother, my mentor and my best friend. I miss you, Mom.

CHAPTER ONE

"I could die right now," my grandmother announced as she clutched her chest with an arthritic hand.

I eyed the scattered crumbs on the plate in front of her and said, "A team of Clydesdales would die if they'd eaten as many donuts as you just put away."

"Yes, but we'd die happy." A broad smile creased Gran's face. "Besides at my age, Laurel, I gotta enjoy life while I can."

Gran was right. Today's excursion to Apple Tree Farm, located in the small town of Camino, fifty miles east of Sacramento, had been a perfect outing. The rolling green hills and valleys, set against a backdrop of the Sierra Nevada mountain range, were famous for their plentiful apple orchards and even more plentiful apple pastries.

While Gran's caloric intake far exceeded mine, I'd still managed to consume one melt-in-your-mouth glazed apple donut followed by a gooey caramel apple. I wasn't complaining, although the waistband of my jeans felt far less accommodating than when I'd dressed this morning.

Gran pointed her finger at me. "You've got caramel stuck to your face."

I stared down my nose but only succeeded in crossing my eyes. She handed me a paper napkin, and I swiped at my nose

1

and cheeks. Just because outings to the area known as Apple Hill made me feel like a kid was no reason to regress to my sticky-fingered, sticky-faced childhood.

Gran popped a final donut chunk into her mouth and smacked her lips. Her gaze roved from the bakery, located at one end of the large red barn, past the produce section laden with bins of colorful apples, pears and pumpkins, finally landing on Ye Old Candy Shoppe directly opposite us.

"Do we have time to get more fudge before Jenna gets off work in the bakery?" Gran asked.

I shook my head, marveling at my grandmother's metabolism then glanced at my watch. "Jenna should be done in ..." I stopped as angry voices assaulted our ears.

Two young men, dressed in red tees emblazoned with the Apple Tree Farm logo, stormed out of the cider house building opposite the bakery. While I didn't recognize the slight dark-haired man, I knew that the tall, hefty blond was Eric Thorson, son of Axel Thorson, the owner of Apple Tree Farm.

Eric's face was as red as the candied apples they sold. He shook his fist at the other teen who reminded me of a young Enrique Iglesias—trouble in tush-tight jeans. Despite being several inches shorter than his opponent, he wasn't backing down from Eric's threatening fist.

I wondered what precipitated their argument and why they'd brought the fight out to the public picnic area. Even though it was nearly five p.m., several families remained seated at rustic wood tables enjoying their delectable purchases. A few people who stood in line to buy the farm's jellies, sauces and fresh fruits, shifted their attention toward the two young men.

"Someone's about to get a whoopin'," Gran said, grinning. "Do you suppose they're fighting over a girl?"

I shrugged. "It's none of our business, although I hope no one gets hurt."

She shifted her gaze to a point over my left shoulder. "Looks like we may be involved whether you like it or not."

"What?" I spun around to discover the last person I'd have expected to join the altercation—my daughter, Jenna.

Her auburn hair gleamed bright red, despite being encased in a hairnet to ensure no errant strands landed on the pastries she sold. With that fiery hair, sparks shooting out of sapphire blue eyes and the supersized spatula in her hand, she resembled an avenging angel.

She hurled herself between the two men, oblivious to possible injury to herself. I jumped up from the bench and joined the fray, thinking that all the two young men needed was a mature adult to calm them down so they could conduct a reasonable discussion. I reached Jenna's side, yanked on her elbow and shoved her behind me. My daughter has four inches on my own five foot four and a quarter, but I had twenty-five (or after today's outing, possibly thirty) pounds to offset the vertical difference between us.

"Mom," Jenna protested as she tried to push through to the young men.

I thrust my arm out to block her movement. "Stay out of this, Jenna." I faced the two aggressors, prepared to mediate their argument.

Eric swung his fist at his dark-haired opponent who ducked and countered with his own blow. *Thwack!*

That's all it took for one forty-year-old mother of two to go down for the count.

CHAPTER TWO

I opened my eyes to a multitude of stars twinkling overhead. Seconds later, the scent of chocolate assailed my nostrils.

I blinked twice. My grandmother bent over me waving a thick chunk of chocolate fudge less than an inch from my nose. When I tried to rise, she shoved me back down onto the grass where I'd apparently fallen, since a few long blades tickled my neck.

Gran grinned, her fillings glinting in the sunlight. "In the old days I'd have used smelling salts," she said, "but I figured you'd respond better to chocolate."

I propelled myself into a sitting position and blinked at the small group of people standing around me. I gently touched my throbbing cheek and winced.

"I'm so sorry, Ma'am," said a male voice to my right. I swiveled my head around.

Whoa. Really. Bad. Idea. A wave of nausea engulfed me, and I sensed the donut and caramel apple I'd eaten earlier careening back up my digestive tract.

On a positive note, that was eight hundred fewer calories to exercise off.

I stifled the urge to heave the best of Apple Tree Farm's delights onto the shoes of the bystanders.

"Tony didn't mean to hurt you, Mom." Jenna crouched next to my side.

4

"It was an accident," said the teen I presumed must be Tony.

"Heck of a right hook, young man," Gran said. "She's going to have quite a shiner."

Shiner? That got my attention. "Do I have a black eye?" I asked. "Does anyone have a mirror I can use?"

Gran and Jenna both said no, but their matching guilty expressions made me wonder. On Monday, I was scheduled to make a marketing presentation at Hangtown Bank in Placerville where I work. The last thing I needed was to present a battered and bruised face to the bank's Board of Directors.

"Tony, get off this property before I beat the crap out of you," Eric said. He squatted next to Jenna and placed his arm possessively around her shoulder.

She shook it off. "Leave me alone, Eric. And stop bullying Tony."

A loud baritone interrupted the teenage soap opera surrounding me. "What is going on here, son?" demanded the angry voice. A few seconds later, an unhappy older version of Eric stood over me. Axel Thorson thrust out a muscular arm and hoisted me off the ground.

"Laurel, what happened to you?" Axel's strawberry blond moustache and beard bristled with indignation.

I glanced at Jenna and Tony. The young man looked petrified. My daughter gave a quick shake of her head, her eyes pleading with me.

"I bumped into something," I muttered to Axel. "Nothing to concern yourself over."

"Tony punched her," Eric snarled. His fists remained clenched, ready for battle.

"One of the boys' arms accidentally connected with my face." Not the best explanation, but my brain wasn't operating at full capacity. Or even half capacity. "I'm sure it wasn't intentional."

"I apologize for their behavior, Laurel," Axel said in a solicitous tone. "How can I make it up to you? Perhaps a dozen donuts on the house?"

My stomach roiled at the thought of more fried sugar, but my grandmother's digestive system was made of sterner stuff.

"Sounds good," she replied. "We'll take a half dozen of your glazed and another half of your cinnamon ones. Or maybe those new vanilla frosted donuts." She smacked her lips in anticipation. "That should speed up Laurel's recovery."

I started to shake my head then realized it would be less painful to go along with Axel's suggestion.

"Thanks for the offer," I said to him.

A relieved expression crossed Axel's face. He addressed the young men. "Eric, go back to the cider house. Tony, to my office. Now."

Jenna protested but stopped when Tony rested his palm on her forearm. She didn't appear to mind Tony's gentle touch. I could tell Eric observed it as well. He stomped over to the cider house, a grim expression on his face.

"Jenna, why don't you take your mother and grandmother to the bakery?" Axel moved closer to examine my injury before adding, "Better get your mother some ice, too."

Gran and I followed Jenna back to the bakery. Since it was past closing time, the barn-like structure was empty. While I tried to think of a tactful way to grill Jenna about the young men's argument, Gran jumped in, feet first.

"Looks like those two young roosters were fighting over you," Gran said, playfully punching Jenna in the arm. "Either of them make your heart twang?"

Jenna blushed and picked up her pace, but that didn't stop Gran's inquisition as she trotted after my daughter.

"The young one who knocked out your mother was kinda hot. What did he do to upset Axel's son?"

"Let's get Mom some ice first," Jenna said. "Then we'll talk. Okay?"

We couldn't argue with her logic. Gran and I plopped into white plastic chairs across from one another at one of the visitor tables while Jenna scrounged up some ice for me and a dozen donuts for Gran.

Five minutes later, I was icing my cheekbone while Gran was icing her taste buds. Jenna refrained from joining her great-grandmother. She claimed that after working weekends in the bakery for three weeks she was "off" donuts for now.

I wondered if that philosophy could also apply to me. Would working at a candy store put me off chocolate? Was that even possible?

My focus shifted to my daughter who seemed intent on tying two straws into a dozen knots. I leaned forward as she spoke.

"Eric's been hassling me ever since I started working here," she said.

"Did you tell Nina?" asked Gran. Nina was a close friend of my grandmother's as well as the manager of the Apple Tree bakery. Because of the older women's friendship, Jenna had landed one of the highly coveted seasonal weekend jobs at the farm. With college less than a year away, any contribution to her slim college fund helped.

Jenna nodded. "Nina told me to avoid Eric, but she said she didn't want to upset the apple cart. Or upset Mr. Thorson, I guess."

"What do you mean, he hassles you?" I asked. "I got the impression Eric likes you."

Jenna rolled her eyes. "He likes me a little *too* much. Eric is supposed to work in the cider house with Tony, but it seems like he's always in the bakery hitting on me."

Gran thumped the table with a gnarled fist—the one not holding the donut. "That's plain wrong. I'll call Nina when I get home. We can't have that boy harassing you."

"How did Tony get involved?" I asked, curious about the young man responsible for the right side of my face now feeling frostbitten. It might be time to give the ice pack a rest.

"Tony and I often take our breaks together. A few days ago, I got so ticked off with Eric that I stormed out of the bakery. Tony could tell something was wrong, so eventually I confided in him. Eric joined Tony and me on our break today. He kept pulling on my hairnet, saying 'Rapunzel, Rapunzel, let down your hair.'" Jenna pretended to gag.

After Jenna's revelation, I was ready to tie up and gag Eric the next time I saw him. I wondered if Axel was aware of his son's repugnant behavior.

Speaking of the owner, another round of raised voices could be heard outside the building. Gran snapped her head around so fast her blond pixie-cut wig slipped to the side, uncovering one of her pointed ears, and giving her the appearance of a tipsy elf. My grandmother began wearing wigs two decades ago with styles ranging from Lucille Ball to Lady Gaga. As far as we knew, underneath her multi-hued wigs, she could be balder than Bruce Willis.

Jenna helped Gran to her feet before she raced off. I rose from my chair and straightened Gran's lopsided "do." We followed my daughter out to the employee parking area.

A Volkswagen Beetle that looked almost as old as Gran peeled out of the lot. It was more of a lurch than a peel as the driver struggled to shift the ancient gears of the rusted yellow Bug. I recognized Tony behind the wheel of the vehicle before he disappeared in a plume of dust down the long gravel drive.

"I'm sorry you were a party to that boy's nonsense," said Axel, a frustrated look on his face. "He's one juvenile delinquent who will be difficult to reform."

"Tony is not a juvenile delinquent," Jenna blurted out. "He's a great guy." Under her breath, I heard her say "as opposed to your son."

If Axel overheard her remark, he chose to ignore it.

"Jenna, your mother has done an excellent job of raising you. Perhaps in time Tony will also become an exemplary citizen. For now, he should be grateful I didn't have the police arrest him."

"Why would you arrest that boy?" Gran asked. "He was only trying to keep your son's mitts off my great-granddaughter."

"I have no idea what you're talking about." Axel looked as confused as I felt. "This has nothing to do with Eric. I discovered Tony has been stealing from me."

CHAPTER THREE

"That's impossible," Jenna cried. "Tony would never steal from anyone."

"Your loyalty to your coworker is admirable." Axel's bushy reddish-blond brows drew together in a frown. "But I'd appreciate the same loyalty to your employer."

"What did the kid steal?" Gran asked.

"Several hundred dollars, according to my son. And this isn't the first time. The cider house receipts were short a few weeks ago, too."

"But, but..." Jenna sputtered, but our conversation was interrupted by the arrival of a deeply-bronzed, middle-aged man sporting the farm's logo shirt, stained jeans and a matching red ball cap. He whispered something in Axel's ear then walked off.

"I'm sorry, ladies, but I need to address a few issues with Brent." Axel thrust his bearded chin toward the man he'd just spoken with. "Enjoy the rest of your weekend." He strode off to a large warehouse across the huge parking lot.

"That's so unfair," Jenna complained. "Tony would never steal."

"I'm sure Axel wouldn't accuse your friend of taking the money if he didn't have proof," I said. "And it could be worse. He could turn Tony over to the police."

"Still sucks," Gran muttered. "I have half a mind to throw away these donuts Axel gave us."

I glared at her, and she smiled at me with frosting-glazed lips. "Don't worry, Laurel, my smart half would never let me do anything so drastic."

On that note, we all piled into my geriatric Prius. During the ten-minute drive down Highway 50 from Camino to Placerville, Jenna lamented about the unfairness of life in general and Axel Thorson in particular. I commiserated with her, but the situation was beyond my control.

When we arrived at Gran's turn-of-the-century Victorian, I noticed my ex-husband, Hank, standing on the front porch, the embodiment of things completely beyond my control. He was dressed in what he took to be sartorial splendor: a clean pressed blue shirt, khaki trousers and a navy-blue print tie. Hank was either going to a wedding or a funeral.

When a powder-blue convertible pulled up to the curb, driven by an attractive longhaired brunette, I realized a third option existed. He was going on a date.

Since our divorce four years ago, Hank had attempted to woo me back into his life. He finally realized a few months ago that we would not be getting back together. Ever. Although it took a long time for the hurt to dissipate, I'd eventually forgiven him for leaving me for one of his clients. We now maintain an amicable parental relationship.

Besides, I'm in a committed relationship with Detective Tom Hunter, although I hadn't seen my honey in over four weeks. In the two short years Tom has worked for the El Dorado County Sheriff's Office, he so impressed the Sheriff that he'd recently been assigned to a joint strategic task force in Reno comprised of participants from law enforcement agencies from all parts of the country.

The case was so super-secret that Tom hadn't spilled any details during our pillow talks. Unfortunately, those conversations only occurred via our phone calls—Tom in his Reno hotel room and me in my lonely king-size bed with my multi-colored cat, Pumpkin. A girl's gotta cuddle something.

Gran greeted Hank, and he bent over to kiss her cheek.

"Hey, Roomie," she said, "looks like you're ready for a hot date." She smirked at him and he winked back. Hank had moved into Gran's house over the summer. The two of them made the original Odd Couple look almost normal by comparison, but their peculiar living arrangement seemed to work for them. Hank, a general contractor, fixed all the things Gran broke on a daily basis. Gran loved to cook and bake, and Hank loved to eat and, well, eat some more.

Jenna exchanged hugs with her father. While the two of them bonded, I stood off to the side, arms folded across my ample chest, watching as the driver of the convertible slid one long, tanned leg out of the car, followed by a matching one. As the woman straightened and smoothed down her snug silk wrap dress, I recognized her as Brooke Martin, a local CPA.

Brooke fluttered slender fingers in our direction. Hank waved back indicating she should join us on the front porch. She sauntered up the driveway looking more like a runway model than an accountant. Not that I was jealous of her tall slim frame. I was perfectly happy with my chubby cheeks and hips.

Yep. Perfectly. Content.

Although I still sucked in my donut-filled stomach.

Brooke smiled at us then moved in for a lip lock that might have gone on forever if Gran hadn't nudged Hank with the pink box of donuts.

Hmmm. This was obviously not a first date situation. I'd have to get the scoop from Gran later on. As Hank reached for the cardboard box, he laid his swamp-green eyes on me and did a double take.

"Laurel, what happened to you?" he asked. "You look like you ran into the wrong end of a fist."

"It was an accident," Jenna said. "Mom's face was in the wrong place."

"Obviously." Hank snickered.

Gran pointed at the donuts. "Axel tried to sweeten the situation."

Hank lifted the cover of the box and reached inside, but before he could grab anything, Brooke pushed his hand away. "We need to get going, sweetie," she said. "The fundraiser begins in a half hour."

Hank reluctantly returned the donuts to Gran before he transferred his attention back to me. "Hey, the four of us should double date sometime."

Yep. Double dating with my ex and his girlfriend was definitely on my top ten list of fun things to do.

Right behind a colonoscopy.

Hank kissed Jenna on her cheek. "I have a meeting in Camino tomorrow so I can stop by Apple Tree Farm and drive you home. Give your mother a break. What time do you get off?"

"They changed my hours for tomorrow." She threw a sideways glance at me. "I work from six until noon.

"Six? In the morning? Are you kidding?" I yelped. "You need your own car."

Jenna beamed at me. "Awesome. How soon can we get it?"

I watched as her father ushered his girlfriend down the driveway before I replied, "As soon as your father can pay for one."

Before the sun rose the next morning, Jenna and I were zipping up Highway 50 for the short commute from our Placerville home to Apple Tree Farm.

I signaled then made a left turn off the freeway followed by another left onto Carson Road. The warning light on my gas gauge turned yellow, indicating a refill would be necessary. I sipped the coffee in my travel mug and pondered the wisdom of driving Jenna back and forth to a job that barely paid minimum wage. But teens must start somewhere, and her paltry paychecks contributed to her college fund. When your daughter maintains an A plus average, she deserves as much assistance as a mother can give. Even if it meant sunrise to sunset chauffeur service.

We pulled into the parking lot, deserted except for a newer model black Mercedes.

I shut off the engine. Jenna rested her head against the passenger window. I couldn't tell if she was depressed about going to work or if she'd fallen asleep. She rolled both shoulders then peered out her window.

"Are we early?" she asked. "I only see Axel's car. We got here fast."

It's easy to make good time when no one else is cruising up the hill at such an ungodly hour. Even God was probably still reclining in bed, swiping at his or her snooze button.

A bright light shining out of the window of the warehouse caught my attention. "Is that Axel's office?" I asked.

"Yeah, although he's not usually here before six. Axel's not so bad. It's his son that's the problem."

Another vehicle pulled into the employee lot. Nina, the bakery manager, stepped out of an older model SUV. Her long gray braid swung down her back as she reached over into the passenger seat. She yanked out a well-worn cloth purse, threw it over her shoulder and slammed the door shut. Nina waved, indicating Jenna should follow her into the bakery.

"I'll see you later," Jenna said. "Assuming I don't get fired, too."

"Honey, don't worry about what happened yesterday. I'll go talk to Axel right now. It might be a good time to catch him before the place fills up with tourists."

Jenna gnawed on her lower lip. "Okay, but don't make him mad. I don't want to lose this job."

"Are you kidding? Discretion is my middle name."

That remark finally elicited a smile from Jenna. She climbed out of the car and followed Nina into the bakery. I brushed my unruly reddish-brown curls in an attempt to make my hair look presentable, then eased myself out of the driver's seat.

Even though the sky had lightened to a pale bluish-gray, it was chilly this early in the day. I shivered and zipped up my lightweight fleece jacket. The cedar-scented air smelled fresh, hinting of autumn's approach. I trotted across the parking lot hopeful Axel wouldn't mind the early morning interruption. He might even have a fresh pot of coffee going. That thought put a smile on my face and increased the speed in my feet.

I reached the large red-sided, metal-roofed structure that housed Axel's office as well as the warehouse. He didn't answer when I knocked so I peeked through the partially open miniblinds. The room appeared well lit but unoccupied. He must be somewhere else in the building.

I contemplated getting back in my car and driving home, but I hated to miss this opportunity to conduct a mother to father discussion about Eric's unacceptable behavior. Maybe I could catch Axel somewhere else on the grounds.

I strolled around the building and spotted a door standing ajar. The interior lighting was dim, and as I pushed on the door, I softly called out Axel's name. No need to startle him.

I walked down a narrow corridor lined with wall-to-wall boxes and empty crates stacked on both sides. It led to another corridor to the right. I called Axel's name again, this time a little louder.

I entered the cavernous storage facility. Enormous bags of sugar and flour were stacked on metal shelves next to supersized boxes of napkins and paper plates. Along with crates filled with apples and pears. A fine dusting of a white substance coated the concrete surface. My size nine Nikes skidded across the slick floor.

I stopped and barely avoided crashing into a large white object sprawled on the floor next to the shelving. Seconds later, I realized I was face to face with Axel Thorson, covered from head to toe with a blanket of powdered sugar.

I cringed as Axel's lifeless blue eyes stared up at me in accusation.

The Donut King was no more.

.

CHAPTER FOUR

I gazed in disbelief at the bakery owner. His hair, moustache and beard, saturated with powdered sugar, gave him the look of a frosted Colonel Sanders.

Unfortunately, this was not a finger-licking moment.

I knelt down and placed a finger on Axel's carotid artery, but nothing pulsed back at me. To be sure, I rested my head on his chest and listened for a heartbeat, but I only succeeded in acquiring a layer of white stuff in my nose. I sneezed and powdered sugar flew everywhere.

Great. I'd probably contaminated a potential crime scene by sneezing evidence all over the place. I stood and surveyed the vast space. Was I jumping to conclusions?

Axel could have suffered a heart attack and accidentally knocked over the fifty-pound bag of powdered sugar from one of the shelves, which broke open after it landed on top of him. But Axel was only a year or two younger than me so that scenario seemed doubtful.

I reached for Axel's hand. It felt ice-cold, even colder than the chill enveloping my entire frame. My eyes moved to a rolling pin resting against the wall. Maybe he'd tripped on the heavy object.

Or maybe someone used the utensil for something other than rolling out pie dough.

My stomach clenched at the thought an assailant could still be on the premises. I scanned the room but didn't detect another presence. Which still didn't quiet my nerves. I reached into my purse, grabbed my cell and dialed 9-1-1, my teeth chattering louder than a band of chipmunks. The dispatcher assured me the ambulance should arrive in less than ten minutes. I told them to notify the sheriff's office as well.

Waiting alone in the vast warehouse did nothing to allay my growing fears, but it didn't seem right to desert Axel. Common decency overrode common sense in this situation. When the sound of sirens finally pealed in the distance, I breathed a huge sigh of relief.

I retraced my steps through the building and ran to the parking lot. I greeted the two paramedics, one of whom I remembered meeting when my grandmother fell a few months ago.

"You look like you've seen a ghost." The expression on the EMT's dusky face grew puzzled when he noticed my white-caked hands and cheeks. "Actually, you look like a ghost. What's going on?"

I haltingly explained the situation, and they took off for the warehouse. By now, the sirens had drawn the attention of the bakery staff. Both my daughter and her boss were headed in my direction.

Jenna reached me first. "Mom, what's happening?" she asked, her eyes wide and frightened. "Are you okay?"

I grabbed her hands, which were almost as white as mine, although her palms were coated with flour. She must have been preparing the first batch of donuts. Jenna's worry made me forget my own concerns.

"I'm afraid something's happened to Axel," I said, wondering how to break the news to them.

Nina placed a powdery palm over her heart, leaving a white handprint on the Apple Tree Farm logo. "Mercy me, will he be okay?"

16

"I'm sorry. He's…" The sound of additional sirens rolling up the long drive drowned out my reply.

Nina's eyes welled with tears. From what I recalled, Nina had run Apple Tree Farm's bakery for over thirty years, starting back when Thor Thorson, Axel's father had been in charge. I wrapped a sympathetic arm around Nina's waist while Jenna peppered me with medical questions, courtesy of watching *Grey's Anatomy* for years. None of which I could answer, or would answer, until the police investigated the scene.

A few minutes later, a squad car and a plain tan sedan squealed to a halt next to my Prius. Two El Dorado County Sheriff's Deputies jumped out of the official vehicle. A female dressed in a practical navy pantsuit, who sported an equally practical short chestnut-brown haircut, climbed out of the other car. She glanced in our direction then spoke briefly to the officers. They approached our small gathering, the two six-foot-plus deputies dwarfing the woman who looked to be close to my height and age.

"I'm Detective Reynolds," she introduced herself. "Who called 911?"

"That was me," I said. "I found the body, I mean Axel, in that building over there." I pointed toward the large warehouse, now bathed in bright sunshine. An ominous gray sky seemed more appropriate for this sad situation.

"You didn't touch anything, did you?"

"Well, I touched Axel," I admitted. "To make sure he was as dead as he looked."

She mumbled something about "amateurs" under her breath before she addressed the two deputies.

Hey, I wasn't an amateur when it came to finding dead bodies. Not that I planned to add that to my Facebook profile.

"Deputy Everett will take your statements," she said to Nina and Jenna. "You follow me," she ordered as she hiked across the parking lot, not even glancing back to see if I was heeding her command. But I was used to following official orders. Most of the time.

I could visualize my detective boyfriend silently shaking with laughter at that comment. I sure wished he was still in charge of homicide instead of away on his secret detail.

Detective Reynolds led the way, and I reluctantly followed after her and the other deputy. They stopped as soon as they reached the open door to the warehouse.

Reynolds glared at my blurred footprints. "What were you doing in this building?"

"I needed to discuss a situation with Axel that involved my daughter."

Her head whipped around so fast I thought she'd get whiplash, although her hair remained smooth and in place. I'd have to find out what products she used. Later on, after she warmed up to me.

Which, given her cheery personality, could take a decade or two.

"What kind of situation?" she asked.

"Axel's son has been harassing Jenna, but she was afraid to mention it to Axel. She didn't want to lose her job."

Reynolds narrowed her eyes, causing me to wonder if Jenna and I had just been elevated to the suspect pool.

"We'll talk more. Stay," she commanded as if ordering a pet spaniel at home.

I stood outside the door while a parade of crime scene techs entered the building, followed by the departure of the paramedics.

How soon would an official contact the Thorson family to inform them of the sad news? It would be horrible if Eric arrived for work and learned about his father's death. And poor Dorie Thorson. What a tragedy to lose her husband so young.

After twenty minutes had passed, I decided I was done playing the waiting game. For all I knew, the detective had forgotten about me. I was concerned about my daughter. The death, a possible murder of her boss, isn't something a teenager encounters every day. Jenna's needs took precedence over the detective's.

I plodded across the dew-laden grass and reached the asphalt parking lot, now filled with additional squad cars and forensic personnel. I waved at a young deputy whose path had crossed mine on a few occasions.

"Ms. McKay, it's nice to see you," said Deputy Mengelkoch. "Well, not really, I mean, it's not that nice," he stammered, his face reddening.

"This isn't how I anticipated my morning turning out either," I said. "It looks like the entire Sheriff's Office is here. Can I speak to my daughter?"

"They should be done interviewing her by now. Go on in."

I thanked him then entered the building. Jenna and Nina sat next to each other at one of the customer tables. I dropped into the seat opposite Jenna. "How are you holding up, honey?" I asked.

"I'm fine," she said, although her red-rimmed eyes declared otherwise. Nina's wrinkled cheeks still bore tracks of her own tears.

"How are you doing?" Nina asked me. "After all, you're the one who found...him." She snuffled and swiped at her eyes.

"Axel looked quite peaceful and serene," I reassured her.

"Everyone loves, I mean loved Axel," said Nina, looking and sounding bewildered by the shocking news. "He was a wonderful boss. When he was younger he worked for his father learning the business from one end to the other, just like his son is doing now."

She sniffed. "Poor Eric. He has big shoes to fill."

Jenna and I exchanged glances, but this wasn't the appropriate time to comment on Eric's wandering mitts. From now on, he'd hopefully be too busy filling those big shoes to waste time annoying the female staff.

I looked around the immaculate bakery and dining area. The entire operation appeared to be sound and well cared for.

"Did Axel have any financial issues?" I asked curiously.

"Not that I'm aware of," Nina said. "That new apple farm next door opened up last year, which means additional competition, but we shouldn't hurt for business. The weather's been cooperative, so despite the drought we've harvested a decent crop this year."

My stomach chose that moment to interrupt our conversation with a growl resembling the roar of a mountain lion. My untimely digestive disruption helped lighten the atmosphere. Both Jenna and Nina erupted into giggles which bordered on the edge of hysteria.

"Would you like one of the day-old pastries, Laurel?" asked Nina. "We save them for the staff to take home."

Before I could reply, Detective Reynolds noisily announced her entrance. Several deputies followed in her wake. Based on the dark expression on her grim face, the discovery of a sugar-coated corpse hadn't sweetened her disposition any.

I had a feeling we were going to need more than a few day-old donuts to turn this detective into a happy camper.

CHAPTER FIVE

Detective Reynolds first addressed Jenna and Nina. "Thank you for your statements. You're both free to leave."

Nina looked confused. "What about the bakery? And our customers? Sunday is the busiest day of the week."

"The bakery is shut down today as are all the shops. We've blockaded the entrance and posted several deputies to ensure no one enters the premises. All vendors and customers will be denied admittance." Reynolds shot a dirty look in my direction. "Obviously we can't have people traipsing all over the place."

"Did you contact Axel's brother, Paul?" Nina asked. "And Axel's wife?"

Reynolds nodded. "They've both been informed."

"How is Dorie doing?" I asked.

"Not well, as you can imagine," Reynolds said curtly, although her tone indicated a trace of sympathy for the new widow. "Ms. McKay, I have a few more questions for you."

She ushered me to a table some distance away from Jenna. Nina indicated she would remain with my daughter while the detective and I chatted.

"So what have you discovered?" I asked.

She stared at me as if I were a bug that had just crawled out of her shoe. "I'm the one who's supposed to ask the questions."

21

Geez. The woman had a chip on her shoulder the size of a woodpile.

"Sorry, my bad, it's just that I've been involved in a few investigations."

She pulled a small notebook from her blazer pocket. "So I've heard."

I shared a conspiratorial smile. "All positive comments, I assume."

"Not really." She frowned. "Let's get down to business. There are smudged fingerprints all over the victim's clothing. Any chance those belong to you?"

Fine. If that's how she was going to be. "I explained that already. I checked to see if I should perform CPR then realized it was too late."

"Right. Now tell me more about this grudge you had against Thorson." She eyed my swollen cheek. "He assaulted you so you tried to get back at him?"

"I didn't hold a grudge against Axel," I sputtered. "I only found out yesterday his son has been hounding my daughter. Eric and another young man named Tony got into an altercation late in the afternoon, and Tony's fist accidentally connected with my face."

I pressed on my cheekbone to illustrate the damage and flinched.

"So this Tony person fought with Eric Thorson. Then what happened?"

"Axel broke up the fight. He sent his son back to the cider house and Tony to his office. A few minutes later Jenna and I overheard a conversation when Axel fired him. Tony sure wasn't happy," I said, remembering the way his *Antiques Roadshow* VW tore down the driveway.

"Unhappy enough to come back and kill his former employer?"

"Of course not." I protested, although I really didn't know anything about the young man. Still, I felt confident my daughter was a good judge of character. Then her remarks sank in.

"So Axel *was* murdered."

The detective tapped her pen against her full lips. "I didn't say that. The medical examiner will make that determination. I'm merely checking into all possibilities."

"Isn't murder usually tied to one of three things: love, money, or revenge? I think they mentioned that on *Castle* the other night," I said, trying to be helpful.

She shoved her notepad back into her pocket and stood. "Perhaps you should switch to the Food Channel and stay away from crime shows. It might be in the county's best interest."

It also might be in my children's best interest since no one would ever confuse me with a domestic diva, but there was no way a cooking show could ever captivate me like my favorite crime shows.

My cell rang and I reached into my purse to grab it. My heart fluttered when I saw the caller's name.

"It's my boyfriend," I said to Reynolds. "Do you mind if I take it?"

"Tell Tom I said hi." She winked and sauntered off.

I clicked the green accept button while processing her curious comment and even more peculiar wink. Maybe she had a tic in her eye. After our conversation, I was feeling a bit twitchy myself.

"Hey, Tom," I said into the phone.

"Hi, sweetheart, I miss you." The man certainly knew how to greet his girlfriend. His soft baritone warmed my heart and... other stuff.

"I miss you, too. How's your case coming?"

His heavy sigh indicated it wasn't coming along that well. "It's troublesome, but that's not why I called. I heard that Axel Thorson was found dead early this morning at Apple Tree Farm. Wasn't Jenna supposed to work there today?"

"She *was* scheduled to work until I stumbled over Axel."

"Oh." Complete silence followed for so long I began to wonder if we'd lost our connection. Then Tom continued. "No one shared that particular tidbit with me. Dare I ask how you managed to include tripping over Axel in your day's activities?"

"You know me. Timing is everything, and I never seem to have it. When Jenna and I arrived a little before six, we noticed Axel's car in the parking lot. After she and Nina entered the bakery, I walked over to Axel's office to discuss something with him."

"And…" he prompted.

"When he didn't respond to my knocking on his office door, I walked around the building thinking he might be in the warehouse." My voice dropped. "And he was."

"I wish there was a way to keep you out of trouble," he mumbled into the phone.

Well, maybe if he wasn't 120 miles away we could do that. Together.

"By the way, Detective Reynolds told me to say hi to you."

"Oh."

"I don't remember her working homicide in the past. Is she new to El Dorado County?"

"The Sheriff recruited her from the Bay Area. We both worked for the San Francisco Police Department at the same time. Last year she was involved in an incident…" he paused. "Anyway, Ali wanted a change from the city. It can be grueling dealing with a hundred plus homicides a year."

"She seems competent." Annoying but competent.

"Very much so. It's a good thing there's no reason for you to be involved." I didn't respond and his volume increased in intensity. "There is no reason, is there?"

"Nope. I'm just an innocent bystander in search of a donut."

"Good," he said. "Let's keep it that way."

An excellent plan. Too bad I had no control over it.

CHAPTER SIX

The drive from Apple Tree Farm to our house was even more subdued than the ride there. Once we arrived home, Jenna announced she planned to nap and then study for her upcoming SAT exam.

I would have loved to squeeze in some nappy time myself, but my mother, Barbara Bingham Bradford, and my stepfather were due any minute with my eight-year-old son. Since I'd been forced into weekend chauffeur duty, Mother had agreed to ferry Ben to his soccer game yesterday afternoon and let him spend the night at her house.

My newish stepfather, retired Detective Robert Bradford, formerly of the El Dorado County Sheriff's Office, had no grandchildren of his own, and he and Ben had become best buds. Since Hank's parents had died more than a decade ago, and my father had passed away when I was only ten, Ben had grown up without a grandfather. The new addition to our small family had been accepted by everyone, including the woman Bradford once treated as his number one murder suspect.

Me.

My head drooped lower than the plants I'd forgotten to water this week. I brewed a fresh pot of coffee to welcome my guests and to wake myself up. I took a sip of the steaming liquid just as the doorbell rang.

As I walked through the family room, I passed Pumpkin napping in her wicker basket. She blinked once then evidently decided that was sufficient feline activity for the afternoon and went back to sleep. Lucky cat.

Mug in hand, I opened the door and greeted my family. Ben graced me with a hug before he ran to the family room and switched on the television. Bradford gave me a peck on the cheek and joined Ben.

"What's the rush?" I asked my tall, slender mother, who as usual looked like she'd stepped out of a Talbot's advertisement, dressed in a matching coral twinset and beige slacks.

"Ben has discovered football," she said with a moue of distaste. "Your Sundays will never be the same."

"It was bound to happen sooner or later. This hasn't been a great Sunday anyway."

"So I heard. We ate a late breakfast at the Cozy Apple Café and all the talk was about Axel Thorson." She sent a horrified look in my direction. "Jenna didn't discover him, did she?"

"No, stumbling over bodies seems to fall under my jurisdiction."

"How on earth did you manage that?"

We entered my kitchen where I poured her a cup of coffee and refilled my own as I shared my macabre morning discovery plus my encounter with Detective Reynolds.

Mother took a moment to mull it over. "Axel is highly regarded around here," she said. "The farm does well, and he's active with the growers association." My Realtor mother was better informed than Google when it came to county businesses. "I've never heard anyone say anything negative about him, although..." She paused for a few seconds. "I vaguely remember someone in the office saying his farm might be for sale."

"I don't see how a sale could have anything to do with murder."

"Are you certain it wasn't an accident?"

"Trust me." I shivered. "The man did not sugarcoat himself."

Mother rose from her chair and walked over to the counter. The sun shone through the kitchen window making her short blond hair glimmer. She picked up the carafe and refilled both our cups before joining me at my aging oak table.

"Despite your unfortunate timing, the detective, hopefully, won't think you're involved." She wrinkled her pert nose at me. "When did they add a woman to the homicide department?"

"About two months ago," Bradford informed us as he entered the room, all six-foot-five inches and 250 pounds of him. He reached into a cupboard, grabbed a chipped red mug, and poured the remains of the coffee before settling in a chair across from me. "They started looking for a replacement when Tom was asked to join that task force. He'd worked with Reynolds in the city before he moved here and recommended her. Said she was terrific."

"He never mentioned her before," I remarked.

"Hard to believe the Sheriff's Office left your name off the new hire memo," Bradford commented.

"Ha, ha, very funny. She's kind of a pit bull. Reminds me of an old bear of a detective I once encountered."

We exchanged grins.

"Tom called to check on Jenna. He mentioned some incident Reynolds was involved in back in San Francisco, but we were interrupted before he could finish. Do you know anything about it?"

Not that it was any of my business, but I didn't usually let that stop me from asking questions.

Bradford shook his shiny bald dome. "Nah, all I heard was that she was on administrative leave from SFPD when they recruited her, and she jumped at the opportunity to move here."

"Hopefully she's as terrific as Tom thinks she is." I also hoped my boyfriend meant that compliment in an official capacity.

"Did Tom mention how his case was going?" Bradford asked.

I stared at him. "He wouldn't say word one to me about it. Do you know what's going on?"

"More or less. It's a big operation, and they may need to recruit some more officers to help out."

Mother leaned over and kissed her new husband on his ruddy cheek. "I'm glad you're retired, so I don't have to worry about anything happening to you."

Bradford stared at his half-filled mug before he looked up, a sheepish expression on his face. "Did you know retirement doesn't prohibit a former officer from acting as a consultant?"

"No," replied Mother in a tone frosty enough to eliminate global warming. "I did not know that. Is there something you'd like to share with your wife?"

Oops. This could be the boomer newlyweds first spat. Should I stay or leave?

"Tom's asked me to work with the task force," Bradford said.

This decision was a no brainer. I got up from the table and left the room.

CHAPTER SEVEN

I bumped into Jenna in the hallway. Ben followed close behind in search of his super-sized playmate. We returned to the kitchen where the silence was as thick as the chili I planned to serve for dinner.

"C'mon, Grandpa." Ben latched on to Bradford's catcher's-mitt-sized paw and tried to yank him out of his chair. "Half time's over. You're gonna miss the game."

Mother flicked her slender hand at her husband. "Go enjoy the game. We will finish this conversation later."

Bradford looked torn between resuming the discussion with his wife and pleasing Ben. The combination of hanging out with my son and watching the game proved irresistible. Based on forty years of my own experience, he probably realized as I did, that it was far better to let my mother cool down before continuing a potentially confrontational conversation.

The two males left the room. Jenna slipped into Bradford's empty seat.

"Straighten up, dear," Mother corrected my daughter. "Posture is everything."

Jenna scowled and slumped further into her chair. "Good posture won't get me into Harvard or bring Mr. Thorson back to life."

Interesting segue from college to Axel's demise.

"I'm sorry you were involved in that horrible situation this morning," I said to her.

"I feel bad for Eric," she said. "Even if he is a butthead. I remember how awful it felt when Dad was in jail. I can't imagine what it would be like to lose a parent, especially like that."

My eyes misted. Across the table from me, Mother's frozen expression thawed several degrees.

"It's a sad situation for the Thorson family and the Apple Tree staff," I replied. "I hope they can solve this case quickly."

"You don't think Tony's a suspect, do you?"

"Do you know any reason why the detectives would think that? Besides the fact he was fired yesterday. That's not a reason to kill someone."

Jenna planted her elbows on the table, rested her head on her palms and mumbled a reply.

I brushed a few strands of her hair behind her ear. "I couldn't hear you. What did you say?"

"He has a record."

I stared at her. "I presume you don't mean a musical record."

She shook her head. "He says it was all a big mistake. He and a friend stopped at a mini-mart last year in Diamond Springs. Tony stayed in the car while the other dude went into the store to get some soft drinks. Instead of getting soda, his friend took some beer without paying. Tony was listening to the radio and claims he didn't pay attention to what his pal threw in the back seat. Tony had no idea he'd stolen anything until the police stopped them. He ended up going to juvie hall."

"Who is this person you're discussing?" asked Mother.

"A young man who works with Jenna," I said. "Or used to work with her before Axel fired him yesterday. Supposedly for stealing."

"I bet it was Eric who took the money," Jenna said, "and blamed it on Tony."

While I admired my daughter's loyalty to her friend, her naiveté was undoubtedly interfering with her normally excellent judgment.

"The police will sort everything out. In the meantime, you need to study for your SAT. Let's concentrate on that for now."

Jenna slid her chair back and grumbled her way out of the room.

Mother waited until Jenna was out of earshot before her inquisition started. "Why would you let Jenna fraternize with someone who's spent time behind bars?"

"Tony came to her rescue the other day when Eric Thorson was bothering her. I'm sure that's the only reason she has a soft spot for him."

"We don't need any boys distracting her right now. Not with those exams and college applications coming up."

I was in full agreement with my mother, a rare occurrence indeed. The sound of two football fans hooting and hollering in the family room indicated the game was over and the Forty Niners had won. Mother picked up our cups, rinsed them out and loaded them in the dishwasher.

"Robert will be in a good mood. I need to talk him out of that foolish idea of assisting your boyfriend." She glared at me.

"Tom doesn't run his staffing needs by me, you know. I think your husband just misses being in on the action."

"Maybe I can find some chores around the house. There are some pictures I need hung and a couple of faucets that should be repaired. Those tasks should keep him occupied."

I doubted if replacing leaky faucets and hammering a few nails into the wall could ever achieve the excitement of a homicide investigation, but I planned on staying out of this discussion.

I had my own "to do" list to work on. It might not involve anything as important as solving a murder, but if I mucked it up, my career would be dead in the water.

CHAPTER EIGHT

A few minutes after eight the following morning, I walked through the glass double doors of Hangtown Bank's corporate office, situated in a nineteenth-century brick building in downtown Placerville. After staying up until two a.m. to complete my marketing presentation, I'd neglected to set my clock radio. I was awakened from a sound slumber by ten pounds of fluff sitting on my chest, and a paw not-so-gently batting an early wakeup call on my chin.

Thank goodness for Pumpkin's early alarm since it took an extra five minutes for me to mask my bruise with several coats of cover-up. The kids cooperated by getting ready without arguing over whose turn it was in the bathroom, and they both made it to their schools on time.

Sherry, the bank's receptionist, glanced at her watch, but she merely smiled and winked at me. Working moms stick together. I was grateful my position didn't require me to be tethered to a headset and switchboard by eight a.m. on the dot every day. Previously I'd worked at the bank in several capacities, first as a branch manager and then as a mortgage loan underwriter. I'd enjoyed underwriting but discovered that I missed the personal contact with bank customers. Sometimes analyzing a seven-hundred-page mortgage loan file just isn't stimulating enough.

When a position in the marketing department opened up six months earlier, I'd jumped at the opportunity to apply for the job.

My supervisor, Bruce Boxer, Vice President of Business Development and Marketing, not only bore a strong resemblance to his canine namesake in appearance, he'd barked at me on more than one occasion.

I'd worried whether marketing would prove to be my *métier,* or turn my life into what the French quaintly refer to as *merde.*

But then Cupid smote him with a perfectly aimed arrow, and Mr. Boxer morphed from a curmudgeon to the most relaxed boss ever. He was currently on a Mediterranean cruise with the new love of his life. Before he left on vacation, he'd begun handing more responsibilities over to me, making me curious if retirement was in his near future.

Which meant a promotion could be in mine. I was working hard to prove I was ready. Hangtown Bank was a well-run and conservatively operated local bank, owned by the same family for over 150 years. It took its name from the few years in Placerville's colorful history when the town had been officially named Hangtown. Established during the California Gold Rush, the community had suffered with villains who attempted to procure their gold the easy way—via holdups and homicide. Fed up with the criminal element, the locals decided one day to mete out their own punishment. The stalwart oak hanging tree became a part of our city's history.

I had barely settled into my economy-version ergonomic chair when Stan Winters, my friend and former underwriting co-worker, ambled in. Although Stan's fashion sense occasionally drifted to something more suitable for the production of *La Cage Aux Folles,* today he could have posed for the cover of *American Banker* in his light gray pinstripe, aqua shirt and matching tie, a newspaper tucked under his arm.

"Hey, looking good," I complimented him. "What's the occasion?"

Stan preened and straightened his tie before sliding into my one and only guest chair. "The El Dorado County Musical

Association invited me to a luncheon today. They also asked me to join their board."

"That's terrific. No one knows more about musical theater than you."

He flapped his wrist at me. "Oh, please, there are probably one or two show tunes I haven't memorized."

He opened his mouth, and I interrupted him before he could belt out "Oh, What a Beautiful Morning." Despite Stan's ability to rattle off the lyrics of every Rogers and Hammerstein musical ever written, he was completely tone deaf.

"You wouldn't believe what happened to me this weekend," I said, in an attempt to divert him from serenading me.

"You found another dead body?" Stan flourished the local newspaper with theatrical zeal, revealing the headline story complete with two prominent black and white photos.

In bold print, the title of the article screamed—*Donut King's Disturbing Death*. Two large photos provided visuals. The photo of Axel Thorson looked like the one he'd used for official functions.

The photo to the right displayed a woman wearing a low-cut saloon girl dress perched on the top of a stagecoach. The caption under the photo read, "Local banker and Wagon Train supporter Laurel McKay makes a chilling discovery."

"Oh, great." I frowned at the paper. "Why did they have to mention me? And where did they get this photo?"

"Your wild stagecoach ride during the Wagon Train Parade last summer led to a wee bit of notoriety," he said. "While I'm never surprised when you stumble over a dead body, how did you manage it this time?" He pushed his wire rims up his nose and examined me more closely. "And end up with a black eye. Tell, sister."

Since I wouldn't get any work done until I answered Stan's questions, I shared everything that happened over the weekend, from the fight between the two teens, to my finding the victim and subsequent discussion with Detective Reynolds.

"Sad situation. You don't think you're a suspect, do you?"

"I think the detective suspects I'm a nuisance, but I barely know the Thorson family."

"I'm not one to sugarcoat the situation," Stan said, while I inwardly groaned at his pathetic pun. "But I don't think you have anything to worry about."

"Good. Because I'm giving a presentation to the Board tonight, and that's my priority for today."

"You're moving up in the banking world. What's your topic?"

"You know how I like to emphasize the Placerville community and its history in the bank's promotional efforts," I began when he interrupted me.

"Like that flyer you designed saying Hangtown Bank wants to rope in your account?" Stan stuck out his tongue and mimed having a noose around his neck.

My cheeks reddened. The promotion Stan referred to had focused on George, the dummy who hangs over the original Hangman's Tree Bar on Main Street, a few doors down from the bank. I thought it a clever way of tying in some Gold Rush history, but my boss wasn't as enamored of my historical creativity as I was.

"That was one of my first efforts. I'm far more subtle now." I shoved a sample of one of the flyers I'd drafted into his hands.

"Nicely done." Stan returned the flyer to me. "I like the idea of the bank sponsoring the annual Apple Tree bicycle race. It's great publicity for Hangtown Bank and the local farms and wineries that participate. You've got a winner there."

"From your lips to the Board's ears." I returned his newspaper to him. "If only my fish-netted legs hadn't landed on the front page of the paper the day I have to meet with the bank honchos."

"Hey, it could have been worse. They might have submitted a photo showcasing your other assets."

Stan was right. During a rowdy real life stagecoach chase, my saloon girl outfit had been seconds away from turning into a YouTube wardrobe malfunction. Today, I'd managed to conceal my Kim Kardashian curves under a boring Betsy Banker black suit. If you look like a professional and prepare like a professional, you can't go wrong.

Right?

Shortly before six that evening, I climbed the stairs to the second floor. I rarely spent time on the plush executive level and those few occasions had resulted in me quaking in my clearance-sale heels. With my first presentation to the bank board due in a few minutes, I was trembling so violently I worried the nineteenth-century building might collapse.

I attempted an internal pep talk by rationalizing that a woman who has faced down a killer or two shouldn't worry over facing a room filled with bank directors.

Although the plus side of facing off against a killer was that you didn't have to worry about your PowerPoint presentation imploding.

My two-inch heels sank into the thick gray carpeting as I walked down the lengthy corridor past sepia photos of Ulysses S. Grant, John Studebaker, Horace Greeley, and other visionaries who had visited or resided in Placerville. Remembering their contributions to society boosted my flagging spirits and helped propel me down the hallway where the open door of the conference room awaited my arrival.

The twelve members of the Hangtown Bank Board mingled with one another near the back of the expansive room where the coffee, tea and pastries were. I'd already drunk enough coffee to flood a Starbucks, so my primary concern was that I wouldn't rattle off my speech at warp speed. Or need a potty break mid-presentation.

The board was comprised of several Main Street store and restaurant owners, an attorney, a doctor, and several commercial farm owners including Walter Eastwood, owner of Valley View Vineyards and Orchard, one of the largest operations. The members came in all shapes, sizes and genders, although thinning gray hair was the most prevalent feature among the men. Some dressed in pinstripes while others wore logo-embroidered polo shirts and khakis.

A younger woman stood in the back of the room conversing with a short, stocky, silver-haired man—Mr. Chandler, the bank president. She appeared close to my age although I didn't recognize her. Her glossy dark hair curled as if she'd spent years perfecting the style and her expert makeup enhanced her café au lait complexion. Her black-and-white geometric print dress completed the picture of a successful businessperson.

Who was she?

I laid the folder containing my presentation and handouts on top of the glossy polished cherry table. Belle, the president's secretary, had promised the projector would be primed and ready for my spiel. Hopefully, I was primed as well.

After a few minutes, the board members assembled around the table. Mr. Chandler greeted everyone then introduced the visitor as Adriana Menzinger, the owner of a marketing firm located in Sacramento. Mr. Chandler announced that after the marketing department's presentation, Ms. Menzinger would discuss the merits of my plan as well as present her own recommendations.

Although Mr. Chandler didn't specifically say the words, it only took me a few seconds to realize that he, and perhaps the board, were considering outsourcing the bank's marketing. Which meant I could be tweeting about my own unemployment in mere days.

Or hours. Talk about pressure.

My face felt hot and flushed. Rivulets of perspiration cascaded down my chest. Either the thermostat was broken or I was experiencing the first hot flash of my life.

I sensed my bangs curling from the unexpected heat wave. I opened the bottle of water at my seat and spilled a few drops on my papers. My preference would be to dump the contents on my head, but instead, I gulped the refreshing water hoping it would diminish the heat overtaking my body.

It didn't help. Just when I felt I'd reached the seventh circle of hell, Mr. Chandler announced it was my turn to speak.

I grabbed my notes and walked over to the LCD projector stationed at the end of the table. Although I'd loaded my presentation earlier in the day, someone must have used the laptop in the interim. As I searched through PowerPoint, my internal temperature increased degree by degree.

The shrill notes of "Shake It Off" caused me to jump. Everyone's eyes shifted to the empty chair where my black purse rested.

Crap. I sprinted around the table, grabbed my handbag and dug deep for my phone. I recognized my daughter's ring tone and assumed she was calling to find out when I'd be home from the afterhours meeting. I breathed a sigh of relief when the clamor stopped as quickly as it had begun. Everyone in the room was staring at me. Could this day possibly get any worse? I received the answer immediately as a new text appeared on my screen.

Mom, I'm in jail.

CHAPTER NINE

As a single mother supporting her family, my career means a lot to me. But nothing tops the safety and welfare of my children. I apologized to Mr. Chandler and the board, indicating I had a personal emergency.

I left the conference room and immediately dialed Jenna's phone. It rang several times before landing in voicemail. For the next five minutes, I repeatedly tried to connect but always ended up with the same result. Squaring my shoulders, I re-entered the conference room and beckoned to Mr. Chandler. He grimaced but remained silent as he followed me out.

"Is there a problem?" the President asked in a curt tone.

I showed him Jenna's text. "I can't reach my daughter. I have to drive to the jail and find out what's going on."

Mr. Chandler had once spent a short and uncomfortable stay at the El Dorado County government-run bed and breakfast. Since I was the one responsible for his eventual release, he responded to the text as I hoped he would.

"You need to be with your daughter. That's your first priority, although your marketing proposal is clearly important to the bank. I'll ask Adriana to go through your presentation then the board can discuss it afterward. She may even be able to make some recommendations. You and I can meet tomorrow to discuss the results."

The odds of Adriana Menzinger supporting my initiative over her own marketing plan were about one in a million, but I had no choice. I thanked Adriana and the board members, grabbed my purse and flew down the stairs faster than Taylor Swift could shake it off.

During my brief drive to the county jail, I speed-dialed both Tom and Bradford, hoping someone official could lend some aid. Neither answered his phone. Not surprising. Tom was embroiled in his own investigation. Bradford could be doing who knows what with my mother. The senior newlyweds continued to enjoy each other's intimate company far more frequently than their Generation X daughter and her boyfriend.

So annoying.

A hundred different scenarios, none of them appealing, flashed through my imaginative brain. Jenna had arranged for a ride home with one of her girlfriends who also planned to attend a special band practice today. Did the girls get into an automobile accident?

There couldn't be any other explanation. My daughter was an A-plus overachiever. How else could she have landed in jail? I made one last phone call asking Patty Swanson, one of the other soccer moms, to pick up Ben from his practice and take him to her house until I could get him.

I drove up the long winding road leading to the jail and pulled into their parking lot. My car slid into a compact space between two Sheriff's Office patrol cars. I grabbed my purse hoping that whatever reason landed Jenna in jail would not require any bail exceeding the twenty-dollar bill in my pathetic wallet. After walking out on the Board of Directors that could be the last remaining twenty in my possession for a while.

The last time I'd been in the building had been to visit Hank during his brief incarceration.

I'd never expected to pay a return visit.

I entered the lobby and explained my situation to the female staffer sitting behind the bullet-proof check-in window. She nodded sympathetically then typed something into her computer.

The hot flash that had previously invaded my body disappeared, leaving behind clammy hands and a chilled sense of disbelief.

"Your daughter is fine, Ms. McKay," she said. "And, for the record, she is not under arrest."

The sigh I let out was loud enough for them to hear back on Main Street. Confusion quickly followed relief.

"I don't understand. Where is Jenna?" My voice escalated until it was as shrill as an *American Idol* reject.

"She's still downstairs in booking. Please wait in the lobby, and I'll arrange for one of the deputies to escort her upstairs."

I tried getting more answers from her, but she was already attending to the lank-haired, sad-faced woman waiting in line behind me.

I plopped into a metal chair that squeaked its disapproval. The chair was probably older than I was. Rumor had it the county would soon build a new jail. At the rate I was visiting the premises, I hoped they'd hire someone from HGTV to furnish the waiting area.

After what seemed like an interminable wait, but was probably only ten minutes, Jenna walked out, her face pale, her expression grim. I recognized the officer accompanying her as Deputy Becker.

When Jenna saw me, a huge smile of relief appeared. It quickly disappeared as she hung back, undoubtedly waiting to see if my response would be that of a loving mom or a judgmental jury.

Her disciplinary sentence could wait until later. I grabbed her slender frame and drew her into the biggest Mama Bear hug I'd ever delivered.

She finally pulled away, tears careening down her cheeks. "Thank goodness you're here. This is the worst day of my entire life."

My daughter was only seventeen. There were plenty of worse days to come, although I had to admit this day would easily make it into my top ten.

Jenna turned to face the officer. "How much longer will Tony have to stay here?"

41

"Oh, he's not leaving any time soon," said the deputy.

"What do you mean?" she asked him. "You can't keep him in jail for an illegal U-turn."

"No, but we can keep him in here for murder."

CHAPTER TEN

Jenna slumped against me, almost knocking the two of us onto the grimy floor. I straightened her up but kept my arm around her in case more shocking news followed.

"You've arrested a friend of my daughter's for murder?" I asked Deputy Becker. I was beginning to feel like I was in the middle of a *Twilight Zone* episode. It was time to cut to a commercial.

"Your daughter was a passenger in a car driven by someone who's recently been under investigation. When he made an illegal U-turn, the officer who stopped him discovered an arrest warrant had been issued two hours earlier."

"You mean she was kidnapped?" That was the only explanation I could imagine for why my daughter had been a passenger in the car of someone with an outstanding arrest warrant.

"No, she wasn't in the car under duress," the officer replied. "I was under the impression Antonio is her boyfriend. Look, I've probably said more than I should as it is."

"But you can't arrest—" Jenna cried out before he interrupted her.

"Please take your daughter home before she says something she regrets and ends up spending the night in juvenile detention."

Jenna seemed to be in shock, so I shoved her out of the jail before she did anything that could lead to an official arrest. She said nothing further as we walked to my car, but she had to know a grilling was in store. Before my interrogation began, I called Patty and told her we were on our way.

Both Bradford and Tom had left messages while my phone was set on vibrate. I'd update them as soon as I had something worthwhile to share. I started the car, checked the rearview mirror to ensure no patrol cars were in my way and turned right for the short drive to Patty's house.

Jenna stared silently out her window. My patience, never a strong suit, had almost run out of gas when she finally opened up.

"Thanks for coming to get me," she murmured.

"Of course, any time," I replied then corrected myself. "Except there better not be a next time. I have a million questions to ask and only a few minutes to get answers before Ben hops in the car. First, who is Antonio and why were you in his car?"

"Don't you remember Tony Perez?" she said. "From Apple Tree Farm? The guy who clobbered you?"

I flinched, remembering the sound and feel of his fist against my cheek.

"Amber and I stopped at Starbucks after band practice and ran into him there. We started talking, and when Amber had to leave, Tony offered to drop me at home."

"Jenna, you know better than to let a strange boy drive you to our house," I chided her.

"He's not a stranger. I've worked with him for the past three weekends. Plus he's Nina's grandson. That should be a good enough reference for you."

"I didn't realize he and Nina were related," I replied. "But still, you and I both heard Axel accuse Tony of stealing money. How can you trust him?"

Jenna threw out her full lower lip, a facial expression I knew too well. "Don't you trust me enough to choose my friends?"

I didn't trust myself to answer her question, so I moved ahead to the question that had been burning neurons in my brain since we'd left the jail.

"Of course, I have confidence in you. But your safety is my highest priority. I don't want you to get hurt."

Ever. Not if I could help it. "What do you think the deputy meant about Tony being held in jail on a murder charge?"

"That's why Tony wanted to talk to me." A couple of stray tears puddled on her high cheekbones. "He was afraid that with Axel's death, he'd never be able to clear his name regarding the cider house thefts. He assured me he would never do anything like that."

Her tears flowed faster than a broken faucet. "Plus it was my fault he got pulled over. We were talking, and he missed the turn on to Green Valley Road. I told him to make a U-turn at the next light. I forgot you can't make one at that intersection anymore, and he must not have noticed the sign. The next thing we knew, a deputy sheriff pulled us over. The officer returned to his car to check Tony's registration, and a few minutes later a second car arrived. They shoved both of us into the back of the patrol car."

She swiped at her tears with the sleeve of her sweater, dotting the pale fabric with blots of mascara. Keeping my left hand on the steering wheel, I reached behind the seat and grabbed a few tissues from the battered box on the floor. My mother might deride my car as cluttered, but I consider it a conveniently-stocked home on wheels.

"The detectives must think Tony returned to Apple Tree Farm that evening or early the next morning to kill Axel," I remarked.

Jenna blew her nose. "Stupid detectives. I wish Tom were here examining the evidence."

That made two of us. Although I wished Tom and I were examining each other.

Focus, Laurel.

"You have to help him, Mom."

"Honey, I can't interfere with their investigation."

"That didn't stop you from helping Dad and Mr. Chandler."

"Those cases were different. Your father is, well, your father, and he needed all the assistance he could get. As far as Mr. Chandler, I had information the police found helpful."

"Fine," Jenna replied in that teenage tone of voice which translated into it not being at all fine. "Then I'll just have to investigate myself."

CHAPTER ELEVEN

We arrived at Patty's house to discover she had already fed Ben dinner, so that was one less item to worry about. My teenage Nancy Drew clammed up for the rest of the ride, although her silence was barely noticeable since Ben chattered nonstop all the way home. I tried to concentrate on his conversation, but my brain shifted into overdrive as I assessed Tony's situation.

Despite Jenna's plea for me to get involved, I barely knew the young man. There was no need for me to meddle.

For a change.

We arrived home and I hit the remote control. The overhead door groaned as I drove my car into the crammed-to-the-ceiling garage of the Craftsman-style house my ex had built fifteen years ago.

Ben unfastened his seat belt and opened the rear door of the car. He reached over and grabbed his stuffed backpack off the floor where he'd dumped it. Jenna eased herself out of the front seat. She stared at her fully loaded brother for a few seconds. Then she shrieked.

"Jenna, what's the matter?" I rushed around the car to her side.

"My backpack," she said, a horrified look on her face.

"What about it?" I looked around for the forest-green backpack in question.

"I left it in the back of Tony's car. When the cops took us to the jail, I forgot all about it." She slumped against the passenger door. "My books, homework and SAT study guide are inside. And I left my oboe, too."

"Where is Tony's car now?" I asked.

She shrugged. "I don't know. I'm sure he never expected to remain in jail. Would they tow it somewhere?"

"I'm as clueless as you are. Let me call Tom and see if he would know." The downside of having a detective boyfriend is his schedule. The upside is an "in" with the homicide department.

Lucky me.

My call to Tom landed in voicemail. It could be minutes or hours before he returned it. I climbed the stairs to my bedroom and changed into a tee shirt and a pair of shorts. Although Ben had eaten dinner, Jenna and I had not. I didn't know about my daughter, but I was starving.

I optimistically rummaged through the freezer and scored a quart of leftover beef stew. Although no one would ever confuse my cooking with Rachel Ray's cuisine, I could whip up a palatable recipe or two.

And there's nothing like a home cooked meal to make up for a brief stint in the slammer. I placed the stew in the microwave to begin the thawing process and pulled some romaine lettuce, tomatoes and avocado from the refrigerator for our salad. My cell phone trilled halfway through my slicing and dicing.

I glanced at the screen and promptly put down my paring knife.

"Thank goodness you got my message," I said to Tom.

"You were babbling," he said, "I mean talking so fast that all I gathered was that Jenna was at the county jail. Is she okay?"

"Not really, but it could have been worse. One of the teens she works with at Apple Tree Farm was arrested for murder this afternoon."

"I heard about that. But how is Jenna involved?"

"Tony was giving her a lift home and then was pulled over for an illegal U-turn," I explained. "Jenna feels it's her fault he was arrested because she directed him to make the turn."

"You should be glad she's not dating this fellow. Or is she?"

"No, although he came to her rescue a time or two at work. I'm sure it's merely a mild infatuation. The McKay women just can't resist a man with dreamy brown eyes, you know."

That comment elicited a chuckle followed by a remark that made my body not only tingle, but I could actually hear bells ringing.

Oops. Merely the microwave dinging and announcing our stew was ready.

"I'm sorry Jenna is involved in this situation, but since she wasn't arrested nothing will show on her record," Tom said. "Why do you need my help?"

"She left her backpack and her oboe in Tony's car. She needs to study for her SAT exam. I was hoping you could use your super powers to help me retrieve it."

"I'll give Reynolds a call and find out where the car was taken. Be prepared though. Her backpack could be considered evidence."

Evidence? Yikes. "Tom, please do something. I don't care what it takes. Jenna needs her backpack. If you think it will help persuade Reynolds, I'll bake some of my toffee brownies for her."

There had to be some way to get into the detective's good graces. And who doesn't love brownies?

"I don't think Ali is big on sweets. She's pretty disciplined about staying fit and..." his voice trailed off as quickly as my annoyance rose. "Never mind. I'll get right on it, Sweetheart."

Nice save, Sweetheart. But I could be magnanimous. After all, Tom had managed to remain my boyfriend through thick and thin, well, at least through thick.

"Jenna and I both thank you," I said. "And I plan on personally thanking you by—" I stopped when Jenna walked into the kitchen.

"I'm waiting," Tom teased.

"Jenna just walked in, so you'll have to wait until you come home. When exactly are you due back here? Can't the other team members keep an eye on the bad guys for twenty-four hours?"

He sighed. "This particular operation is proving larger and more complicated than we anticipated. I'll try to get some time off this weekend. I want to see you and of course spend time with Kristy. She doesn't understand why she has to live with her grandparents while I'm up here."

"I'll try to arrange a sleepover at our house for her," I said, my voice softening. I realized that Tom, a widower, was not only missing his girlfriend, but also his only child, his eight-year-old daughter Kristy.

"A sleepover is a terrific idea," he said. "And maybe someday we'll all...hey, a call came in. I have to go, but I'll handle Jenna's problem as soon as I can."

Okay. Tom would hopefully take care of that problem. All I had to do was arrange a couple of sleepovers.

One with children.

And one without.

CHAPTER TWELVE

As I replaced the phone on the receiver, Jenna glanced up from dishing the stew onto two plates. "Your face is all red. Are you okay?"

I grabbed a napkin and fanned myself. "Must be a hot flash."

Or a flash of the hots. I opened a drawer and brought out utensils for each of us. Next stop: the refrigerator to cool myself off. Milk for Jenna and a well-deserved glass of chardonnay for me.

Although, after a day like today, an entire bottle was justified.

We sat at our kitchen table and chewed our dinner in silence. I'd interrogated Jenna enough this evening. She was undoubtedly still stewing over her missing backpack and trying to come up with a backup plan for her homework.

"Mom, what if—?" Jenna's question was drowned out by the sound of our landline ringing. My fork clattered onto the plate as I raced to answer it before the caller hung up.

"That was quick," I said, recognizing Tom's cell number. "Good news?"

"Not exactly," he replied. "Or to be more specific, not at all. Reynolds considers the backpack evidence."

"That's ridiculous. She's just being a Class A b..." I said, but he cut me off.

"No, she's being a Class A detective."

"Why would Jenna's backpack be considered evidence?"

He sighed one of those heavy "why-doesn't-my-girlfriend-understand-me?" sighs into the phone. "Let's just say Reynolds needs to consider everything associated with a person of interest."

"What does that have to do with Jenna?"

"Since Jenna works at Apple Tree Farm, had an issue with Thorson's son and has been associating with their primary suspect, she *is* a person of interest."

"That is plain ridiculous. Reynolds' policy might make sense when dealing with homicide on the streets of San Francisco, but it's far different here."

"Murder is murder. All detectives have their own way of investigating a crime of this magnitude. Reynolds is very thorough. I can personally attest to that."

Thorough in what, is what I wanted to know.

I jumped when someone tapped me on my back. "What's going on?" Jenna whispered. I shook my head and started up the stairs. Tom and I needed to finish our conversation without any interruption from the subject of said conversation.

I shut the door to my bedroom and flopped down on my bed.

"So what am I supposed to do?" I asked Tom. "Just sit on my hands until Reynolds drives up to the high school, cuffs Jenna and carts her off to jail?"

"Don't you think you're being overly dramatic?"

"No, I'm acting like a concerned mother."

"Look, I need to get going. Please don't do anything to tick off Reynolds. This situation should be resolved in a day or two. In the meantime, maybe some of Jenna's friends can help her out and lend her their textbooks or something."

I only wished it were that easy. But in ten years' time, Tom would become familiar with the extent of his own teenage daughter's homework. Until then, Jenna and I would try to get by without alienating any El Dorado County homicide detectives.

That could be the toughest assignment yet.

The next day I arrived at work a few minutes early. Rather than upset Jenna further, I'd kept Tom's update to myself. I merely shared that he was working with Reynolds to resolve the situation.

I'd written a note to her counselor explaining her predicament, hoping to alleviate her teachers' immediate concerns. Her calculus and AP English teachers had taught her previously when she was a freshman, so they already knew what an excellent student she was. Her physics teacher was an unknown entity at this point. Since the school year had only begun a month ago, he might not be as enamored of her as most of the faculty.

Which reminded me, I wondered how enamored the Hangtown Bank Board was with my marketing presentation. I'd spent many hours on that project and hoped Adriana had done it justice. There were no messages from Mr. Chandler, so I didn't know whether to be relieved or concerned.

As I debated whether to call Mr. Chandler or fetch a cup of coffee from the break room, my cell rang. I dug deep into my purse to retrieve it. My initial hope that Tom was on the line vanished when I recognized Gran's ring tone.

"Is everything okay? Why aren't you in class?" I asked, surprised by the early morning phone call. Gran's Tai Chi sessions began at eight a.m. on Tuesday and Friday. It was rare for her to miss one.

"Something's come up that's more important than me pretending I'm a white crane spreading my bat wings. I got us a case."

"A case of what?"

"A mystery. You know, a case for us to solve."

I rubbed my right ear wondering if my hearing was starting to go.

"Gran, you're not making any sense."

"Girl, you got to get with the program. You remember my friend, Nina, who runs the Apple Tree bakery?"

"Of course, she's Jenna's boss."

"Well, her grandson is that young man who decked you last Saturday. Remember him?"

"Yes, unfortunately." I involuntarily stroked my injured cheekbone, which remained a sickly shade of chartreuse and purple under the thick beige foundation I'd been applying every morning. "Jenna informed me yesterday that he's related to Nina. But what does this have to do with you and me?"

"The cops arrested him last night for supposedly murdering Axel Thorson."

"I'm aware of that, too."

"His arrest just about broke poor Nina's heart. That's why she hired us."

The more Gran talked, the more confused I became.

"You mean she wants us to work in the Apple Tree Farm bakery?"

"Of course not. She wants us to find the real murderer."

CHAPTER THIRTEEN

"Gran, have you been nibbling on your neighbor's medicinal brownies?" I asked.

"Don't be silly," she said. "We need to stay sharp if we're going to solve this case. What do you think of the name TWO GALS DETECTIVE AGENCY?"

"I think..." I paused to contemplate the title. It wasn't half bad. "I think the Sheriff's Office would not appreciate our interfering in their investigation."

"What they wouldn't appreciate is you showing them up again."

I chuckled thinking that I wouldn't mind solving the case and wiping that patronizing look off Detective Reynolds' face. And I certainly didn't want my grandmother investigating on her own. The words *discretion* and *tact* were not among her colorful vocabulary.

"I'm lunching with Liz today, so I'll put out some feelers," I said. "Maybe she can get some information from her hubby."

"Good idea," Gran replied. "Either Brian or one of the other deputy district attorneys should be involved already."

"Let's keep this between us, okay?"

"Got it. I'll keep it on the down low for now."

Which meant every one of Gran's cronies in her garden club and the historical society would know what we were up to within twenty-four hours. You could tweet, tumble and stumble all you wanted online, but for efficient reporting, nothing beat the local GrannyFeed.

I heard Hank yelling in the background. That reminded me of something I'd been dying to ask my grandmother.

"Say, Gran, how long have Hank and Brooke been dating?"

"Long enough for him to tiptoe back into the house at four this morning. Do you want me to ask him for some particulars about their relationship?"

"Nope." I had no desire to learn about any of my ex's particulars. He could do whatever and whomever he wanted.

My office phone rang so I told Gran I'd get back to her that evening. Even before I picked up the receiver, I recognized the extension belonged to Mr. Chandler's secretary.

"Hi, Belle," I chirped into the phone hoping my upbeat tone would produce an equally positive reason for the call. "What's the good word?"

"Mr. Chandler would like to see you upstairs." Although she didn't specifically state it, Belle's clipped words implied my presence was required immediately.

"Can I stop and get some—?"

"Now."

Okey dokey. I hoped Mr. Chandler knew how risky it was to carry on a conversation before I'd integrated some caffeine into my system.

I trudged up the stairs to the executive level, a lined yellow legal pad in hand, prepared for the worst. It was probably just as well I hadn't drunk any coffee because my heart rate had accelerated to two hundred beats per minute.

Well, not quite, but it sure felt like it.

I rounded the corner and entered the long gray-carpeted corridor leading to the president's office. Belle's desk sat directly across from Mr. Chandler's office. As usual, she was impeccably dressed in a tailored, wrinkle-and-spot-free suit. I often wondered if she stored a secret stash of suits in the bank's vault in the event she ever spilled on herself.

Belle pointed toward her boss's office, so I proceeded into the chief honcho's lair. His mahogany desk gleamed in the morning sunlight, the expansive surface marred only by a computer and a silver-framed photo. Mr. Chandler was of the school of thought that an immaculate desk reflected the embodiment of an organized mind.

I personally felt that the bigger the mess on a desk, the bigger the brain sitting behind it, but that was a minority opinion on this hallowed floor.

Mr. Chandler seemed engrossed with whatever he was viewing on his monitor. I tiptoed into the office and quietly settled myself into the well-padded chair that was far more comfortable than the single visitor chair in my own office.

I glanced at the family photo of Mr. Chandler, his wife, Dana, and their college-age son. Despite moving in different social circles, well, technically, I didn't move in any social circles, Dana and I had become friends after a ballroom dance debacle resulting in two murders. Extricating both Chandlers from an awkward as well as perilous position had earned me extra brownie points.

Mr. Chandler switched his piercing gaze from the computer screen to me. Based on his stern façade, I might need every one of those brownie points to keep my job.

Imagine my surprise when his first words were, "Nice job on your presentation."

"Thank you," I replied, attempting to appear nonchalant. "I'm glad the board was pleased with my recommendations."

His gaze shifted left—never a good sign. I uncrossed and re-crossed my legs, wondering if there was a "but" in my immediate future.

"They were," he said, "for the most part. But Adriana Menzinger's proposal also impressed them."

My hands tensed their grip on the wooden arms of my chair as I leaned forward. "May I ask what exactly Adriana is proposing?"

He fidgeted with his dark green Mont Blanc pen before replying.

"I have complete faith in you, Laurel, so I expect you to keep this information in strict confidence."

I nodded. Discretion was my middle name—usually.

"Due to the recent hacking invasions of some of the largest banking institutions in the country, the Board decided to upgrade the security of our own internal system. We feel we have no choice but to implement controls of the highest level for our bank clients."

I nodded again. I certainly had no issue with their decision.

"These upgrades will cost in the neighborhood of several million dollars. We never anticipated that expense when we approved the budget last year, therefore we need to slash costs in other areas."

"I applaud the board's proactive stance," I assured him, although at the same time wondering why he was sharing such confidential information with me.

"You might want to hold off clapping for now. One of the areas under review is our marketing staff. The board is considering outsourcing all future marketing efforts."

It didn't take the IQ of Stephen Hawking to add up Mr. Chandler's comments and figure out where this conversation was headed.

"But, but…" I stumbled as I tried to come up with an alternate plan—one that did not involve eliminating my position. I loved my job and felt that I'd finally found my true calling.

"Next month's agenda will include a decision on this topic. In the meantime, you can continue with your bank-sponsored events, the Apple Gala and the Apple Tree Bicycle Race, etc. The Board will analyze your promotions' financial impact on the bank and assess whether they've helped to increase our customer base."

His comment mollified me. For about two seconds.

"Simultaneously, Menzinger Marketing will release their own social media program aimed at bringing in new business customers to the bank. Their concentration will be directed toward potential clients located in the El Dorado Hills Business Park."

I processed the information. The El Dorado Hills area located next to the Sacramento County line was comprised of a substantial number of lucrative internet start-ups.

"I planned on making business development calls in Camino this week. Do you also want me to meet with El Dorado Hills businesses?" I asked, not certain whether I wanted an affirmative answer since I had no idea when I would find the time.

"No, stick with these projects for now." Mr. Chandler stood, which meant our brief meeting was adjourned. I muttered a goodbye and exited his office. Belle was absent from her desk, so I wouldn't be able to pry anything out of her. Not that she would let me. No one would ever accuse Belle's loose lips of sinking ships.

Or banks.

I spent the next hour working on my marketing plan. If I could engage with the owners of the largest apple farms and wineries in the Camino and Pollock Pines area, the deposits I brought in might exceed the numbers attributed to Menzinger's efforts. Given my paltry salary, it was difficult for me to believe outsourcing would be less expensive than retaining an in-house marketing department, but I wasn't in charge. Unfortunately.

By noon, my brain cells as well as my stomach felt depleted. I was thankful Liz had arranged lunch today. My British friend was the perfect person to cheer me up.

Liz and I had both attended the University of California at Davis. We met at a fraternity party when our dates decided to drink themselves into oblivion. The exchange student from Kent, England, and I bonded on the three-mile hike back to campus. We'd remained best friends for the past twenty years, through my fifteen-year marriage to Hank and subsequent divorce, to her multiple relationships over the years and recent marriage with Brian Daley, an El Dorado County Deputy District Attorney.

I grabbed my purse and strolled past the gray tweed cubicles housing the mortgage underwriters. I stopped to greet my former co-workers since there was a distinct possibility I could land back in the underwriting trenches if my marketing efforts didn't work.

Once outside the bank, a cerulean blue sky sparkled above the pastel clapboard buildings lining both sides of the street. A few months earlier, *Parade Magazine* had listed Placerville's Main Street as one of the Top Sixteen Main Streets in America.

You couldn't beat the combination of historical buildings, pine-tree covered hills, Hangtown Creek, and Davey "Doc" Wiser's stagecoach which offered free rides on holiday weekends.

I strolled past Placerville News Company, founded in 1856. At Renfros, the local bridal shop, I stopped to admire a strapless empire-waist wedding gown in the window that would fit me perfectly. I sighed, wondering why the likelihood of me finding another dead body was higher than of me getting married again.

I crossed the street and entered Cascada, one of my favorite local dining spots. I took off my sunglasses and peered around the spacious brick-walled dining room. No sign of my friend. Liz owns a plush full-service spa in El Dorado Hills, fifteen miles west of Placerville, so she could still be cruising down the highway. My phone yelped and I reached into my purse. Her text apologized, stating she'd arrive in ten minutes.

Which in "Liz Minutes" meant closer to twenty. The host offered to show me to a table, and I decided to take him up on his offer. I could use the extra time to doodle more marketing ideas. As I followed him, I looked around to see if there were other familiar faces in the room. The two occupants of a table not far from where the host seated me were a surprising combination.

Adriana Menzinger's shiny dark bob practically caressed Walter Eastwood's thick white thatch of hair as they conversed closely in soft voices. The marketing guru and the apple farm titan looked as thick as thieves. What were the two of them plotting?

A romantic rendezvous?

Or worse—the murder of my marketing position.

CHAPTER FOURTEEN

I dropped my linen napkin on the table and stood. If anything underhanded was going on between Adriana and Walter that could eventually impact my employment, I planned on discussing it with them this second. They didn't call me Forthright Laurel for nothing.

Well, no one actually referred to me as Forthright Laurel, thank goodness, but that was beside the point. I scooted past two occupied tables and nonchalantly strolled over to the couple.

Adriana glanced up and greeted me with a smirk. "Nice to see you again, Laurel. I assume everything is okay since ..." she sent a sideways glance to Walter, "your hasty departure from the board meeting yesterday."

"Everything is fine," I assured her. Rather than beat around the bush, I decided to jump over the ten-foot hedge the board had constructed between Adriana and me, turning us into competing marketers.

"Thanks for taking the time to review my presentation. I look forward to your comments and recommendations, should you have any."

She rested her hand on top of Walter's weathered palm and smiled sweetly. "There is one tiny issue that concerned both of us."

I felt my frown lines permanently embedding themselves in my forehead as I wondered what she referred to. "Nothing critical, I presume?"

Walter motioned to the empty seat across from him. Liz wasn't here yet so I decided to join them. If I needed to tweak my marketing plan, the sooner I began the better.

Walter spoke in a mellifluous basso. His voice was so mesmerizing, I wondered if he ever participated in local theater productions. Unfortunately, his lyrics were not as appealing as his tone.

"Some of the board members," Walter expounded, "feel it would be inappropriate for a suspect in a murder investigation to be involved in promotional activities associated with our bank."

"But I'm not a suspect in Axel's murder," I objected. "I merely found his body."

He peered at me over the semi-circle of his reading glasses. "Well, it's all relative, you see."

I stared at the two of them with my mouth hanging open and nary a bite of lunch in sight. Walter's theory of relativity wouldn't pass muster with Einstein, and it certainly didn't work for me.

"If every time I stumbled over a corpse…" I blurted out just as my tardy luncheon companion arrived to save me from further embarrassment.

"Adriana, I adore your new haircut," Liz cooed at the black-haired beauty.

Adriana fluffed her hair appreciatively and replied, "Liz, your stylists are the best. That's why I keep coming back."

"Your hair is so thick and beautiful," Liz simpered. "They love working with it." I mentally gagged at my friend's over-the-top compliment. She twisted slightly and winked at me.

Okay, there was a method to my friend's sucking up to her client. I could go with the flow. For now.

"Are you and Laurel working together on a marketing project? If so, you're lucky because Laurel is the best." Liz beamed at me, and I mouthed a grateful thanks back to her. "She's absolutely brilliant."

Adriana leaned back in her chair as if re-assessing my marketing skills. She whispered in Walter's ear and waited while he nodded a reply.

"We had some initial concerns about Laurel being a suspect in the Thorson murder," Adriana said, "but I'm sure we can work things out."

"You don't have to worry about that," Liz said. "What's far more likely is that Laurel will figure out who murdered Axel. Right-o, luv?"

I vigorously nodded an affirmative "Right-o" back at my pal.

Walter threw me an appraising look. "Do you think there's a serial killer out there targeting apple growers?"

Seriously? Did he think someone armed with a truckload of powdered sugar was lying in wait for an opportunity to knock off the apple orchard owners one by one?

"Walter, seriously?" Adriana asked, mirroring my own thoughts. "I'm sure Axel's murder is unrelated to our community."

"You never know," he replied, his expression somber. "There's a lot of money at stake. Something like this could put a big crimp in the tourist trade. Look what happened last year with the King Fire."

Walter made a good point. The 100,000 acre King Fire had raged more than ten miles away from Camino, but its enormous mushroom cloud of smoke had kept many tourists away until it was completely contained a month later.

"I say," asked Liz, who now occupied the fourth chair at the table, "what about the annual Apple Gala? My Sassy Saloon Gals are supposed to perform at the event, and it's normally held at Apple Tree Farm. Do you think it will be cancelled this year?"

"Walter already contacted Axel's widow," Adriana replied. "Dorie's agreed that, for this year, the Apple Gala will be held at Valley View Vineyard and Orchard."

"Poor thing," I said. "I wonder how she's doing."

"Not at all well," Liz said. "She cancelled her hair appointment yesterday. Said she wasn't up to it. I offered her a complimentary pumpkin facial, but she turned it down. Can you imagine?"

I performed an inner eye roll at her comment. My best friend believed most problems could be cured by a visit to her salon.

Liz must have heard my eyes rolling around. "We could eliminate half the wars in the world if people could find a way to alleviate their tension."

Rather than listen to a diatribe on the mental and physical benefits of a seaweed wrap, I switched the conversation back to the original topic.

"The Apple Gala is a big event," I said. "Do you need any help promoting it?"

"Adriana says she has it covered." Walter threw a wide smile at the marketer. "She told me by the time she's completed her promotion of the gala, it will be known as the 'must attend' social event of the year."

Adriana tittered at his compliment. "Menzinger Marketing aims to please. We are a full-service company, you know."

Liz and I exchanged glances. I, for one, did not know what Adriana Menzinger's full-service marketing company provided, but I had a feeling Walter Eastwood would soon find out.

CHAPTER FIFTEEN

Liz and I finally excused ourselves. After that lengthy conversation, only thirty minutes remained of my lunch break. The last thing I needed on my employee record was a black mark citing overly long lunch hours.

The table where the host had previously seated me was currently occupied, so we moved to a vacant table in the back of the restaurant, far from Adriana and Walter's curious eyes and ears.

With little time to eat and talk, I settled for the chef's daily special of a grilled salmon salad. Liz ordered the same. The server assured us she would deliver our meals in five minutes or less. We waited for her to leave before I updated Liz on the murder investigation and my personal life, which as usual, were not mutually exclusive.

By the time I explained how I'd stumbled upon Axel's corpse, why my daughter was a person of interest in a murder investigation and the reasons for my marketing career slowly imploding, Liz had finished her salad and was wiping her lips with a cloth napkin.

Since it's difficult to chat and chow down simultaneously, my plate of food remained virtually untouched. I thanked our server who returned with not only our bill, but also with a square white takeaway box for my entrée.

Liz grabbed the check. I reached into my purse for my wallet, but she swatted my hand away.

"You have enough on your plate," she said, "including your lunch. This is my treat." When I started to protest, she shushed me. "It's the least I can do for you."

It was? And why was that? What kind of escapade would Liz attempt to talk me into this time?

"I'm not donning that Saloon Gals get-up for the Apple Gala," I warned her.

She chuckled as she handed her credit card to the server. "No worries. Amy delivered her son in July, and she's already back performing with the troupe."

"Really? She's back to her pre-pregnancy weight this quickly? Shoot, it took me over…" Actually, I still hadn't lost all of the weight I'd gained from Ben's pregnancy. And at the rate I was going, Ben would be enjoying his own children before I did so.

"Amy is nursing the baby, so your costume fits her fine." Liz fiddled with her clunky gold bracelet, twisting a miniature windmill charm, a souvenir from one of her many European trips, around and around.

"Spill it please, before you rip that charm off."

"I'm that obvious?" she asked, and I nodded. "All right. I hate to mention this, but my problem ties into your current problem."

"Which one?"

She chuckled. "That would be funny except it really isn't. My problem is tied to Axel's death. He agreed to let me open a spa store on his premises."

"Really? That's awesome." I reflected on the various outbuildings comprising Apple Tree Farm. "Where were you locating your store? Aren't the current vendor stalls all occupied?"

"For now. You know the vendor who sells the weather vanes? Or, tries to sell them. They haven't been very successful. When I approached Axel with the idea of selling my natural beauty products, he was all for it."

"I think it's a great idea, but hasn't *Weather Vainery* been there for years?"

"Years and years," Liz replied. "But weather vanes aren't so popular any more. At least, not in this century."

Or any century, I privately thought. Weather vanes are lovely to look at, but who wants to climb up a roof to install one? Especially in our county where many houses are built on steep hills.

"Axel charged a monthly fee for the space," Liz explained. "But he also participated in the vendors' profits. Zero sales equals zero profit for him. He was about to replace her with a new vendor when I came up with my proposal."

"How come you didn't tell me about it?" I was somewhat hurt Liz hadn't asked for my valuable advice—such as it was.

"You're always so busy in the fall with your kids' school activities that I didn't want to bother you with it."

Her explanation somewhat mollified me, especially after I glanced at my watch to discover I was already ten minutes late. "I need to get back to the bank. Now. What's the favor you want?"

"Last Friday night, I stopped by Apple Tree Farm after everyone was gone. Axel told me to leave my merchandise in his office. He said he would take care of storing it. You know my products don't come cheap."

That I did, and I would be forever grateful that I received the girlfriend discount in order to keep my soon-to-be-middle-aged face wrinkle-free and glowing.

"I left the boxes with him, so there's about six thousand dollars' worth of Beautiful Image cosmetics stored somewhere on his premises. Axel planned on telling Vanna, the owner of Weather Vainery, to vacate by the end of the day this past Saturday. That would give me time during the week to set up my own shop. It was a perfect plan, except for..." her voice trailed off.

Except that one of the parties to her verbal contract would not be able to execute his half of the deal.

Ever.

CHAPTER SIXTEEN

I raced back to the office after promising Liz I'd try to use my Apple Tree Farm connections, which so far only consisted of my daughter and her boss, Nina, to locate her valuable merchandise.

I reflected back on my discovery of Axel, coated in powdered sugar from head to toe. It could have been worse—we'l, not for Axel, but for Liz, if the killer had chosen to cover the orchard owner in cosmetics that sold for $100 per ounce. Liz advertised that her Beautiful Image line could completely rejuvenate the user, but even these products had their limitations.

A field trip to Apple Tree Farm seemed in order for a myriad of reasons. Since I'd already planned on visiting several orchard and winery owners to discuss the bank's current promotions, I could attempt a little investigating on the side.

It felt good to have a plan. Tomorrow I would help Liz with her missing inventory, chat with Nina about her grandson's arrest, sell bank services to potential clients, and possibly solve the murder.

Plus treat myself to a caramel apple.

Now this was the way to multitask.

I arrived at the bank the next day prepared for the worst but hoping for the best. My "To Do" list ran two pages, with the first item practically screaming at me, reflecting Jenna's shrill pleas to retrieve her backpack from Detective Reynolds.

Based on my daughter's comments, we held a similar opinion of the detective, and it wasn't particularly complimentary. Rescuing Jenna's backpack from the evidence room would hopefully calm my daughter. Between school, her looming SAT exams and worrying about the fate of Tony Perez, Jenna seemed stressed enough to combust.

I dialed the Sheriff's Office and asked to speak to the detective. She answered the phone in standard cop form.

"Reynolds."

"Um, hello, it's Laurel McKay," I said, wondering if the intimidating detective would ask for further identification such as rank, serial number and murder victim.

"Yes?"

Geesh. You'd think she was being charged by the word.

"I'm calling about my daughter's backpack and oboe that she left in Tony Perez's car. Jenna desperately needs the contents for her schoolwork and band practice. I can't think of any reason why you would need to retain it."

"Perhaps that's because you're a banker and I'm a detective."

Or perhaps it's because you're a bitch.

Uh, oh, I didn't really say that aloud, did I?

"I do whatever needs to be done to solve my cases, Ms. McKay," she replied.

Time to backpedal. "Yes, I've heard you have an excellent record of clearing cases. The Thorson family is lucky to have you in charge of this investigation."

Based on her next comment, my saccharine sweet compliment had been digested and approved.

"We haven't discovered anything incriminating in your daughter's backpack," Reynolds relented.

"Of course, you didn't. Jenna had nothing to do with the murder. And I highly doubt Tony killed Axel either. He's just a kid."

"Tony Perez is eighteen years old. No longer a kid."

"Do you really have enough evidence to keep him in jail?" I asked.

"That's for the judge to decide, isn't it? I'll let you know when we're ready to release your daughter's backpack."

The sound of the dial tone indicated the detective was done for now.

I, on the other hand, was just getting started.

An hour later, my four-cylinder Prius chugged up Highway 50 toward the area known as Apple Hill. A few puffy clouds floated overhead, more decorative than functional. The rain our drought-ridden state desperately needed didn't appear to be in the immediate forecast.

My bank business development calls today would include Apple Tree Farm, Walter Eastwood's Valley View Vineyard and Orchard, and two new venues that had opened a year earlier. Their owners had moved from the Bay Area, as had many of our newer residents, to enjoy pollution-free air, beautiful scenery, reasonably priced housing, and a low crime rate—the best of small town living.

After a brief drive, I turned off the freeway onto Carson Road. My intention was to stop at Apple Tree Farm first and chat with Nina, assuming crime scene tape no longer crisscrossed its entrance.

When I arrived, I was surprised to discover the gravel driveway of the farm not only welcomed the public, but the parking lots were filled from one end to the other with cars, trucks, vans, and tour buses. Throngs of visitors are common on weekends, but this amount of activity seemed unusual for a weekday, especially in September. October was usually the busiest month for the apple farms.

Were the cars full of tourists seeking apple goodies and local crafts, or were they crime show aficionados in search of cheap thrills?

I snagged a parking place at the rear of a weed-filled lot that seemed a quarter mile from the bakery. Although my three-inch wedges made me feel taller and more confident in the office, navigating overgrown weeds while wearing my cute shoes was not a confidence booster. Next time I made the rounds of potential apple grower clients, I would wear practical shoes.

By the time I reached the bakery, the line for the order window wound around the tables and out the open door. Shoot. How would I snare Nina for a short conversation about her grandson? She was undoubtedly elbow-deep in flour, producing donuts by the dozens.

I glanced over to the arts and crafts building located across the parking lot. The seasonal vendors who operated from open-air stalls didn't seem as busy as the bakery, so I drifted past jewelry, stoneware, and framed photos featuring local lakes and the nearby Sierras. Customers chatted with sellers of Christmas ornaments, children's calico bonnets and dresses, New Age CDs, and purses.

My own battered black Coach purse, a birthday gift from my mother several years ago, exhibited substantial wear and tear, so I stopped at Glenda's Leather Goods to look for a reasonable replacement.

My personal preference is a handbag with lots of inner and outer pockets. That way I can ensure that I will *never* find my keys when I need them.

I selected a reasonably priced black leather purse engraved with an intricate scroll on both sides. I poked through the interior––a slot for my iPhone, a small zippered compartment for my lipstick and a large pocket that could hold oversized sunglasses. How clever of them.

The stocky blond storeowner, her name emblazoned in sequins across a hot pink tee shirt, walked over to help me. "Isn't that the best bag?" she said. "That inside pocket is the perfect fit for almost any sized gun. Whatcha carrying, hon? A Glock, Sig Sauer?"

My eyes opened as wide as the purse I'd been pawing through. The only weapon I carried was a mini aerosol hairspray. I could probably subdue an assailant at a distance of, oh, four feet.

"Wow. A purse that doubles as a holster," I said to Glenda. "Who knew?"

She laughed and swatted me on the back. "Aren't you a pistol?"

In my book, better to be a pistol than to carry one, so I probably didn't need any of Glenda's leather wares. Since I hadn't seen her products in previous years, I asked how her business was doing.

"We've only been open since Labor Day," she said, "but in the past three weeks I've sold a bundle of those handbags. After Axel's murder here last weekend, I'd expect sales to increase even more. A woman's got to protect herself."

"You think Axel's murder was a random attack?" I asked her.

"You never know what kind of crazies are out there. Just the other day some fruitcake complained he didn't like the newfangled donuts Axel started selling this year. Maybe the murderer is a traditionalist."

I was having a difficult time following Glenda's line of thinking and wondering if the woman hung out with a few too many fruitcakes herself.

She must have noticed the confused look on my face because she explained, "Axel decided to change up the menu and add chocolate-sprinkle and powdered sugar apple donuts this year, instead of just the usual glazed and cinnamon crumb versions the farm's been selling for the past thirty years. Some folks just don't like change. Could be someone wanted to stop him."

While I doubted an anti-powdered sugar serial killer was running amok, she was right on one count. Someone wanted to stop Axel from doing something.

And they had succeeded.

CHAPTER SEVENTEEN

I said goodbye to Glenda promising to bring my weapon next time, so we could determine the best purse to conceal my artillery. If nothing else, it would hide my chocolate stash from the prying eyes and hands of my youngest.

My morning coffee demanded a pit stop so I wandered over to the rustic restrooms. After completing my mission, I was attempting to wash my hands under a cold trickle of water when someone walked out of the adjoining stall.

"Nina, I was hoping to talk to you," I said. "The line at the bakery seemed to go on forever. I worried we wouldn't have an opportunity."

She swiped a wet hand at her gray braid, which threatened to take a bath in the sink, and reached for a paper towel before addressing me. When she turned, I was startled to see new deeply etched lines in her face.

A couple of tourists, identifiable by their turquoise sequined tee shirts that screamed *we whine for wine* plus matching sequined visors, entered the restroom. Nina motioned for me to follow her out of the building. She led me up a small incline to a grassy area with a few picnic tables scattered around. She sank onto a bench and indicated I should join her. I walked around the table and sat on the weathered wooden surface opposite her.

She blew out a breath and folded her hands together.

"Tough week," I said to her.

Nina nodded. "The worst. It was bad enough learning Axel was dead, but when they arrested Tony, it became a complete nightmare."

"I thought you might quit, but Gran said you're staying on."

"It was the least I could do for Dorie. They're releasing his..." her voice faltered, "her husband's body today so she's busy planning the service. I thought she would close the place down, but Brent, the farm manager, and Eric talked her into keeping the farm open."

"I can't believe the size of the crowd here today."

"Ghouls," Nina exclaimed, her voice and body radiating disapproval. A family of four walked past sending us curious glances.

"Hungry ghouls," I said, hoping to lighten her mood.

She sniffed. "We should charge double. At least, make money off of them."

"How's Tony faring?"

Nina slumped in her seat. "That poor boy. He's never had it easy. My daughter, Rosie, got pregnant her senior year in high school then died giving birth to Tony."

"Oh, how horrible," I responded. What a tragedy.

Tears careened down Nina's cheeks. I dug into my purse for tissues for both of us. I should buy that pistol tote bag. It had pockets big enough to store a drawer full of tissues.

Nina lifted the bottom of her apron and rubbed at her eyes. She smoothed the wrinkled cloth before continuing her sad story. "I can't even describe the anguish I went through. But life has to go on, and a new life needed my love and attention."

"Did you raise Tony?" I asked.

She nodded. "Never expected to raise a child in my," she made air quotes, "golden years."

"What about Tony's father?"

She turned a bleak gaze at the tall conifers surrounding us, lost in her memories. I waited, not wanting to interrupt her thoughts. She suddenly grabbed hold of my hands.

"Virginia said you would find Axel's killer. Someone has to because the police don't seem to care they have the wrong person in jail."

"Gran is a lot more optimistic about my sleuthing abilities than I am."

"I think she plans on helping you." That thought finally painted a smile on Nina's wan face.

"So I've been told, but I really wouldn't know where to start. The last time we spoke, you didn't have any idea who could have done this. Now that you've had time to think it over, has anyone come to mind?"

Nina propped her elbows on the table and her arthritic hands, with their oversized red knuckles, under her chin.

"I hate to point fingers at anyone, but Axel got into a huge argument with Brent, the farm manager, the middle of last week."

"Do you know what the argument was about?"

"No, But Axel's face was so red I was concerned he might have a heart attack or something. Unfortunately, I only heard part of their discussion."

"A disagreement doesn't automatically mean a motive for murder," I said.

"Maybe not," Nina replied. "But the one thing I did overhear was Axel threatening to fire Brent."

CHAPTER EIGHTEEN

We had a suspect!

Not a particularly good one since Brent hadn't been fired last week as Apple Tree Farm's manager.

Would the situation be different if Axel were still around? I decided to add Brent to the list of people I wanted to chat with today.

Nina needed to return to the bakery, but she promised to let me know if someone else popped up on her suspect radar. If anyone had an interest in finding Axel's killer, it was the bakery manager. Otherwise, her grandson could end up in prison for the rest of his life.

Newly motivated, I wondered if any of the other vendors had useful information to share. I smiled at the balding man who offered a selection of wooden toys. I lifted up a carved replica of a Model T Ford, but grimaced when I saw the price tag, which was more than I spent on groceries for the week. I put it down thinking that Ben would probably only use the well-crafted item as transportation for his Marvel characters as they departed on their latest superhero mission.

I'd come back the next time I received a raise. Assuming I still had a job deemed worthy of a salary increase. Which meant I'd better finish my detecting so I could complete my sales calls.

An empty stall stood between the toy vendor and Silken Treasures. The silk-screened apparel was also outside my budget, but that didn't keep me from salivating over the brilliant colors and patterns of the scarves and blouses.

"Can I help you?" asked a tall, willowy blond as I reluctantly put aside a multicolored scarf that brought out the color of my eyes.

"Possibly." I pointed to the vacant cubicle next to her. "Is that stall available to rent?"

"I don't think so," she said, "although now that Axel is gone..." A wistful expression crossed her face. "The previous vendor packed up her supplies late on Saturday after he gave her notice."

She abruptly began straightening a rack of scarves although they looked fine to me.

"I think I remember that vendor," I said. "Was she the one who sold the weather vanes?"

"Tried to sell. People weren't exactly standing in line to buy them. Axel offered the stall to some fancy spa owner from down the hill is what I heard." She sniffed, evidently not a fan of fancy spa owners or people from down the hill.

Wait until she got an earful of my friend's posh voice. Liz had discovered that her "Queen Elizabeth" accent went a long way toward selling overpriced cosmetics.

I leaned closer. "I bet the weather vane lady was upset. Wasn't she here for years?"

"You better believe Vanna was pissed. Last Friday I was in the ladies room shortly after she and Axel had their conversation. I overheard her tell someone she'd like to stick a weather vane up his—" She theatrically flung her arm out and not so elegantly pointed to her behind.

"Do you think Vanna was angry enough to kill Axel?"

"We all say stupid things like that every now and then, but I can't imagine her acting on her emotions." Having realized she'd probably said more than she should, she excused herself to talk to a more appealing customer. One holding a wallet in her hand.

I mulled over the information I'd gleaned in a very short visit. Despite the fact Axel was well-liked in the community, he'd managed to upset his own applecart by angering both his farm manager and one of his vendors.

Not to mention the anti-powdered-sugar nut whom Glenda mentioned earlier. Could a deranged donut aficionado have done the dastardly deed?

Or had I been reading too many culinary cozies?

The rest of my afternoon proved a complete bust. Brent was away for the afternoon so I couldn't ask him about Liz's supplies or his relationship with Axel. And evidently apple farm owners don't hang around their orchards all day counting bushels of apples, waiting for bank personnel to drop by and woo their deposits away. I left my business card with cashiers at three venues and arrived at the bank empty-handed.

Except for one pink cardboard box of donuts for the break room. A little donut love goes a long way with our staff.

My office voicemail included some good news and some better news. Detective Reynolds informed me Jenna's items had been released. I could pick them up at the Sheriff's Office.

The better news was from another detective. Tom said he could manage to get away from the task force for a few hours Thursday night. Was I available?

Was I ever! Neither kids nor killers could keep me away from my honey.

Now wasn't that a country song just waiting to get wailed?

CHAPTER NINETEEN

They say a year in a dog's life is equivalent to seven years for humans. These past four weeks away from Tom felt like six months to me.

I walked into the bank on Thursday, my lips humming "Satisfaction" while my body hummed a refrain of its own in anticipation of tonight's duet. Tom planned on driving directly to my house where we would spend several hours together, but he also wanted sufficient family bonding time with his daughter before she went to bed. I'd made my own family bonding arrangements for my children—quality time with their grandparents whether they wanted it or not. Sometimes it felt weird for my mother to be my confidante when coordinating one of my infrequent rendezvous with my boyfriend.

With a cup of lukewarm coffee in hand, I bumped into Stan halfway down the corridor leading to my office. Although his version was somewhat off-key, he seemed to be humming the same Rolling Stones tune as I was earlier. His toothy grin sparkled a good morning to me, a strange response in itself since mornings and Stan have never been compatible.

"You certainly look chipper," I said to him. His smile widened as he executed an abrupt U-turn and followed me down to my tiny office. I stowed my purse, pressed the on button for my computer and settled into my chair.

"You won't believe my news," he said.

"Try me."

"Remember on Monday I attended that luncheon for the El Dorado County Musical Association?"

"Right. Sorry I was so nervous about my presentation that evening I forgot to ask how it went. Are you going to join their board?"

He nodded so vigorously his wire-rims slid down his pointed nose.

"I'm not only going to serve as a director, but they cast me in the upcoming show."

I lifted my newly tweezed brows at him. "In the show? Like on a stage? In front of people?"

He frowned at my less than enthusiastic response. "No, in front of cats and dogs. Of course, I'll be performing in front of an audience. I'm going to be a shark."

Ah, that explained it. "They're putting on *The Little Mermaid?*"

Stan looked even more puzzled than I felt. "You need to get out more, Laurel. I'm playing one of the Sharks in *West Side Story*. Leather jackets and tight pants. *Très* butch."

As far as I was concerned, it would take more than slicked-back hair, tight jeans and a leather jacket for my friend to morph into a believable gang member, but as long as he and the director were happy then so was I.

"I'll have to practice every evening since the show starts in less than two weeks," Stan explained. "One of the chorus members dropped out so they were really in a bind. Zac, the director, said he'd spend as much time with me as necessary."

Stan stopped to fan his face with his palm. Then he blushed.

Okay, now I got it. "So what's Zac like? Is he one of those Harvey Fierstein types?"

"No, more like Colin Farrell but sexier."

"Tough gig," I said drily. Stan laughed and within seconds we were both engulfed in hysterics. It had been a long time since Stan had been attracted to anyone. Hopefully the feeling was mutual.

The manager of the underwriting department walked past my office and glanced at the two of us. Stan leapt out of his chair and left for his cubicle. While he hadn't completely embraced the Sharks' swagger, his step was buoyant. Perhaps a star would be born.

The rest of my day crawled by. Drafting flyers promoting the bank's hot mortgage products couldn't compete with my even hotter daydreams about my upcoming date with Tom. I'd worried that by spending so much time apart, Tom's feelings for me might have cooled as much as the temperatures in the Lake Tahoe basin.

But since I had enough heat coursing through my body to melt a glacier that should be sufficient for the two of us.

Jenna texted to tell me she'd be staying after school. She needed to make up for missing band practice earlier in the week. She also informed me she'd arranged a ride to her grandparents' house in El Dorado Hills so I didn't need to provide chauffeur service. Jenna ended her message with a smiley face. I wasn't certain whether her emoticon was aimed at me and my date tonight, or whether she was pleased to be participating in band practice now that she had her oboe back.

I felt blessed that my children approved of my boyfriend. For several years after our divorce, Jenna maintained hope that her father and I would eventually get back together. She finally realized that although Hank and I could remain friends and supportive parents, we were not meant to live together.

My cell rang as I was placing it back in my purse. The raucous sound of "Applause" by Lady Gaga reverberated off the walls of my tiny office.

"Hi, Gran." I reduced the volume on the phone since Gran's conversations tend to be at decibel levels more suited for an amphitheater.

"Did you figure out the killer yet?" she squawked.

I moved the phone a few inches away from my ear. "Gran, this isn't a one-hour crime show. Of course not."

"Nina said you and her talked for quite a while yesterday. You must have come up with some suspects other than her grandson by now."

"A few people seemed angry about some of Axel's business decisions, but that's not necessarily enough motive to kill someone."

"Harrumph. Looks like I'll have to take over surveillance. Give me some names and addresses, and I'll tail them. See what they're up to."

"Your red Mustang isn't the best car to use if you're going to follow someone."

Her earrings jangled against the receiver. "Good point. Maybe I should rent something that'll blend in. Like one of those big ole SUVs that are always hanging on my bumper when I drive around town."

Gran might own a sporty cherry-red, eight-cylinder convertible, but she still drove like a little old lady. And her family was grateful she did.

"Look, I have a date with Tom so I'll be tied up tonight. Please don't do anything foolish."

"Hey, I saw that *Fifty Shades of Grey* movie with my Red Hat ladies. Don't you go and do anything foolish yourself. Or, at least, nothing I wouldn't do," she cackled.

I wasn't certain what my grandmother would do should she manage to rope some old gent into her bed. And I definitely wasn't going to ask.

"Jenna is working at Apple Tree Farm on Saturday. Why don't we plan an investigatory expedition then?"

"Okay," she said, sounding somewhat mollified. "I'll expect a total update from you tomorrow, of course."

"About my investigation?"

"Nope, about your date!"

CHAPTER TWENTY

What was that famous phrase frequently quoted? Something about the best laid plans of mice, men and horny women going awry?

Tom called around four with a travel update. Naturally, I chose that moment to take a break and missed his call. His message stated that a meeting had gone longer than anticipated, but he should arrive at my house by 6:30 p.m. at the latest.

I pride myself on my ability to go with the flow, so I texted him back saying I would be waiting for him with open arms. And open chardonnay. After all, it's not the quantity of time, but the quality of said time.

My plan was to make the most of every second.

By 6:20, I was ensconced in a wing chair in the family room watching the news. I'd dressed in a long-sleeve, turquoise scoop-neck top and matching print skirt—casual yet feminine and somewhat flirty. My matching lacy lingerie was one hundred percent flirty.

I was taking my first sip of chardonnay when the doorbell rang. I placed my goblet down on the end table and hurried to answer the door, my leather-soled sandals sliding across the slick wood-planked floor of my foyer. I felt elated yet also nervous. A month apart can be hugely detrimental in a budding relationship.

I unlocked the oak door and it whooshed open, banging against the wall. We stood face to face, smiling like two lovesick teens.

The breeze ruffled Tom's chestnut-brown hair. In the past month, he'd grown a beard and added a large earring in his left ear, giving him the dashing look of a pirate. Or a rock star. His hot chocolate brown eyes remained the same—tender and loving.

Tom's gaze raked over me from my bangs to my painted toes, searing me with heat and anticipation. He threw his arms around me, lifting me almost a foot so we were practically at eye level. I clung to him, my emotions jangling like a jar full of pennies.

Tom set me down and proceeded to kiss me in such a way that if I'd been wearing any socks, he would definitely have knocked them off. He nuzzled my neck, his kisses drifting lower and lower until...

My home phone rang, startling both of us. I reared back and knocked Tom into the wall. Frustrated by the interruption, I was tempted to ignore its demanding ring, but my maternal instincts kicked in and I ran to grab it. My mother's number showed on Caller ID.

"Sorry, Mother could be calling about the kids," I said to Tom.

I picked up the receiver. "Hi, Mom. We're kind of busy here. Are the kids okay?" I asked, hoping she would get my subtle hint.

"So I gathered," Mother replied testily, "from your heavy breathing."

"Is there a problem?"

"I'm not sure. We seem to be short one grandchild."

"What?"

"Jenna still isn't here. Didn't you say she was getting a ride to our house after band practice? She should have been here by five at the latest."

My heart plummeted down to my tile floor as I looked at the rooster clock in my kitchen. It crowed out the fact that it was nearly seven p.m. "She should definitely have been there by now. Did you try her cell?"

"My call went directly to voicemail."

"Omigod. I wonder if she's been in an accident. Jenna didn't tell me who was driving her to your house."

"Maybe she and her friend stopped for a bite to eat."

"I suppose that's possible. She also might not have turned her phone back on after band practice."

"I'm sure everything is fine. Don't worry. We'll handle it. You just have—fun."

"Thanks," I said, wondering how she expected me to have "fun" and not worry about my missing daughter. Life was so much easier when my kids were still in droopy diapers. After we hung up, I called Jenna myself but also ended up in her voicemail. I left a brief but demanding message for her to call me. At once.

Tom joined me in the kitchen. He leaned against the tiled counters, a concerned look on his face. "What's wrong?" he asked.

"Jenna was supposed to go to Mother's house after school so we, um, I mean you and I could..." I paused, feeling my cheeks redden until they matched the teapot sitting on my stove. "Anyway, she texted me that someone would drive her there after band practice. But she still hasn't arrived."

I gazed at his toned six-foot-three frame then grinned ruefully. "A hug from you might help, but I'm afraid we'd get distracted."

"Family comes first," he replied. "What can I do to help?"

"I'm sure it's nothing. She's probably forgotten about the time. But..."

"But that's not like Jenna, is it?" he asked, confirming once again why my heart belonged to this man. He not only knew how I operated, but also understood my teenage daughter.

"No, it's not, which is why I'm worried. She's always so conscientious about her studies, and it bothered her that she was behind in her schoolwork because of her backpack being held at the Sheriff's Office."

I began chewing on my fingernails, a sign of my own stress. Tom reached over and clasped my palms in his large and comforting hands. "Don't destroy your nails. I have something better for you to gnaw on."

He walked out of the room, and I heard the front door open then bang shut. While I gnawed over his comment, he returned with a box of chocolate truffles in his hand.

Does this man know me, or what?

He untied the bow secured around the box, opened it and handed it over to me. I reached for a truffle and popped it into my mouth. I smiled as the rich dark chocolate tickled my taste buds. Not quite the orgasmic experience I'd been anticipating all day, but it was probably as good as it was going to get tonight.

Tom reached over and wiped a speck of chocolate from my cheek. "So what do you want to do?"

What I wanted was to rip his shirt off, but I knew that option was no longer on tonight's agenda. I sighed. "I'll call Jenna's friends. See if they know where she went. And with whom."

"I'll call the Sheriff's Office to see if any accidents or other unusual occurrences have been reported."

We grabbed our respective phones and placed our calls. My first three calls were brief and revealed nothing. On my fourth try, I finally received some useful intel. Jenna's friend, Ashley, who also participated in the marching band, noticed Jenna talking to Eric Thorson a few minutes before band practice. But she hadn't paid attention to where Jenna went once practice ended.

Tom must have noticed from my expression that I hadn't succeeded in tracking her down. He completed his own call then wrapped his arms around me. While his strength provided comfort and support, he still couldn't allay my concerns. Probably silly of me to worry about her, but I came from a long line of worrywarts.

"I'm going to call my folks and tell them I'll be late," he said. "I don't want to leave you until Jenna is located."

"You need your time with Kristy," I replied. "It wouldn't be fair for me to take you away from your daughter. Jenna will show up…" I gulped, "eventually."

We both jumped when my cell trilled "Before he Cheats" by Carrie Underwood. Tom looked startled at the song choice, but on the day I chose my family and friends' cell phone theme songs, I was particularly annoyed with my ex-husband.

"Hank, what do you want? We have a crisis here."

"Are you missing any red-headed daughters?" he asked.

"What? Yes. Do you know where Jenna is?"

"She's here at the house with Gran and me."

"What is she doing there? Why didn't she call me or Mother? She was supposed to be at their house hours ago."

"She lost her cell," he replied. "Here's Jenna now. I'll let her do the explaining."

While I waited for her to get on the line, I pointed at my phone and mouthed Jenna's name to Tom. He smiled and gave me a thumbs-up.

A subdued Jenna got on the line. "Hi, Mom."

This was not the time to yell at my daughter, so I attempted to remain calm. "Why aren't you at your grandmother's, honey? We've been going crazy looking for you."

She sighed an Oscar-worthy sigh. "I screwed up. Can we talk about it when I get home? Dad said he'll drive me there."

"Okay, I can wait until then for your explanation. But it better be a good one."

Jenna mumbled something into the phone. Seconds later, her father was back on the line.

"Can you tell me what Jenna's been doing?" I asked him.

He paused for a minute. "Let's just say she was trying to follow in her mother's footsteps."

CHAPTER TWENTY-ONE

Once Tom heard that Jenna was fine and would arrive shortly with her father, he prepared to take his leave. Tom and Hank hadn't exactly bonded. Hank had an annoying ability to appear on the rare occasions when Tom and I were together. Or it could possibly be due to Tom arresting my ex-husband four months earlier.

"Sorry about ruining our date," I apologized to Tom as we stood together in the foyer, his arms around me.

"I'm glad I could be here to support you," he replied. "And there's always next time."

"Now that you mention it, when will you be home again? Are you almost done with the task force?" I reached up and stroked his bushy beard. "Does your new Paul Bunyan look have anything to do with work? Or are you aiming for a spot on *Duck Dynasty*?"

Tom laughed, his teeth gleaming white behind his dark beard.

"Yes, I grew this facial hair so I could go undercover. Which means I don't know when we'll wrap up this case. I'm meeting Bradford in the morning to discuss the investigation with him."

"Make sure Mother isn't around when you two chat. When Bradford first discussed helping you, she looked ready to blow an entire fuse box."

"One of the reasons Bradford would be valuable to us is that he has experience, but since he's not currently on the force, he hopefully won't be recognizable." Tom rubbed his beard. "I'm hoping for that type of anonymity as well."

"Dating a cop has some serious drawbacks. I'm going to worry about you until you're back safe and sound where you belong."

"Now you can relate to how I've felt in the past when you went chasing after killers. Good thing I don't have to worry about you getting mixed up in Thorson's murder." He peered down at me. "I don't, do I?"

"Nope, there is no reason for me to be involved." Although I could guarantee my grandmother and Nina held a different opinion. But Tom had his own worrisome case to attend to. He certainly didn't need to brood over my activities.

Tom's taillights were a distant gleam when I noticed headlights approaching my house. An older black Ford F-150 roared up my driveway. Hank's ancient truck needed some muffler work. Jenna jumped out of the passenger side, grabbed her backpack and oboe, and made her way to the front door where I stood, arms folded. Hank trailed in her wake.

With her long-lashed eyes downcast, Jenna attempted to brush past me, but I was heavier and definitely angrier.

"March into the kitchen, young lady," I said. "We are going to talk."

Jenna mumbled something about visiting the bathroom first, so I gave her permission to complete that mission. Hank joined me in the foyer.

"Okay if I stick around for your inquisition?" he asked. "Jenna may need some moral support."

"Sure. Whatever." I walked away, and he followed me into the kitchen.

"Am I interrupting something?" Hank pointed to the two empty wine glasses on the counter next to the sink.

"Nope." My ex didn't need to be informed about my love life—or lack thereof. Jenna trudged into the kitchen looking like she was headed for the guillotine. She sat in one of the empty chairs, folded her arms on the table surface then rested her head on top of them.

"Jenna, do you want some water or something to eat?" My first concern was her health and safety. Then her interrogation could begin.

"No, Dad fed us."

"Us?" My eyebrows and voice both lifted.

Jenna threw her father a look, but he chose to ignore her. Instead, he opened a glass-fronted cabinet and pulled out a wine glass. He poured himself a glass of chardonnay from the open bottle sitting on the counter.

"Hey," I protested. It always annoyed me when Hank made himself at home. Just because this had been his home at one time.

"No point having it go to waste," he said. "Want some?"

I said no and turned back to my daughter. "Explain."

"Okay. I ran into Eric Thorson before band practice today. Even if he's been a jerk, I still felt bad about his dad, so I wanted to see how he was doing."

I nodded, pleased with my daughter's solicitousness.

"When I brought up the subject of Tony's arrest, Eric went off on me. He said terrible things about Tony and told me he was going to fire Nina. That it was all her fault his father was dead."

"What? That doesn't make sense."

"He was acting all crazy. Shouting and scaring me." She trembled in recollection. "I finally told him I had to go to practice and said goodbye. Eric left to meet his mother at the funeral home."

"People grieve in different ways," I explained to Jenna. "Eric most likely feels angry about his father's murder, so it's not surprising he's lashed out at Tony, especially if he assumes Tony killed Axel. I'm stunned that he wants to fire Nina though. She's worked at the farm even longer than Eric's father. It won't be easy finding someone to step in and manage the bakery."

"When I told Tony what Eric threatened, he freaked out."

"How could you talk to Tony?" I asked. "He's in jail."

Jenna slowly shook her tangled curls. "Not anymore. They released him late last night. I guess they didn't have enough evidence to keep him."

"And you know this how?"

She hung her head so low her heart-shaped chin rested on her chest. I leaned over the table and lifted her chin up until her eyes met mine.

"Tony called me this afternoon and said they let him go. Then he asked for my help."

"What kind of help?"

"To prove he's innocent."

CHAPTER TWENTY-TWO

"Jenna, what were you thinking?" I asked. "You can't get involved in a murder investigation."

"See, I told you," Hank interjected. "Following in her mother's footsteps."

Jenna and I both glared at Hank who mimed zipping his lip. Hah. We'd see how long that would last.

"Start at the beginning and don't stop until I say you're done," I ordered her.

Jenna's words rushed out as she explained how Tony had left a message for her while she was at band practice. When she called him back and shared her conversation with Eric, they agreed to meet. Tony picked her up from the high school and together they devised a plan.

Since Axel had fired Tony so abruptly the previous Saturday, Tony still retained the key to the cider house. Jenna occasionally worked the six a.m. shift so she possessed a key to the bakery. The two teenagers decided to team up and visit Apple Tree Farm after it closed. She knew Eric and Dorie would be occupied at the funeral home, so they didn't have to worry about any family members discovering them.

"Jenna, what is wrong with you?" I asked, horrified by her admission. "That's breaking and entering."

"Technically, it's not," Hank inserted into the conversation. "They both had keys."

I leveled a look at him.

"But it was still a really bad idea," he told her. "What if someone caught the two of you?"

My mind reeled from Jenna's disclosure. "So what happened? And how did you end up at your father's house tonight?"

"We arrived at Apple Tree a little before six. They'd placed a sawhorse at the entrance, I guess to keep people out at night, but we moved it just enough for Tony's car to get through. He has one of those old VW Bugs so they don't take up much space."

"Weren't you worried some of the staff might still be there?" I asked.

"We figured if anyone saw us I could explain that I left my phone in the bakery last weekend."

I nodded. Not bad, although I hoped my hitherto honest daughter wasn't acquiring a new skill set of devising white lies.

"Tony wanted to prove he didn't steal any money, and I hoped we'd find clues as to who killed Axel." Jenna's eyes locked on mine. "I thought you'd be proud of me, Mom. Plus it would provide a topic for my college essay on why I want to be a criminologist."

Oh, dear. I was such a bad role model for my children.

"Honey, I'm proud of everything you do, usually," I replied. "But not this time. This was a stupid and reckless stunt. And even if Tony is Nina's grandson, you barely know the boy."

Her full-lipped mouth set in a firm line. "Gran said I have good instincts. Said maybe she'd change the name of your detective agency from TWO GALS to THREE GALS. How come you didn't tell me you formed a detective agency?"

"We did not form a detective agency," I said through gritted teeth. I would be calling my grandmother immediately after this conversation. "So did you find anything to help clear Tony's name?"

Jenna's face brightened briefly before it clouded over again. "Yes, well, maybe. We ran across a daily log of sales volumes and dollar totals, but it didn't really tell us anything. Then I decided to go through the trash can."

"That was smart," Hank said.

I wished he would stop encouraging Jenna in her investigative pursuits.

"Smart but messy. Lots of sticky napkins coated with cider." Jenna shivered. "I hope it was cider. I didn't discover anything inside the garbage, but Tony noticed a yellow sticky note stuck to the bottom of the can."

"And?" I had to admit her story intrigued me.

My dramatically inclined daughter perked up now that two parents were riveted to her words. "The sticky was addressed to Brent, the farm manager," she explained.

"I've met him," I said. "So what did the note say?"

"It said—BRENT, MEET ME 6 AM SUN RE THEFT." Her eyes sparkled. "And it was signed AT."

Jenna seemed so excited about her discovery I hated to burst her bubble.

"What do you and Tony think that note meant?" I asked.

"Well, at first we got excited thinking Axel was accusing Brent of stealing the money from the cider house. Then we realized that theory didn't make a lot of sense. Why would Brent bother to steal a few hundred dollars? But since their meeting would have been the day after Axel fired Tony, he must have discovered something important. Maybe after Tony drove away on Saturday. We just don't know what it was."

"Did you check out the bakery, too?"

"We locked up the cider house and were ready to hit the bakery next when Tony noticed Brent's red camper truck on Carson Road about to turn down the drive. We jumped in Tony's car and took off."

I mulled over the extent of their investigating. The sticky note wasn't sufficient evidence to prove Tony wasn't stealing, nor would it clear him as a killer. But since he no longer resided in the county lockup, the District Attorney must not have a strong enough case to prosecute. Yet.

"Where's your phone?" I asked.

Jenna slumped in her chair, her long legs stretched in front of her. "I must have left it on the counter. When Tony spotted Brent's car we took off. I grabbed my backpack but forgot I'd taken my phone out in case I needed to photograph some evidence."

Jenna's penchant for crime shows had paid off. She was smart enough to realize the importance of recording proof of Tony's innocence. Unfortunately, she'd now provided Detective Reynolds with new evidence.

My maternal side warred with my disciplinary side. Should I hug my daughter or ground her for a few weeks? Or years?

Her heart was in the right place even if her head wasn't thinking clearly. "You are incredibly lucky you weren't caught," I said. "But how did you end up at Dad and Gran's house?"

"Tony's car broke down just as we entered the Placerville city limits. He coasted until he could find a safe place to pull over. We called Dad and asked him to come get us."

"Where's Tony now?"

"He's at Gran's house waiting for Nina to pick him up," Jenna said.

Knowing the way my grandmother operated, she was probably trying to talk Tony into joining her new firm—now named THREE GALS AND A GUY DETECTIVE AGENCY.

I couldn't decide how to deal with Jenna's extracurricular activities, so I told her to go to her room while her father and I discussed the situation. She left the kitchen without food and without protest. Seconds later her bedroom door slammed shut.

"What should we do?" I asked Hank.

He shrugged. "Jenna's a good kid. And she means well. You can't blame her for having a big heart and trying to help someone."

"She's lucky this didn't turn out worse. What if Tony is Axel's killer?"

"C'mon, do you really think Jenna's instincts are that far off? Tony looks like a nice enough kid."

I sighed. "Yes, he does, but isn't that what they said about Ted Bundy and Jeffrey Dahmer?"

CHAPTER TWENTY-THREE

Given Jenna's exemplary record, Hank and I decided to let her off the hook with a strict warning to leave the investigating to the authorities. Her priorities were school and the SAT. No other distractions, especially teenagers who resembled celebrity heartthrobs.

Hank left around eight, a few minutes before Mother arrived with Ben. I sent my son up to his room to don his pajamas. Jenna clomped down the stairs and joined Mother and me in the kitchen.

"Am I grounded?" Jenna asked me.

"You certainly should be, young lady," Mother chastised her. "Worrying me to death. I swear I sprouted ten new gray hairs while I waited for you."

Jenna and I stifled matching smiles. The odds of my mother and her stylist allowing one gray hair to mar her platinum coiffure were slim.

"I'm sorry. I didn't mean to upset you," Jenna apologized. Her eyes widened suddenly. "What about my phone? How do I explain leaving it in the cider house?"

"Good question," I said, stumped for a minute how to solve that problem. "I guess I could drop by Apple Tree Farm when they first open. I'll claim your phone belongs to me." I eyed my daughter. "And since I'm footing the bill, it does."

"Have I told you lately you're the best mother ever?" Jenna threw her arms around my neck nearly suffocating me in her exuberance. Considering her light disciplinary sentence, she was right.

The next morning, I woke Jenna fifteen minutes earlier than usual so she could make both kids' lunches. I might as well take advantage of my daughter's apologetic state since it wouldn't last for long. I dropped the kids off at their respective schools then drove up to Apple Tree Farm yet again.

The previous evening, I'd called Nina to explain Jenna's phone dilemma. She promised to go into the cider house and retrieve it before Brent or anyone else noticed it on the premises.

While en route, Nina left a message stating the phone was in her possession. Once I'd recovered Jenna's cell, I could visit some of the other farms on my list.

I drove down the long road leading to Apple Tree Farm. It was still early so only a few cars were parked in the visitor lot. I pulled into a compact spot, grabbed my purse and slid out of the driver's seat, slamming the door behind me. The black flats I wore crunched their way across the graveled lot. Inside the barn-like structure, the tables and chairs remained empty except for Detective Reynolds and Axel's widow, Dorie Thorson.

They both glanced in my direction as I hustled across the floor. Although I wanted to pay my respects to the widow, the last thing I needed was an early morning grilling from the detective. Reynolds evidently didn't feel the same. She beckoned me over to their table. "Ms. McKay, please join us," she commanded.

I gazed longingly at the bakery counter where Nina stood, her left hand clutching my daughter's cell, her eyes fearful. I sent her a reassuring smile and joined Dorie and the detective.

Reynolds patted the chair next to her as if she were my new BFF, wanting to catch up on our gossip. I glanced at my watch before sitting down. Reynolds noted my movement. "In a hurry?" she asked.

"I need to make some sales calls, but I can spare a couple of minutes." I switched my attention to Dorie. "I'm so sorry for your loss. How are you holding up?"

The new widow resembled a pale imitation of her normally bright-eyed, blond perky self. She blinked twice, but her eyes remained dry. I imagined she'd cried gallons of tears in the past week.

"I'm okay," she said, although her appearance belied her words. "A lot of decisions need to be made about the operation of this place, and I'm not used to making them."

"Hopefully Nina and Brent can provide some guidance for you," I said.

Detective Reynolds shifted her attention to me. "I didn't realize you and Nina were such good friends."

"Oh, um, yes." I said, wary of anything the detective asked me. I decided it couldn't hurt to elaborate. "She and my grandmother have been pals for years."

Reynolds merely nodded, but Dorie perked up and asked, "How does Jenna like working in the bakery?"

Other than the early hours, Dorie's son harassing her and Axel dropping dead last weekend, Jenna liked it just fine.

"She enjoys the customer contact."

"That's good," Dorie replied. "I was worried she wouldn't come back to work this weekend, and we're short staff. Emily gave her notice yesterday. Said she was afraid there was a serial killer out to get all the employees. And, of course, Tony's no longer employed here."

"It's such a heartbreaking situation," I said. "You must be wondering who could have done such a thing."

"I've wracked my brain trying to think of anyone who wanted Axel dead." Dorie looked at Reynolds. "I was surprised you arrested Tony. I don't know the young man very well, but it's difficult for me to imagine him murdering Axel just because he was fired."

"People don't always act rationally," said Reynolds. "Especially angry young men."

I chose to ignore the detective's comment and continue questioning Dorie until someone stopped me. "Did Axel have issues with any of the other orchard owners?"

Dorie looked down at her manicured fingernails. "Not really. More and more apple farms are opening, so it's become more competitive in recent years. Plus everyone is concerned about the drought. Axel was trying to form a consortium of orchard and vineyard owners who would work together to manage our resources more efficiently."

"You mean like sharing them?" I asked.

She shrugged. "Axel never really discussed the business with me. But he thought the farmers could save money if they worked together."

Detective Reynolds finally inserted herself into the conversation. "Did other farm owners agree with your husband's ideas?" she asked.

Dorie chewed the lipstick off her lower lip while she contemplated. "I don't think Walter of Valley View Vineyard and Orchard was interested in participating. He owns one of the largest farms in the county and figures he can do whatever he wants. Axel used to say Walter's ego was bigger than the giant pumpkins in his pumpkin patch." She blushed. "Sorry, that wasn't very nice."

I patted her hand. "Anything you say is helpful to the investigation. We have to make sure the right person is arrested for your husband's murder."

"No," Reynolds barked at me. "*I will ensure the killer is arrested.* Your job is to make sure your daughter stays away from my investigation. No more nighttime forays messing with my evidence."

"What?" I tried to maintain a poker face although I wondered how Reynolds found out about Jenna's expedition.

"A deputy saw Antonio Perez's car pull out of Apple Tree Farm last night. His VW is fairly recognizable and so is your daughter's fiery mane of hair. Do you know what they were doing here after hours?"

I thought fast. "I think Tony wanted to talk to his grandmother." It wasn't the best excuse but, hopefully, Nina would back me up if questioned.

Reynold's cell rang before she could comment. She peeked at the number, smiled then glanced at me. She stood, hit the answer button and greeted the caller with a loud, "Hi, Tom," before walking to the other end of the building.

I frowned but decided to take advantage of her absence to finish my conversation with Dorie.

"Do you plan to run the farm yourself?" I asked her.

"I don't know what to do. Eric is pushing me to let him take over the management, but my son is barely making passing grades at school right now. He doesn't need any other distractions. I'm working my way through the books, but I think Axel's CPA, Brooke Martin, will need to help me make sense of them."

"I know the property has belonged to the Thorson family since the nineteenth century, but I assume selling is an option."

"That's a possibility, although Axel would have hated for us to sell. My husband held a sixty-percent interest, and his brother owns the other forty. Do you know his brother, Paul? He has a life coaching practice in Placerville."

"Maybe Paul can manage the operation," I suggested.

Dorie laughed so hard that tears flowed down her rounded cheeks. After a while, I couldn't tell if she was crying or laughing. I ran to the counter, grabbed some napkins from the holder and handed a stack of them to her.

"I'm sorry," she apologized. "My emotions are bouncing all over the place, not to mention my hormones. The thought of Paul running this place set me off. My brother-in-law couldn't manage a lemonade stand, much less an operation of this size."

"So he's a life coach without a clue?"

She erupted into another fit of giggles. "Oh, my. What you must think of me. Let's just say that Paul is more of a," she made air quotes, "'visionary' or thinks he is. Their father used to say Paul was all vision and no common sense. Or work ethic. That's why his dad gave Axel the majority share of the farm."

American River College Library

On the other side of the room, I noticed Detective Reynolds stuff her phone in her pocket. She walked toward us, a satisfied smile on her face.

"Did Axel and Paul get along?" I asked Dorie, throwing in one last question before the detective stopped me.

"Most of the time," Dorie replied. "Paul doesn't make much from his profession so this farm provides the majority of his income. We haven't even discussed the business end yet. There have been too many other decisions to make."

Dorie abruptly stood. "And I better get busy making those decisions. It was nice seeing you, Laurel. Thanks for cheering me up."

I started to rise, but Reynolds placed a palm on my shoulder silently encouraging me to remain.

"So what did you ladies discuss?" she asked. "You *will* share anything promising that you learn, correct?"

"Of course." I sent her a wide-eyed innocent look I knew wouldn't possibly fool her. "I always do."

"That's not exactly what Tom indicated to me on the phone right now." She smiled like a cat that had just gobbled a cage full of canaries.

"Did you need his advice to help you solve this case?" I lobbed my own verbal shot back at her.

"No, quite the reverse. We're meeting to discuss how I can assist him with his task force. Once I solve this case, I can join his team. The two of us worked very well together back in San Francisco."

"How nice," I said evenly.

"I particularly enjoy doing undercover work with Tom," she purred. "It can be so rewarding."

CHAPTER TWENTY-FOUR

I maintained my cool and merely said, "Tom is such a professional. The sooner he wraps up his case, the sooner he'll be home with me and our families. Thanks for helping him out."

My response rendered Reynolds speechless, so I decided to escape while I could. When I rose from my chair, my movement finally sparked the ignition switch on her vocal cords.

"I'd like you to answer a few more questions."

The smell of hot apple cider and fresh-baked cinnamon donuts wafted toward our table making me salivate.

"If you want me to provide cogent answers then I'll need a serotonin infusion," I said.

Reynolds looked confused until I pointed to the counter where a short line of hungry customers waited. She narrowed her eyes and muttered, "Doesn't look like you've had any shortage of serotonin lately."

Grrr. "I thought police officers always include a daily supply of donuts in their diets." And if anyone needed sweetening, it was this detective.

"We're more enlightened these days. But if you must have a donut, please don't let me stop you."

After her scathing remark, I almost changed my mind except that I still needed a subtle way to retrieve Jenna's phone from Nina. I grabbed my purse and stood behind the other patient patrons. When I reached the open window, I ordered two donuts and a small cider from Nina. She discreetly slid Jenna's phone under the bag. I scooped them up and covertly stuffed the items in my large tote.

I set my cup of cider on the table, plucked one of the donuts out of my purse, placed it on a napkin and waited for Reynold's grilling.

She eyed the cinnamon-coated treat with an expression that looked more like donut envy than carbohydrate repugnance.

"Ms. McKay, I feel we may have started off on the wrong foot," Reynolds said in a tone that would have sounded apologetic if it had come from anyone else. I nibbled on my tasty pastry waiting for her to shove said foot into her full-lipped mouth again.

She said, "I realize that finding the victim makes you feel like you have a vested interest."

"I didn't know Axel well, but it was still a shock to discover him," I said. "Of course, I want his killer found and brought to justice as soon as possible. I'm also concerned that you consider my daughter to be a person of interest."

"I don't have children of my own, but if Jenna were my daughter I'd be very concerned about some of the decisions she's making."

Nothing like dissing my daughter to raise my maternal hackles. "Jenna is a straight A student. She would never get involved in something dangerous or stupid. She's never even given us cause to ground her."

Although at the rate she was going lately, that could change any day now. While I didn't agree with Jenna's recent actions, I understood her reasoning. My eldest had always held a soft spot for underdogs. I remembered one time when my seven-year-old stood up to a fifth grade bully twice her size who'd picked on a boy in her class with a facial disfigurement. I couldn't fault her then and I wouldn't fault her now.

"Jenna merely wants to ensure no innocent parties are wrongly accused. After all, you locked up Tony Perez when you didn't have sufficient evidence."

Reynolds face turned an unattractive aubergine. She looked angry enough to chew my head off.

I reached into my purse and dropped the second donut in front of her. She pulled it out of the bag and chomped half the donut in one bite.

Better the pastry than me. As a peace offering, a donut worked well.

"Our department has accumulated a significant amount of data in this case. Just because the judge chose to let Mr. Perez out of jail at this juncture does not imply he is innocent. Does your daughter know he had an assault charge leveled at him when he attended Independence High?"

I didn't know whether Jenna was aware of Tony's assault charge, but her mother certainly had not been informed. I raised an eyebrow and asked the detective to elaborate.

"We learned about the incident through our discovery work. It's the reason the school expelled him. Did you know he also has a juvie record?"

"I knew he and a friend were arrested for stealing alcohol, although he told Jenna he was unaware of his friend's intent," I said. "Were there other occurrences?" If Detective Reynolds unfurled a long list of Tony Perez's adolescent crimes, then Jenna would not only be grounded, she'd be sent to a nunnery for the remainder of her senior year.

"No, that's it." The detective sounded disappointed that Tony hadn't racked up a lengthy criminal history. Then she elaborated, "That we've uncovered. But once these adolescents get involved in a gang, anything can happen."

Gang?

Why did I have a feeling the detective wasn't referring to the Apple Dumpling Gang?

I was definitely Googling nunneries the minute I returned to the office.

105

CHAPTER TWENTY-FIVE

The detective's cell blared before I could glean more about Tony's checkered past. She crammed the remainder of the donut in her mouth while she listened to the person on the other end, mumbled a goodbye and left.

What was that all about? Well, despite all indications to the contrary, the world of crime did *not* always revolve around me. Something was going on, but it was her problem, not mine.

My gaze strayed to the bakery counter where Nina frantically attempted to bake donuts, serve customers and make change. I hoped she'd get some relief soon. Much as I wanted to discuss the detective's inference about Tony being a gang member, it looked like that item was off the agenda for now.

I glanced at my watch, blinked and took a second look. Surely, it wasn't ten a.m. already. I better kick my legs and my car in gear and get over to some of the farms on my list before everyone disappeared. Based on past experience, trying to arrange a Friday afternoon meeting could be more difficult than planning a date with Tom.

I walked to my car, now surrounded by hundreds of vehicles and slid into the driver's seat. I pulled out the official El Dorado County guide to the fifty plus farms and wineries in the area. Although I'd stopped at all of the well-established apple farms on numerous occasions over the years, a few new ones had sprouted up that I'd never visited. It couldn't hurt to pay a brief business development call.

In my world, marketing and mystery solving weren't mutually exclusive activities. They practically went hand-in-hand.

My first stop would be Valley View Vineyard and Orchard. Walter was the first owner in the area to combine an ongoing apple farm with a vineyard. Tourists from out of state often think Napa Valley is the only place to go wine tasting in California, but the wineries in El Dorado County produce award-winning wines year after year. The elevation in Camino, ranging from 2,500 to 3,500 feet altitude, is not only perfect for growing apples and pears. It's also excellent for syrah, zinfandel and a number of other varietals.

Walter had recently completed the addition of a new tasting room and an events center. They were located a short distance from the original bakery and the produce shop that had been in existence for more than twenty years. The events center would host local fundraisers, weddings and any party that someone with unlimited funds and fantasies could dream up.

I hoped the owner would be on site today. If I wanted to keep my job, getting the backing of the bank board member/orchard and winery owner was essential. As I drove up the newly paved road, I marveled at the changes Walter had initiated since I'd last stopped by. The wine business must be doing very well if he could afford so many major improvements.

I parked the car and debated which building he would most likely hang out in. It was a little early for wine sampling, but at this time of day the Mediterranean-style stucco tasting room would likely be less crowded than the bakery and produce area.

When I stepped out of the car, the sun blazed down on the asphalt and on me. I took off my linen blazer, laid it on the back seat of the car and let the rays fill me with my daily quota of Vitamin D. After a few minutes of eighty-plus degree heat, I looked forward to the cool temperatures of the tasting room.

I lucked out. Walter stood behind the long mahogany counter that covered half of the room, chatting with a couple of tourists holding wine glasses in their hands. As I debated my best approach, an employee placed a logo-etched glass in front of me and filled it with some kind of white wine.

I picked it up and unthinkingly sipped from the goblet before I remembered I was on official bank duty. Well, one sip couldn't hurt. Plus it would be rude not to sample their product when the owner stood a few feet away from me.

Since Walter was occupied with customers, I wandered around the room, noticing how carefully they'd arranged their retail merchandise. I lifted a crystal goblet, one of a set of four, and examined the base of the glass for the price. Ouch! No wonder this farm was so successful. I could have sworn T.J. Maxx carried a similar set for ninety percent less. Although this glassware was probably of much higher quality.

Probably.

The couple Walter had been conversing with finally left the tasting room, leaving him, an employee and me.

"Mr. Eastwood, you've made some amazing improvements to the property," I said cheerfully.

He blinked before finally recognizing me. "Oh, yes, Ms. McKay from the bank." He looked down at my glass. "You're out wine tasting by yourself?"

"Oh, no, of course not. I'm working today." I practically threw my glass at him, spilling the remainder of the contents all over the counter. The last thing I needed was for Walter to tell the bank president his marketing director was a lush.

I grabbed a few paper napkins and attempted to clean up my mess while I chatted with him. "So many people have commented on your wonderful wines that I wanted to sample one while I waited. Do you have a few minutes to discuss the Apple Gala with me?"

Walter hesitated then nodded. "Sure. C'mon down to my office." He walked around the counter then motioned for me to follow him. A short hallway off the tasting room led to two closed cherry wood paneled doors. He opened the door at the end. I followed him into a small but comfortable office. A large window overlooked acres of vines bursting with plump purple and pale green grapes.

Walter's desk resembled mine, except his piles were taller and covered every inch of the wood surface. The stack of files and brochures teetered precariously. I worried that if I breathed heavily, the files would tumble down. I could literally be buried under paperwork.

Walter addressed the situation by grabbing all three stacks and creatively rearranging them on the carpeted floor. He chuckled at my expression.

"Don't worry. I know exactly what's in every pile."

I smiled in response. "We all have our own methods of organization."

"Yep. So what kind of help do you need with this big shindig we're putting on?"

Good question. Now I needed an equally good answer.

"You know, of course, that the Thorson family originated the event twenty-five years ago."

He nodded. Of course, he would know that.

"Since this year represents the gala's silver anniversary, Hangtown Bank decided to co-sponsor the event and pay tribute to Axel and his family."

"Be a bit difficult to do that now," Walter said wryly.

I couldn't tell if he was being sarcastic or merely realistic so I barreled on.

"Everyone appreciates you stepping in and holding the gala here. I would still love to acknowledge Axel and the Thorson family at the event, in some way. If that's okay with you."

Walter tipped his chair so far back it collided with the bookshelves behind him, sending a pile of stuff crashing to the floor.

He shook his head at the mess. "It may be time to hire a secretary." He peered at me. "Are you looking for a new job?"

Nope. At least, I hoped not. And even if I was, it would not be as his file clerk.

"However you decide to pay homage to Axel is fine with me," Walter said in answer to my earlier question. "His wife must be going crazy trying to keep the place going. Axel kept his operation pretty close to his vest."

"I spoke with Dorie earlier today. She's got her hands full managing it. Plus some of her staff quit. Worried about their own safety."

"You can't blame them if they're concerned about a killer being on the loose. I heard the Sheriff arrested someone but then let him go."

"I doubt that young man murdered Axel." I secretly thanked Walter for providing me with the opening I'd been seeking. "You've known Axel for a long time. Can you imagine anyone who would have done something so horrible?"

Walter started to lean back again then thought better of it.

"Not really. Axel is, I mean, was a great guy. Hard worker. Honest to a fault. Difficult to believe anyone would up and kill him. I don't know if this has any bearing on what happened, but Axel struggled after last year's season got off to such a slow start due to the King fire. He wondered whether to diversify like I did. Since his income came solely from Apple Tree's fruit crops and the fall tourist trade, his revenues were way down. Plus he'd built a new house for him and Dorie that cost a bundle. I'm pleased I decided to expand into the wine business so we can stay open year round."

"Apple Tree Farm has been in business for forty years. The Thorson family must have encountered rough times before."

Walter shrugged. "There's always stuff that needs to be repaired, improved, modernized. People buy property up here thinking they're going to be gentlemen farmers, sitting on their front porch watching the dollars roll in. Then they're surprised by how much work there is. Axel confided his new house cost more than he anticipated because Dorie kept coming up with bigger ideas. I told him to talk to Hangtown Bank about getting a loan, but I don't know if he contacted them or not."

I didn't know either, but I could definitely find out. The one thing I knew for certain was that financial troubles occasionally lead to other troubles.

Like murder.

CHAPTER TWENTY-SIX

While my conversation with Walter offered insight into the Thorson family's financial situation, he provided zero assistance on the upcoming gala. As far as Walter was concerned, all we gals, referring to Adriana and myself, had to do was make him and Valley View look good. And raise money for the beneficiary of the fundraiser.

A piece of cake. Okay, not really, but a piece of cake did sound appealing. It was a crime to visit the quaint apple orchards and bakeries and not stop to sample some of their delicacies, but I'd already exceeded my carbohydrate quota with that delicious donut this morning.

I met with three more farm owners, all of whom seemed interested in my presentation. On my way back to the office, I stopped for a drive-through chicken salad, dressing on the side, and an iced tea.

Back at the bank, I chomped on my salad while retrieving the numerous messages on my office phone. The loan department wanted my help marketing a new mortgage product, the savings department needed an ad for a new high-yield CD, and the manager of a new Amador County branch requested a flyer promoting their grand opening.

And the board thought my job could be outsourced to an outside firm? Not hardly. Speaking of that outside firm, my final voicemail was from Adriana Menzinger requesting a meeting this evening. She evidently did not have two children awaiting her arrival at home on a Friday night.

As I debated which call to return first, my cell blared "Rule Britannia." I grabbed my phone and greeted Liz.

"Did Adriana call you?" Liz asked. "She wants to get together with us tonight."

"She left a message about a meeting. What's this about?"

"Adriana wants to discuss the gala. She said even though Walter Eastwood agreed to move the party to his venue, nothing has been done yet. She knows I'm in charge of the entertainment, and you're handling the event for the bank, so she thought we should brainstorm tonight. At Sienna."

I loved Sienna Restaurant in El Dorado Hills, but dinner there didn't fit into my dining budget. Her next words clinched the deal.

"Adriana's treating."

Five hours later, Adriana, Liz and I sat in a comfortable corner booth in the elegant Tuscan-themed restaurant. My daughter was still trying to work back into my good graces, so I'd co-opted her to babysit her brother. She acquiesced without a squawk. Despite this being a business meeting, I intended to enjoy the food, ambiance and company.

Technically, Adriana and I were competing against one another, she for the bank's business, and me, for my job and financial welfare, but that didn't mean we couldn't engage in a cordial working atmosphere.

We concentrated on the first order of business, choosing our wine and placing our dinner orders. I leaned back into the cushions, which were comfy enough to enjoy a nap, something I sorely needed after my early Apple Hill foray, followed by punching out enough flyers to bring in droves of new customers to every department of the bank. My left sandal slipped off my foot. I wiggled my toes and decided to free my right foot as well.

I smiled with pleasure, which Liz immediately noticed.

"You look quite content, luv," she said. "Have you solved Axel's murder already?"

A startled expression crossed Adriana's face. "You're seriously looking for his killer? Are you nuts?"

Well, that was one way of looking at it. How lovely of her to share her opinion with me.

"Laurel excels in solving crimes," Liz defended me. "She's the Jessica Fletcher of Placerville."

I smiled modestly although I would have preferred Liz comparing me to someone a few decades closer to my age, such as my current favorite TV detective, Jane Rizzoli, of *Rizzoli and Isles*.

Adriana narrowed her dark, heavily-lined eyes at me. "It must be difficult to keep up with your marketing responsibilities if you're always off chasing murderers."

I stiffened my spine but kept my tone polite. "I'm excellent at multitasking. Just call me a Renaissance woman."

She smirked as she eyed my curves. "I can see that. Michelangelo would have loved your—look."

The server chose that moment to deliver the bottle of wine we'd ordered. Good thing he didn't bring it sooner because I might have dumped my glass on the marketing maven.

A complete waste of chardonnay.

Liz interceded before we could come to verbal blows. "Shall we divvy up the responsibilities for this apple bash? Since I'm already arranging for the Sassy Saloon Gals to perform, I'll find out if anyone hired a band."

"Excellent," Adriana said. "After my lunch meeting with Walter, I put together a plan utilizing social media and my other media connections. I placed an ad in the local papers and dropped flyers all over town. Since the marketing is taken care of that just leaves food and drink."

She snickered. "That should be right up your alley, Laurel."

My glass of wine maneuvered itself mere inches from Adriana's white eyelet top. Liz jabbed her elbow in my ribs. I scowled at her but decided to sip my wine rather than waste any of it on Adriana's apparel.

"Who did they hire to cater the event?" I asked.

"Serenity Thorson," Adriana replied. "Axel's sister-in-law."

"Does she own a catering company?" I asked, unfamiliar with her name.

"She opened her bakery, Serenity Sweets, on Main Street a couple of months ago. It specializes in gluten-free and vegan items. Next to the Lifestyle Center they own. They teach yoga, tai chi, healthy living, etc."

"Doesn't Paul Thorson also do life coaching?" I asked. "I've always wondered what exactly life coaches do."

"Maybe you should make an appointment with him. You never know when you might need some advice on your lifestyle, or," Adriana paused briefly, "potential career changes."

Despite Adriana's insinuation, I was pleased with her remark. For the first time tonight, she'd provided me with some worthwhile advice. I might not need any life coaching myself yet, but Paul Thorson could easily shed some light on his brother's murder.

And possibly throw in a gluten-free cookie or two.

CHAPTER TWENTY-SEVEN

Saturday morning, I drove Jenna to Apple Tree Farm. Her shift ran from nine until five, a more reasonable timeframe than the previous week. Dorie sent a grateful smile in our direction when Jenna walked in. At first, it surprised me to see the widow behind the bakery counter until I realized she needed to augment her depleted labor pool. And keeping busy probably helped.

My second stop would be to drop off Ben at my grandmother's house. Ben and Hank planned on a day of fishing, an excellent father/son bonding experience. I wouldn't mind a relaxing day sitting on a shady riverbank, catching up with one of my favorite mystery authors, but I'd promised my grandmother we would investigate today, and I doubted she would let me forget it.

I parked on the street in front of Gran's house. It looked like she was entertaining three generations since Mother's white SUV was parked in the driveway, pristine as usual. Sometimes I wondered if my mother purchased a "buy one hundred car washes, get one free" coupon from the local Suds & Shine.

My hip brushed against the Prius, which after traveling up and down graveled roads this week, looked less like periwinkle and more like gray. I wiped a smudge of dirt off my black jeans while I waited for Ben to collect his fishing paraphernalia: a miniature version of Nemo he intended to use for bait and his lucky Forty Niner baseball cap. As we walked up the sidewalk, I noticed Hank had repaired some of the cracks previously eroding the front walkway. I could fault my ex for many things, but he certainly knew his way around a tool chest.

I banged the shiny brass knocker on the newly painted red front door. When no one answered, I pushed on the door and it opened with nary a squeak. Voices echoed from the kitchen. Ben darted in while I dawdled behind. I'd spent many weekends at Gran's house when I was a child, while my mother, a new widow, put in long hours attempting to make a success of her new career in real estate. Every corner of the stately Victorian contained poignant memories of a young girl's dreams.

The aroma of fresh coffee put a spring in my step as I entered Gran's homey kitchen with its flower-sprigged blue wallpaper and kitschy décor. Three adults were comfortably seated in captain's chairs around Gran's maple table. Ben hovered over his father, ready to set off on their expedition.

The grown-ups greeted me with smiles, all of which faded when they discovered I'd arrived empty-handed.

"Where's our goodies?" Gran complained. Her penciled brows displayed her displeasure.

"Did you leave the box in the car?" Hank asked. "I don't mind getting it."

"No one gave me a donut order, and I decided I've eaten enough apple-filled dough for the week." For the year, for that matter.

Gran peered over her trifocals and shot me a dirty look.

"I need to talk to Serenity Thorson, the caterer for the Apple Gala," I said. "She owns that new bakery on Main Street that specializes in gluten-free options. We could try out some of her stuff. It would be healthier for us."

"I've made it to eighty-eight with a healthy dose of gluten every day," Gran grumbled. "I don't need to change my diet now."

"I read about their new venture," Mother said, "but I haven't had an opportunity to check it out. I'm curious to see if they can make a success of it in Placerville."

"I was surprised the bakery is doing the catering. Usually Bob's BBQ handles that event," I said. "Although Serenity is married to Axel's brother and Apple Tree Farm was originally hosting the event."

"Tragic thing, Axel's murder," Hank chimed in. "He dumped a pile of money into that warehouse expansion he did last year."

"You bid on it, didn't you?" I asked him.

He nodded. "Yeah, but Dundee Construction got the bid. Axel's business must be booming if he could afford to do all that upgrading plus build that new mansion of his."

"According to Walter Eastwood, Axel struggled to stay profitable this year."

"Maybe he planned on expanding into winemaking or something besides the apple business," Hank said. "That warehouse is big enough, plus I think he added a climate-controlled room."

"That warehouse is huge..." My voice trailed off when I remembered my last visit to the enormous building. "I can't believe it's been less than a week since I stumbled over the poor man."

"I'm worried about Jenna working there," Hank said. "Do you think it's safe for her?"

I exhaled before answering because I'd also considered his question. "I'm not crazy about her situation, but with several thousand people coming and going, she should be fine. I told her she can't work any early or late shifts though."

"I hope you also informed her to stop playing Nancy Drew," Mother said.

"Yeah, one meddler in this family is enough," Hank said.

Three generations of icy blue eyes stared at him.

"For your information, Hank, me and Laurel started our own detective agency. And my sharp-eyed great-granddaughter might come on board, too."

This time a duet of "What?" from Mother and Hank blasted my eardrums.

"We got a case," said Gran with a smug smile on her face. "With a retainer and everything."

Really? Our client was *paying us* to meddle?

"Ma, don't be ridiculous," my own mother protested. "You can't open up a detective agency at your age." She sent me the look that used to terrify me when I was a teenager. And still did. "Laurel, stop encouraging your grandmother with this hare-brained idea."

"We'll just see about that," Gran fired back. "I expect you'll be eating your words when we find the killer."

Mother rolled her eyes but restrained herself from further comment.

"Where's Grandpa?" Ben asked. "He's supposed to go fishing with us."

Mother stiffened. "He also decided to play detective for a few days."

"Hah. No wonder you're in such a pissy mood," Gran squawked. "Your hubby's deserted you."

"I am not in a p-bad mood," Mother replied. "But I don't understand why Robert let himself get dragged into this undercover operation." She pointed an agitated index finger at me. "It's your boyfriend's fault. Encouraging my husband to partner with him again."

"I had nothing to do with that decision. I've barely spoken to Tom lately." Or kissed him. Or indulged in any shade of romance.

"I don't understand why Robert can't enjoy his retirement like the other seniors in our community. I told him to join Serrano County Club and take up golf. But he claims that whacking a tiny white ball isn't nearly as much fun as searching for a killer. Men!"

Gran wrinkled her forehead. "Do you think they could use my help on this task force? Maybe as a decoy or something?"

Four voices shouted out, "No." Even Ben recognized Gran's suggestion was a bad idea.

"You might get hurt, Granny G," he said, his face solemn. "That would make me sad."

She leaned over and plopped a soft kiss on his freckled cheek.

Hank pushed his chair back and stood. "Time for us guys to get on the road. Barbara, I hope you can keep these two out of trouble today."

Trouble? Us?

All we had on today's agenda was visiting a bakery that specialized in healthy foods. We couldn't possibly get into trouble.

CHAPTER TWENTY-EIGHT

Mother insisted on driving us into town, which was fine with me. I spent enough hours playing chauffeur. Plus the seats of her SUV were cushier than mine. Serenity Sweets was located in a historic brick building near the eastern end of Main Street. The rear of the building abutted Hangtown Creek, which in the fourth year of the California drought held barely a tablespoon of water.

We parked in a small public lot a block away from the restaurant. Pedestrians clogged the sidewalk, a common sight on Saturday. Placerville offered excellent antique stores, vintage clothing shops, wonderful dining, and historic "must see" tourist attractions including Placerville Hardware, the oldest hardware store west of the Mississippi.

We strolled down the sidewalk toward a royal blue awning with Serenity Sweets scrolled across it in an elaborate gold font. I pulled open the glass-paned door and motioned for Mother and Gran to precede me.

The scent of coffee mixed with other aromas, fruity as well as chocolate, permeated the small store. The glass cases were partially filled, or partially empty, depending on your perspective. Late stragglers like us would have to make do.

A petite young woman with a modified pixie haircut—short in the back with a sweep of long burgundy bangs covering one eye, walked out from the back. She wiped her hands on a blue apron that matched the awning out front and asked if she could assist us.

"Yep." Gran pointed at the display cases. "Whatcha got for normal folks to eat?"

I doubted the adjective *normal* had ever been used to describe my grandmother, but I interpreted her request for the clerk.

"What my grandmother means is do you have anything that's not gluten free?"

Gran nodded, her platinum Marilyn Monroe wig wobbling in unison. "Yep, we want something sinfully sweet."

"I would like to try some of your healthier options," Mother said. "Can you tell us more?"

Despite an explanation that involved a considerable amount of gum chomping, the helper's descriptions were specific enough to suit the two women. And me. But I was an easy mark.

We each ordered something different. I chose a coconut vegan scone, and Gran and Mother decided to be adventurous and try some gluten-free options. They sat at a white wrought iron table with four matching chairs while I paid for our order.

As the teen counted out my change, I inquired if Serenity was around. She nodded, closed the register and went into the back. A minute later, a woman in her late twenties or early thirties joined me. Her raven black hair was styled similar to her assistant, although her bangs formed a short thick fringe across her smooth forehead, highlighting sculpted cheekbones and a pair of curious jade green eyes.

"Laurel McKay," I said, reaching over to shake her hand. "I'm on the Apple Gala committee. I understand you're catering it."

"Oh, right. Adriana mentioned your name to me. We have everything under control so you don't need to worry. Would you care to see our menu for that night?"

"Yes, thanks." I didn't want to mention that I'd fretted about her trying to force feed a BBQ-loving rural community into dining from a vegan buffet. She motioned for me to join my family while she printed a copy of the menu.

The coconut scone was delicious enough for me to consider going vegan. Their coffee tasted rich and smooth, some type of Fair Trade beans they blended themselves. I had to admire the couple for taking the initiative to open a restaurant that promoted good health as well as fair wages.

Serenity joined us at our table. She handed me a copy of the menu and stood there waiting while I perused it. The menu featured a variety of dishes, some vegetarian, some not, but overall something for everyone. I breathed a sigh of relief and passed it back to her.

"Does it meet with your approval?" she asked, her eyes twinkling and her lips curved in a half-smile.

"Completely. Your food will be the hit of the party. It looks so good you may be stuck catering this affair for years to come."

She laughed. "That is very sweet of you to say. Our restaurant and catering business are brand new to this community, so I certainly hope we're successful. We were anxious to prove to Axel we could handle an event of this size."

"I'm so sorry for your loss," I said. Mother and Gran joined the condolence chorus and invited her to sit with us.

"It's been tough on Paul." Serenity slid into a chair. "He's six years younger than Axel and idolized him growing up. We've only been married a few months, so I didn't get to know Axel very well. Or Dorie yet, either," she added. "They were busy with the orchard operation plus building their new house. And Paul and I have been working nonstop to get the Lifestyle Center up and running."

"I'm sure Axel and Dorie were helpful in supporting your new endeavor," Mother commented.

A flash of anger briefly marred Serenity's classic features. "Families can be complicated. They don't always see eye to eye on things."

Gran snorted. "Hah. You got that right."

Mother glowered at Gran before continuing. "Such a difficult time for you and your husband."

Serenity nodded, her fingers pulling apart the paper napkin in her lap. "We're just trying to hold it together."

"Your brother-in-law was so well respected in this town," I said, hoping to prompt some inside information from Serenity. "It's hard to believe someone would murder him in such a bizarre fashion."

"I've always said *sugar can kill,* but I certainly didn't imagine that scenario." Serenity stared at me. "Wait a minute. You're the one who found Axel, aren't you?"

I nodded. "It was awful."

"Did you notice anything unusual while you were there?" Serenity asked, her eyes wide and curious.

"Like what?"

"Oh, just wondering if the killer left any clues. Maybe it was some type of cult killing or something."

"Nothing other than poor Axel buried under several inches of powdered sugar. I wish I'd been more observant at the time because the detectives don't seem to be getting very far with this case."

"That's why we're on the trail of the killer." Gran zeroed in on the bakery display cases. "We might need more replenishment, though, before we set out on our investigation."

Serenity's eyes grew so large they resembled giant green marbles. "You're trying to track down the murderer? By yourself?"

"Laurel here is gonna help, and so is my granddaughter. She's working undercover inside the Apple Tree bakery looking for clues."

"Jenna is not part of this agency," I said to Gran before turning to Serenity. "I mean, there is no agency."

"I certainly won't feel comfortable until the murderer is found," Serenity exclaimed. "Paul is worried someone might have an axe to grind against all the family members."

"Any particular reason why he feels that way?" I asked.

She took another napkin from the container and began shredding it. I hoped they got a discount on their paper products. My favorite stress buster is mangling paperclips, but I try to economize by reusing the same one.

"Paul thought Axel might have gotten involved in something he shouldn't have."

I leaned closer ready for the scoop, but the door opened and several couples entered the store. Serenity stood and said, "I'd better go help my assistant."

"What about Axel? What did he get involved in?" I asked, not ready to let her off the hook she'd just dangled in front of me.

"Does it really matter now that he's gone?" She shrugged and disappeared behind the counter.

Heck, yes!

CHAPTER TWENTY-NINE

The three of us finished our morning snack then stood on the sidewalk discussing how to spend the rest of the day. Gran wanted to don her deerstalker hat and track down suspects.

There was only one problem with that suggestion—we didn't really have any.

"What do you mean we don't have no suspects?" Gran thrust her fists on her skinny jeans-clad hips.

"What we have is a lot of 'what about' and 'what if' scenarios, all based on secondhand gossip," I said.

"That's good enough for me," she replied. Gran began ticking off names on one liver-spotted digit after another. "There's Paul Thorson. He and Serenity started this new business that probably required a bunch of money up front. Didn't Dorie say the brothers owned Apple Tree Farm together? Who gets Axel's share now that he's gone? Dorie or Paul?"

"Good point," My mother seemed surprised by Gran's analysis. "That should be the first item we research. What about the widow? Any reason Dorie would kill her husband? The spouse is always a suspect."

"She is such a nice woman." I sighed. "I can't imagine her killing Axel."

"Wives can be driven to murder and usually for a good reason," she muttered to herself.

I chuckled at Mother's comment, obviously directed at her husband's new undertaking.

"Okay, we need to check out Dorie's alibi," I said. "Anyone have any idea how we do that?"

"Will Detective Reynolds share information with you?" Mother asked me.

I snorted. It was unlikely Ali Reynolds wanted to share anything with me other than possibly my boyfriend. But that would be over MY dead body. "I doubt if she'll tell me anything. Tom mentioned that Axel was killed around midnight, so Dorie could easily have snuck out of the house without Eric hearing her."

"Or, vice versa." Mother and I both grimaced at the horrible thought that Eric could have killed his father.

"Okay, that's three," said my efficient elderly partner. "Who else we got?"

"I need to talk to Brent, the farm manager," I said. "Nina mentioned that he and Axel argued a few days before the murder. Plus there was that mysterious sticky note Jenna and Tony found in the cider house. Maybe Axel caught Brent embezzling money."

"He sounds like a possible suspect. But is that it?" Mother sounded disappointed by the brevity of our "persons of interest."

Gran pointed in the direction of the one-hundred-year-old, stately white courthouse. "What about her?"

Mother and I wheeled around to search the sidewalk. I shaded my eyes and squinted. I finally recognized Gran's target far ahead of us.

"It's Vanna, from Weather Vainery. Great catch, eagle eyes," I said to my grandmother. "She needs to be on our list."

"Hurry up and catch her." Gran motioned at me. "Your mom and I will be right behind you."

I started to protest then realized she was right. Plus I had a coconut scone to burn off. I could have doubled as a Forty Niner halfback as I zipped down the sidewalk, evading tourists to the right and left, trying not to lose sight of the stocky woman hauling a shiny green object that was almost as big as she was.

As I drew nearer, I slowed to catch my breath. One of these days, I needed to get back to Zumba class. Best exercise ever for building up stamina and burning off calories.

And lately I was low on stamina and high on calories.

Vanna stopped for a minute and rested the heavy item against the window of an antiques store. By the time she lifted it up again, I'd reached her side.

"Can I help you with that?" I offered.

She set what looked like a unicorn-shaped weather vane back down and frowned. "Do I know you?" she asked.

"We've met at Apple Tree Farm in the past. I've always admired your craftsmanship." Which was true. I just couldn't see paying hundreds of dollars for something no one could see except the occasional hawk flying over my roof trolling for dinner.

At my mention of the farm, her face darkened. "That place. I'm not surprised someone tried to sweeten Axel up. Ungrateful man." She grabbed on to her weathervane and shuffled down the sidewalk. I wasn't letting her go, not with that kind of lead-in to my inquiries.

"You don't sound surprised about Axel's murder," I said. Elated was more like it.

She halted, practically stabbing a passerby with the unicorn's horn. "The man kicked me out of my stall last week. For no reason at all. Shoot, I've operated my business in that same spot for longer than he ran the farm. No good son of a..." I cut her off before she could elaborate any further.

"Do you have any idea who would want Axel dead?" Besides you, I felt like adding.

She scrunched her snout-like nose. "Who did you say you were again? Are you a detective?"

"Yep, we're detecting this here case," said a raspy voice behind me. The rest of the agency had arrived.

"Oh, hi, Virginia," Vanna said to Gran. "How did you get involved in Axel's murder?"

"Nina Perez, his bakery manager, hired us to prove her grandson didn't kill Axel."

Vanna looked confused for a few seconds before she burst into laughter.

"Ha, ha, you made my day," Vanna said, wiping her eyes. "What's the name of your agency? Senior Snoopers?"

Gran looked miffed but merely replied, "Why don't you make *our* day and give us some clues." She looked Vanna up and down. "Did you do him in?"

Vanna stared at her. "You're kidding, right?"

"Yes, she is," I quickly reassured her. "Always making with a joke. Right, Gran." I nudged my grandmother so hard she fell against my mother.

"What she meant to say," Mother gently intervened, "is that being the perspicacious person you are, perhaps you've pondered over some potential suspects."

I wasn't perspicacious enough to follow Mother's alliterative query, but Vanna stopped glowering at us.

"You know, I have thought about it," Vanna admitted. "Axel wasn't all bad. But he seemed real stressed lately. Always looking for ways to make more money. Axel said I wasn't bringing in enough to suit him."

"But you're so talented," gushed Mother, proving why she excelled as the number one real estate agent in her office. She could suck up with the best of them.

Vanna smiled so wide she displayed enough gold fillings to make a bracelet. "Thank you. I pride myself on my expertise, although I fear weather vanes aren't quite the hot commodity they used to be."

Such as back in the Revolutionary War?

"Okay, let's get back on track here," Gran interrupted. "So, Vanna, you got any suspects for us or not?"

Vanna shot Gran a frustrated look. "I don't know if this will help, but I complained to my loan processor about losing my concession at Apple Tree, worried about its impact on me refinancing my home loan. She mentioned that Axel had applied for a loan himself. A big one."

"At Hangtown Bank?" I asked, surprised I hadn't heard anything from Stan, my spy in the loan department.

"No, I'm getting my mortgage with Sierra Mountain Lenders, over on Placerville Drive. My loan officer is Amy Dunnett, in case you want to talk to her."

"That is extremely helpful of you," Mother said. "And if your refinance doesn't work out, I'd be delighted to list your property for you."

Ka-ching! Mother was never one to let a potential client slip through her elegant fingers.

"Um, sure," Vanna replied. "Glad I could help. Okay, gotta run now." She patted the shiny brass tip of the unicorn's horn. "This big fella is going to his new home at Golden Star Gallery. Where the owners appreciate my artistry."

We said goodbye and good luck then headed for the parking lot.

"I wonder how big of a loan Axel applied for and if he got it," I mused. "He must have struggled to keep the business going."

"It certainly sounds like he was experiencing money issues," Mother agreed.

"It's not that complicated," Gran scoffed. "What goes out needs to be less than what's coming in. Plain and simple." Spoken like the bookkeeper she used to be.

"Too bad he didn't have you on his team," I said to Gran. "You might have saved him from his financial issues."

She nodded. "Yep, but it's never too late to have TWO GALS DETECTIVE AGENCY on your side. In fact, I just came up with a slogan for us."

"Slogan?" Mother and I simultaneously cringed.

"Don't waste your dime. Have us solve your crime."

CHAPTER THIRTY

We drove back to Gran's house energized by the prospect of multiple missions. Mother would attempt to learn more about Axel's financial state. With an Outlook contact list that could rival the Kardashian family's network, she should be able to discover more about his current state of affairs prior to his demise.

Gran used to play bridge with Axel's mother but hadn't seen her in ages. She would pay a condolence call on Carolyn Thorson and chat her up. Gran felt bad she hadn't kept in touch so she could kill two birds with one visit. Carolyn might have personal insight into Axel and Dorie's marital life and some knowledge of what was going on behind the scenes at Apple Tree Farm.

Since I planned to pick up Jenna from her afternoon shift, I was assigned the task of speaking with Brent, the farm manager. I also wanted to locate the cosmetics Liz had left with Axel. My friend would be devastated if someone accidentally tossed out thousands of dollars of her products.

The minute Mother parked the car on Gran's driveway, we jumped out, three generations of women who all needed to pee.

What a family legacy.

Mother's cell rang, and she waved us ahead while she answered it. Her initial perky greeting quickly reversed into a series of abrupt staccato responses. It didn't take a detective to detect trouble brewing on the home front.

Gran and I went in separate directions. Once we took care of business we met up in the kitchen. Mother joined us a few minutes later. Based on her demeanor, her call had not ended in a satisfactory manner.

"What's wrong?" I asked.

"My husband," she emphasized his spousal status, "called to inform me he is packing a suitcase and driving up to Reno to assist your boyfriend."

"Is that all?"

"All?" she screeched. "Do you have any idea how risky this operation is? Robert is going undercover."

Gran sat down at the kitchen table and scratched her knobby chin. "That's like hiding an elephant in a parrot cage."

I stifled a chuckle at Gran's analogy, but she was right. My six-foot-five stepfather didn't blend in anywhere except maybe a Big and Tall store. "I'm sure Tom won't use Robert in any capacity that would be too dangerous," I said, attempting to soothe my mother. "You can't blame your husband for wanting to help. He spent his entire life as a public servant, trying to make this community a better place."

"As do I when I try to find the perfect house for someone."

"I'm sure all your clients are appreciative of your real estate acumen. Just like the citizens of El Dorado County are grateful to Robert and Tom for keeping this area as crime-free as possible."

Mother sniffed but remained silent.

"He'll be fine." Gran patted Mother's hand with her own. "They'd need a tank to take down your husband."

Mother had to chuckle at that remark, and we joined in. She left a few minutes later saying she needed to kiss her husband goodbye before he set off on his mission to save the world from evil, one criminal at a time.

Gran called Carolyn Thorson and arranged to visit her in an hour. I glanced at my watch. Nearly two. More than enough time for a little detecting. Nina had assured me Brent would be working today. It would help to learn why Axel threatened to find another manager.

I hopped in my car, drove past Gold Bug Mine and turned on to Highway 50. Lines of cars claimed both lanes, but they maintained the speed limit, so it only took a few minutes longer than usual to arrive at Apple Tree Farm. Today the parking gods smiled on me. A truck pulled out of a space in front of the bakery just as I drove up.

I entered the bakery building. Jenna stood at the pastry counter handing a pile of bills and change to a customer. Close to fifteen people waited in Jenna's line, as well as the line of a new counter clerk I recognized as Rose Margolis. Rose and I had attended high school together. I decided to greet both of them later when the line of customers subsided.

I wandered over to the cider mill hoping to locate Brent, but instead found Eric. Only one person waited so I stood behind him. After he paid for his gallon jug, I moved up to the counter.

"Hi, Eric," I said to the young man. "How are you doing?"

"Oh, hi, Ms. McKay. Okay, I guess. Just trying to help my mom keep the farm going."

"Well, I'd love to buy a half gallon of your delicious cider." I grabbed my wallet while he pulled the apple cider from their oversized refrigerator. "I also need to talk to Brent about something. Do you know where I can find him?"

Eric scowled. "Brent and Tony are in the warehouse unloading supplies."

"Tony is working here again? Are you sure?"

Eric threw me one of those disgusted teenage looks. "Yeah, we've lost some staff, and my mom hired him back." He swore under his breath.

"How nice of your mother to give Tony a second chance."

"Yeah, a second chance to steal from us." Eric shoved the cider at me and grabbed the five- dollar bill in my hand. "That's going to change when I take over."

He yelled "Next" to the person behind me. Okay, I guess we were done here. I returned to my car and deposited the jug in the back seat; I needed my hands free for eating.

I mean sleuthing.

I headed toward the warehouse, analyzing Eric's last remark. It probably made sense for the heir apparent to want to assume control of the business. I wondered how his uncle and mother felt about that. And their current farm manager.

As I reached the warehouse where I'd discovered Axel's body, a sense of déjà vu filled me with dread. But despite my trepidation, questioning Brent was a priority.

The large wooden doors were propped wide open. Both Brent and Tony unloaded supplies from a truck backed into the building. I could only imagine the quantity of flour, sugar, cinnamon, and shortening they purchased in order for Nina and her staff to make their heavenly pastries.

I yodeled a hello as I approached the men. Tony must have recognized me as Jenna's mother since he waved and smiled.

"This area isn't open to the public," Brent said as he walked toward me, his work-roughened hands shooing me away.

"Nina sent me to speak with you." I nodded at Tony, still not overly enthralled with the young man and the activities he'd persuaded Jenna to participate in.

"Does Nina need some supplies?" Brent asked.

Did she? Considering the number of patrons roaming the grounds, she probably did.

I emphatically nodded as I tried to convince myself as well as Brent. "She told me to have Tony bring a bag of..." I scanned the burlap bags stacked well over my head. "Sugar. And flour. And cinnamon."

Brent screwed up his face at my order. "Must be doing a good bit of business in the bakery. Okay, boy, take your grandma her supplies. But come right back. Don't stop to gab with those cute gals at the counter."

I seconded that motion, although a wee bit of gabbing would give me more time alone with Brent.

Tony flashed a Crest-white grin, probably relieved for the short break. He loaded the heavy bags into a covered golf cart adorned with the Apple Tree logo and set off for the bakery. Brent moved away from me and reentered the warehouse. I was right behind him.

He pivoted and suddenly we were nose to nose. "Is there more?" he barked. His clothes smelled like stale tobacco so I retreated a few feet.

"A friend of mine, Liz Daley, the owner of Golden Hills Spa, left some supplies here last Friday. Axel had arranged for her to take over the spot that Weather Vainery used to occupy."

"That Vanna," he snorted. "She couldn't sell those lame ass vanes if her life depended on it."

"Right. I guess that's why Axel decided to give Liz the opportunity. With his demise, I understand it's somewhat uncertain whether Apple Tree will stay in business. Liz asked me to find the Beautiful Image cartons. Her cosmetics are quite valuable, and she'd hate for them to get mislaid or thrown away."

Brent's thick graying brows drew together, and he moved closer. "What do you mean Apple Tree Farm might not stay in business? Who did you hear that from?"

I moved away. "Several people mentioned it to me. I can't remember offhand who it was."

"Did Dorie tell you she's selling the place?" he asked.

"Not exactly. But this place is a huge operation for her to manage. Maybe she would be better off selling it and living on the equity."

"She's got me to manage it for her. If she'd let me. The woman's sticking her nose all over the place. She's gonna ruin everything."

I nodded sympathetically. "I agree. She should be relying on you more. After all, you were Axel's right-hand man."

"You got that right."

This conversation was all very interesting, but I hadn't learned anything useful so far. It might be time to up my game.

"So, considering your close relationship with Axel, how come he threatened to fire you?"

CHAPTER THIRTY-ONE

Brent backed away, stumbled over a burlap bag and landed with his legs splayed on the cement floor. I reached out a hand to help him, but he declined and quickly stood.

"You're just full of questions, aren't you?" He snarled at me as he brushed off his jeans.

"There are always questions when a murder has occurred. And since I'm the one who found Axel, I certainly have some." I put my palms up. "Not that I'm accusing you of anything. Someone mentioned your conversation with Axel."

"You mean that old bag overheard us talking," he muttered, "and sent you over here to pry."

Yep, that was pretty much it.

I switched to a different tack. "Why don't you tell me what the discussion was about, and then I'd be willing to put in a good word for you with Dorie."

"I don't need any help from you or any other meddling busybodies." He took a couple of steps in the opposite direction then turned back to face me.

"Okay, I might as well get it off my chest so you can leave me alone."

Brent's easy acquiescence surprised me, but I waited to hear what he had to say.

"Axel and me didn't always see eye to eye on some of the operational stuff," Brent drawled. "Nothing out of the ordinary though."

"I can see how that could happen," I encouraged him. "Axel probably had his mind set on doing things a certain way."

Brent relaxed his shoulders at my comment. "Right. As the farm manager, I'm supposed to have the authority to manage everything. Especially with Axel all tied up building that ritzy new mansion of his."

I nodded, growing more and more curious about the Thorsons' new home. It sounded gorgeous. But this was not the time to get distracted. I had questions, and Brent was finally supplying answers.

"So I decided to change suppliers." Brent pointed toward the rows of shelving, loaded with bags of staples, which looked sufficient to make the fifty thousand plus donuts Nina told me they sold every month. Considering over a million tourists visited the Apple Hill area every year, that number wasn't entirely out of the question. "And improve the bottom line."

"Why would a change in suppliers bother Axel? Especially if it helped to reduce expenses?"

Brent shrugged. "Never said. Just told me he was the boss and to go back to using the vendors we used before. Or else."

"So you did."

He shoved his hands in his pockets. "Right. Now, if you don't mind, I have work to do." He strode off to the depths of the warehouse without giving me a chance to utter my thanks for the information he'd shared.

Lost in thought, I strolled back to the bakery. Brent's explanation made sense, sort of. Axel had developed excellent relationships with all of his vendors over the years. He wouldn't appreciate Brent changing them while he'd been distracted building the new house. Even if it did help the bottom line.

Or did it? Maybe Brent switched vendors to help *his* bottom line. Now that would definitely be grounds for Axel to terminate him and report him to the authorities.

But was Axel's threat sufficient reason for Brent to terminate his boss? Permanently? What kind of money were we talking about here?

Why was it the more questions I asked, the more questions arose? And how could I let Brent walk away without locating Liz's supplies?

The flashing lights of an El Dorado County Sheriff's vehicle pulling into a parking space across from the bakery distracted me from my reverie. Detective Reynolds jumped out of the car and rushed into the bakery. The expression on her face was not the look of a donut-seeking detective. Young Deputy Mengelkoch was right behind her.

I sped up, my heart racing almost as quickly as my red sneakers. Why wasn't Tom ever around when I needed his support? Wasn't that the whole point of being in a relationship? Having someone to hold your hand when times were tough?

I blew out a breath. Everything was probably just fine. Reynolds couldn't possibly intend to arrest Jenna. A high-pitched scream that sounded remarkably like my daughter echoed from inside the building. Tourists munching on their apple-filled treats paused to look around.

I sprinted around a baby carriage and vaulted over a crate of apples a startled tourist dropped in front of me, barely managing to avoid sideswiping an elderly couple leaving the bakery.

Cinnamon-scented chaos greeted me inside. People swarmed in all directions, some trying to get out of the way, others moving closer to the action. One crabby customer continued to stand at the window demanding that someone hand over her donuts.

I sighed in relief when I saw Jenna was fine. Then I noticed the tears streaming down her flour-mottled cheeks as she stood with her arm around Nina. The older woman looked ready to collapse as Detective Reynolds snapped a pair of handcuffs around her target.

Tony Perez.

CHAPTER THIRTY-TWO

The sea of tourists parted as Reynolds and the deputy led their silent captive out of the bakery. I followed them since nosiness is one of the required attributes of the TWO GALS DETECTIVE AGENCY. Plus, as far as I knew, the suspect's grandmother was still our client.

"What are you doing?" I called out to Reynolds.

"Our job," she replied. "Step back, Ms. McKay, or we'll also take you in, for interfering with an arrest."

The detective shoved Tony into the backseat of her car. Deputy Mengelkoch tried to control the crowd, some of whom probably thought this was a new reality show—CSI: Donut Detectives. Reynolds backed up the car, barely missing a teen snapping photos with his phone. The young man spun around and took a few shots of me. I covered my face with my hands. The last thing I needed was to make a social media splash tonight.

The deputy jumped into the passenger seat. The car crawled down the road as Reynolds attempted to avoid knocking over any curious tourists. Through the side window, Tony sent me one last pleading look before he bowed his head.

I returned to the bakery. Dorie and Jenna stood on either side of a sobbing Nina. A "temporarily closed" sign had been placed in front of one of the bakery windows, but Rose's window was now elbow-deep in hungry patrons.

Jenna flung her arms around me. "Mom," she sobbed.

"It will be okay, honey." I patted her back but had no idea whether my statement would prove to be true or not. She finally released me, and I was free to speak to the other two women.

"Nina, did the detective say anything to you?" I asked.

"Nada," she sniffed. "Tony delivered those supplies you requested for me." She quirked a silvery eyebrow at me. "He was on his way back to the warehouse when the detective arrived."

"Can they do that?" Dorie asked me. "Arrest Tony a second time?"

"Yes, they can. They must have found additional evidence against him."

"But he didn't do it," Nina cried. "It's not possible. I know it."

"Can you call Tom?" Jenna asked. "Please."

I whipped out my cell, but as usual my call went directly to Tom's voicemail, so all I could do was leave a message. A rather surly voicemail, I admit, which was not my intent. The combination of my frustration with our relationship and fear about Tony's arrest colored my tone.

Dorie went back into the bakery to help out at the counter. Nina didn't seem to be in any condition to wait on people unless you enjoyed eating donuts decorated with teardrops. I used a tissue to wipe the mascara-stained tears from Jenna's pale cheeks and sent her off to help Dorie. Serving customers should provide a temporary distraction for her.

I asked Nina if there was someplace we could talk, where we didn't have to worry about anyone eavesdropping or snapping photos. A grieving grandmother should not be considered camera fodder for the paparazzi.

Nina led me past super-sized stainless mixing bowls and enormous rectangular fryers, to the rear of the bakery kitchen where a grouping of four straight-back wooden chairs were set around a small square table.

"Can I get you any water?" I asked. "Or a donut?"

She shook her head, her gray braid swinging in all directions. "No, I'm okay. Tony's arrest was such a shock to my system. I thought everything would be fine once they released him."

"It looks like you better hire a lawyer for him."

"But how will I pay for one?" Her face crumpled and she looked like she would tear up again.

"Don't worry about that. If you can't afford an attorney, they'll assign a public defender to his case." I patted her hand while I assembled some questions of my own. "Nina, since they arrested Tony again, they must have new evidence against him. I take it he doesn't have an alibi?"

"After Axel fired him, Tony said he cruised around for a while then grabbed a burger at a drive-through. Eventually he calmed down. He told me he drove back to Apple Tree to talk to Axel about the missing money, knowing that Axel frequently worked late. Axel's car was in the parking lot, but his office was dark. Tony assumed he'd gotten a ride with Eric or Dorie. When Tony arrived home, my bedroom door was closed so he figured I was asleep and didn't call out."

Not much of an alibi. In fact, none at all.

"Detective Reynolds must be zeroing in on something other than motive. I can't imagine Tony killing Axel just because he fired him. I can understand him being angry about Axel's decision, but murder would be an extreme reaction, wouldn't it?"

"Tony has a bit of a temper," she admitted, "but it disappears as fast as it flares up. He hates bullies and was kicked out of high school after he punched a punk who wouldn't stop picking on an autistic kid. He's working on his temper, and I can assure you Tony would never kill Axel. Never, ever, ever."

"Tony certainly has his grandmother in his corner. But, what if in a fit of anger, your grandson grabbed a rolling pin and assaulted Axel?"

She latched on to my hands, squeezing them tight. Nina was several decades older than me, but her years working in the bakery led to muscular arms far stronger than my banker biceps.

"Tony would never have murdered him," she said. "Axel was his father."

CHAPTER THIRTY-THREE

Whoa! I sure didn't see that one coming. Axel was Tony's father? Who knew? Actually, that was a very good question. Who did know? And did the answer have anything to do with Axel's murder?

"How long has Tony known Axel was his father?" I asked Nina.

"Not much longer than I've known," she replied. "Tony started working here right before the farm opened for Labor Day weekend. A few weeks ago Axel and Tony were rearranging some boxes in the fruit bin area. They discovered they were both color-blind. I watched them laughing as they compared notes about the problems they encounter getting dressed. I could tell the similarities didn't end there. Although Tony inherited Rosie's dark eyes and hair, they share an identical cleft chin and a few mannerisms that I never noticed until they were working side by side."

"Did you know Rosie dated Axel?"

Nina sighed. "Rosie never disclosed the name of Tony's father. She said it was her first and only sexual experience, and I believed her. But it only takes one time to make a baby, doesn't it?"

Poor Nina. Losing her daughter could have crushed her spirit, despite the entry of her new grandson into the world.

"Did Tony ever question you about his parents when he was younger?"

"When he was little, I told him both his parents died right after he was born. As he grew older, he naturally became more curious. When his fifth-grade teacher assigned the family tree project to his class, I finally admitted I had no idea who his father was." Nina's eyes met mine. "His tree only had branches on one side."

My heart filled with sorrow as I reflected on the pain Nina endured on a daily basis. But didn't she say Tony recently learned about his father?

"When did you tell Tony about your discovery?"

"I kept silent for a while, but I'd watch them together whenever I could. I was struck by how their movements and gestures resembled one another. One night after closing, I bumped into Axel and blurted out my suspicions."

"Was he stunned?"

"To put it mildly." She grimaced. "At first, he denied it. Said it wasn't possible. Case closed. So I drove home and tried to forget about it."

"That must have been difficult."

"Impossible. But then I noticed Axel watching Tony, too. One day, about a week before his death, he asked me to come to his office."

Nina lowered her voice and I moved nearer, not wanting to miss a word.

"Axel confessed to secretly dating Rosie nineteen years ago. Thor Thorson had hired Rosie to help out at the candy shop. We were both pleased because Rosie planned to attend college, and we struggled to get by. Every extra bit of income was a godsend."

I could certainly relate to her financial struggles. The joy of having an academically-gifted daughter was tempered by the frustration of not being able to give her every opportunity to pursue her dreams.

"I'd noticed Rosie and Axel chatting now and then," Nina continued, "but the teens who worked at Apple Tree were a nice bunch of hard-working kids and they got along well. Axel was a college sophomore so he was a couple years older than most of them. He'd drive up here on the weekends to help out. His father always planned on leaving the business to his sons."

"So when did Axel and Rosie..." I couldn't use the term "hookup" in front of Nina, but she knew what I meant.

"From what he told me, I gather the two of them met after her school got out, at the library or a fast food restaurant. They'd spend a few hours together. Then one evening things progressed..." She threw up her hands. "Well, you get my drift."

I certainly did. There would be no more Tony and Jenna after-school outings. I didn't want any Romeos interfering with my Juliet's college plans.

"Anyway, to make a long story even longer," she said with a sigh, "Axel said Rosie stopped taking his calls. The next semester he transferred to Berkeley. Out of sight, out of mind. He met Dorie a few months later. They began dating and got married the following summer." Nina spread her arms out wide. "Then Eric was born and that was that."

Well, not quite.

"When did Tony learn Axel was his father?"

"Axel wanted to have a paternity test completed before he told his family. He implied Rosie might have had another lover, but I nipped that thought immediately. Still, I considered it a fair request and agreed to wait until we had scientific proof. I retrieved samples of Tony's DNA from his hairbrush. Axel arranged a rush order to have the test completed by a private company."

"It made sense to tread carefully. But what happened?"

"Eric's been on Tony's case ever since Tony started working here this fall. I don't know why unless...," Her gaze veered in the direction of the counter clerks, one pretty, auburn-haired teen in particular. "Anyway, he seemed intent on making Tony's life miserable. Maybe Eric noticed the similarities between Axel and Tony as well. Tony became so frustrated he told me he was going to quit. I just up and told him that Friday night before Axel was killed that Axel might be his father."

"What did Tony say?"

"He was stunned at first. Then kinda miffed Axel hadn't stayed in touch with my daughter after he transferred to Berkeley. But after a long tearful conversation, Tony seemed pleased that his father was alive despite the peculiar circumstances. I told him not to say anything to anyone until Axel discussed it with Eric and Dorie. Tony understood the announcement would be a shock to the entire family."

"Did Eric somehow find out Tony was his brother?" I wondered if that was the reason for their altercation that Saturday.

"Tony told me Eric accused him of being a bastard and a thief, but I don't know if Eric discovered Tony was his half-brother, or if he was angry with him for other reasons. He laid into Tony and they took their fight out to the parking lot."

The fight I mediated with my face.

"After Axel sent Tony to his office, Tony let his temper get the better of him."

"Can you imagine how Tony felt," I asked her. "Learning that Axel was his father and then getting fired by him?"

Nina's expression turned to stone. "Axel handled it all wrong. Especially when he believed Eric's accusations that Tony was a thief."

Poor kid. "You don't think Tony came back with the intent to harm Axel?"

"It's just not possible," Nina murmured, more to herself than to me. I looked up when I heard footsteps approaching us.

Dorie drew out an empty chair at our small table. "I'm not cut out for this," she complained as she fell into the chair and stretched her legs.

"Nina, I don't know how you've managed to stand on your feet all these years." Dorie slumped lower before she sprang up. "Oh, saints, listen to me blubbering about myself. How are you doing, and what on earth are you going to do about Tony?"

Nina and I exchanged looks. It didn't sound like Axel had shared the discovery of his newfound son with his wife. And it wasn't my position to inform Dorie. Or Reynolds. It was up to

Nina to disclose the relationship to the widow and the detective. Unless the detective had already discovered the connection.

I sighed. I had a feeling that piece of information would NOT be helpful in proving Tony's innocence.

CHAPTER THIRTY-FOUR

Nina left to assist the bakery clerks while Dorie took a break. There wasn't much I could do until Jenna's shift ended so I decided to make the best of it.

"Dorie, did Axel ever mention any problems with Brent? Or any of the suppliers Brent worked with? Brent mentioned he and Axel had a minor disagreement, but they'd worked it out."

She leaned over to remove one flour-caked black suede ballet flat then the other. She examined the shoes then tossed them onto the floor.

"These Pradas are goners," she said, her lips curling in displeasure. "I guess I better wear something more practical if I need to keep helping at the bakery. Are you looking for weekend work, Laurel?"

Uh, that would be a negative. Chauffeuring Jenna back and forth was proving to be way more work than I'd envisioned when she applied for this job. I shook my head and repeated my previous question before Dorie got distracted once again.

She stared at her shoes before responding. "I'm afraid I've spent so much time in the past six months decorating our new house that I didn't really pay any attention to the farm. I certainly didn't need to before Axel died."

I hated to pry, but I was positive Dorie wanted the right person behind bars as much as Nina wanted her grandson released from jail.

"Why don't you think about it and let me know," I said. "It could be important."

She squeezed her eyes shut then opened them wide. "I do remember Axel got all bent out of shape a few weeks ago. He was working on his inventory, making sure they had all the supplies they needed before the October burst of customers. The quantities on hand didn't add up. That's one of the reasons he was working so late that night." Her voice and gaze drifted off, and she looked like she was a million miles away. Or perhaps only wished she was.

I hated to keep hammering at her, but I needed to learn more about the missing inventory. "Do you remember anything specific?"

She shrugged. "Not really. You should ask Brooke Martin. She's the accountant for the farm. Axel said he was going to run some numbers by her." Dorie's eyes widened in horror. "Unless someone stopped him before he could do it."

I would ask Brooke. Just because the CPA was dating my ex didn't mean I couldn't be objective about her input.

I glanced at my watch. Nearly closing time. Dorie stood and stretched, then left to assist at the bakery counter. I walked over to the open area where a few customers loitered, arms full of produce, jellies and homemade syrups. I snatched a bottle of cinnamon-apple pancake syrup and a jar of pear-apple butter. A grim-faced Brent helped at one of the registers. He seemed more intent on getting rid of the customers than luring them into buying additional items.

I switched to his line. He grunted when he saw me, totaled the items and stuck out his hand. I reached into my wallet for my credit card and handed it over.

"Say, Brent, I still need to find my friend's Beauty Image products. Can I go through the warehouse some time?"

"Nope. Too dangerous. I'll take a look once I'm done here. Give me your phone number, and I'll let you know when I find them."

Well, that was better than nothing. I wrote my number on the back of the receipt and handed it to him. He waved me on and began checking out the customer behind me. I strolled over to my car, dumped my purchases then went back to see if Jenna was done for the day.

Jenna waved at me from behind the counter and indicated I should wait for her. I plopped into a plastic chair, willing myself to sit quietly and meditate. As usual, my overactive brain had its own ideas.

Why would Brent say it was too dangerous for me to look through the warehouse? Did he fear I'd spot something he'd concealed? One thing was certain, it had definitely been dangerous for Axel to be in the warehouse the night of his murder.

CHAPTER THIRTY-FIVE

During the drive back to Gran's house to pick up Ben, the conversation between my daughter and myself was punctuated with yawns. Despite her fatigue, Jenna wanted to know how I planned to get Tony released from jail. I could tell from her comments that Tony had not disclosed anything to her about his paternity. I told her the entire agency, that is, Gran and I, were devoted to getting him released. Therefore she need not get involved. Jenna's priorities were school and her SATs the following weekend.

We arrived at Gran's, and I pulled up behind Hank's black truck. Surprise, surprise, Brooke's Miata was parked at the curb. I flicked away any jealous thoughts that might be circling. Hank had just as much right to a fulfilling relationship as I had.

I just wished Tom and I were together fulfilling each other right now!

Jenna and I eased out of the car and strolled down the sidewalk. We let ourselves into the house. Laughter echoed from the kitchen, and we headed in that direction.

Hank, Ben, Brooke, and Gran were seated around her maple table. Brooke's dark hair brushed Ben's cheek as he demonstrated something to her. My heart plummeted before it stabilized back into neutral.

Hank looked up at my approach. "Hi, honey," he said.

Both Brooke and I glared at him. "Whoops, force of habit." Hank turned to Brooke. "Sorry, honey."

I groaned inwardly and chose to ignore my ex, usually the safest option. I circled the table, stopped behind Ben's chair and ruffled his already tousled cowlicks. "How was the fishing, sweetie?"

Ben flung his slightly sunburnt arms out, practically whacking Brooke's perfectly shaped nose. "I caught two fish," he exclaimed, "and Brooke caught four. Dad didn't get none."

"Dad didn't get any," I corrected Ben.

"That's what I said." Ben turned a puzzled look at me. I decided the grammar police could take the day off. I walked to the cupboard and grabbed a glass. While I filled it with tap water, I casually addressed Brooke. "I didn't realize you would be joining the boys today."

She glanced at Hank then back at me. "It was sort of a last minute decision. Hank mentioned they were going to Ice House Lake, and I decided I could use a few hours break from work. I hope you don't mind?"

"Oh, no, of course not." How could I possibly be upset when she was being so darn nice? Plus she was keeping Hank out of my hair. She deserved brownie points for that alone.

I slid into the empty chair next to Gran and tried to think of a subtle way to discuss Axel Thorson's financial situation with his accountant. Gran leaned over and whispered into my ear, "Got some goods on the Thorson family." Since Gran's whisper is a shade softer than maximum volume on my TV, everyone at the table heard her comment.

"What do you mean?" asked Jenna. She stood behind her father, her palms resting on his shoulders.

Gran leaned forward, her grin as wide and mischievous as a tipsy Cheshire cat.

"I drove over to Axel's mother's house," she explained. "Wanted to share my condolences with Carolyn."

"Granny G, you're even sneakier than Mom." Jenna grinned and her brother hooted.

Gran elbowed me. "I've got a few decades on your Ma. But she's not doing too bad herself."

Gee, thanks for the compliment. If Gran wasn't careful, I'd resign, and she'd have to rename the firm ONE OLD GAL DETECTIVE AGENCY.

"I learned some stuff, although..." She looked at me and then over at Brooke. "We can talk later."

Brooke smiled uncertainly, possibly sensing she was now the elephant in the room. My hope was that she was a CPA with an elephantine memory of facts and figures, some of which she'd offer to share with me. She shoved her chair back and stood. "I should probably go."

"No, that's okay, you're part of the..." My voice tapered off. Brooke wasn't part of our dysfunctional family yet. And I wasn't privy to Hank's thoughts and desires. She was, however, part of my investigation.

"Dorie Thorson told me to contact you," I said to Brooke. "Nina told me she'd overheard Axel threatening to fire Brent, but she didn't know why. I questioned Brent today, and he claimed they merely had a difference of opinion over which suppliers to use. Dorie thought it was a more serious disagreement. That her husband suspected Brent of stealing some of the farm's inventory. Maybe selling it himself. Did Axel ever discuss this with you?"

Brooke steepled her fingers under her chin and looked around the room, probably trying to decide how much information she could share.

"I'm not completely clear how you're involved with Apple Tree Farm," she said. "Did Dorie hire you to help her manage the operation?"

Not exactly, although she did offer to let me work in the bakery. I wasn't certain if donut selling equated with a management position.

"We're working on solving Axel's murder," Gran chimed in. "We know that young kid didn't off him. So Laurel and me is helping poor Dorie out."

"You can call Dorie and ask her," I assured Brooke. "But the sooner we all get some answers, the sooner we determine who Axel's killer is."

"And can get Tony out of jail," Jenna said. "Please help."

Three generations of McKay females surrounded the CPA, our identical baby blues solidly fixed on her. I wasn't certain she would budge. Then Hank whispered in her ear.

She giggled and slapped at his hand. "Fine. I can see I'm outnumbered here. But please do not share this information with anyone."

"Scout's honor," Ben piped up, reminding me that little ears are sometimes connected to big mouths. We sent Ben into Gran's den to watch TV behind closed doors.

I figured I'd get the investigative ball rolling. "Did Axel mention any issues with Brent such as theft or anything of that nature?"

She nodded. "This will probably all come out eventually, but Axel had huge fiscal issues. Last year's tourism drop coupled with that money pit of a house practically bankrupted him. He took out a short-term loan on the farm last year that matured a few months ago. The lender threatened to begin foreclosure proceedings, so Axel was desperate to pay it off before he lost Apple Tree."

"That would be such a blow to his mother," Gran muttered. "Losing the family farm because he got too big for his britches building that McMansion of his."

"Do you think Dorie realized what was going on?" I asked Brooke.

"I don't know her that well. Axel was kind of old-fashioned about the business. He didn't want to worry Dorie's 'pretty little blond head,' as he put it. But he let her have her way about most of the decisions for the new house. She claimed she had better taste, and he didn't have time to choose home decor."

"Great taste doesn't always equate to smart decisions," Hank said. "I see this stuff happening all the time. People spend hundreds of thousands of dollars over their original budget. All of those upgrades and extras add up." Hank clasped Brooke's hand and winked at her. "That's why I like to date smart women." Then he winked at me.

Gack! Although Hank's comment about overspending homeowners made sense.

"Poor Dorie," I said. "First she lost her husband. Now she might lose the farm and possibly her new house."

A newcomer entered the discussion. "Did Axel have life insurance?" asked Mother as she entered the kitchen.

"I'm glad you're here," I said. "Everything okay with your hubby?"

"Men." She looked exasperated. "I sent him off to play cops and robbers."

"Barbara, it's nice to see you again," Brooke said to Mother. "And that is an excellent question for Dorie."

I mentally added following up on Axel's life insurance bequest to my "to do" list.

"Back to Brent's possible thievery," I said.

"Sorry, I got distracted," Brooke said. "Axel's situation is complicated. He didn't mind when Brent initially changed suppliers. Brent's been helping manage the farm for ten years, so Axel left that area under Brent's control. But when he became desperate for every possible cent to pay down the loan, Axel analyzed the numbers more closely. He counted the inventory himself and told me the numbers weren't adding up."

"Was Axel going to fire that thief?" Gran asked.

"He was ready to although he didn't think he could run the place all by himself. He'd even asked his brother to help out, but Paul said he was too busy with his new, um, business."

She snorted unbecomingly, and I found myself liking her despite my initial reluctance.

"I'm not sure a life coach is the best choice to run a huge business operation," I said tactfully.

Gran stood and patted her flat rump with both hands. "Carolyn told me her younger son couldn't find his…" Noticing Jenna's rapt attention, she stopped in the middle of what I imagined would have been a highly colorful description. As a senior in high school, Jenna had certainly heard far worse from her classmates.

And, to be honest, from her great-grandmother.

"What else did you learn from Carolyn?" asked Mother.

"Well, I gather Paul is not averse to asking his mother to lend him money," Gran replied. "The only problem is that repayment doesn't occur as frequently as the borrowing does. Paul was positive his new center, his coaching combined with their classes and Serenity's bakery, would be a huge success. Carolyn said her son truly is a great salesman. Could sell a herd of cows to a vegan. He just can't manage a business to save his life."

"Did Carolyn help fund Paul's center?" I asked.

"Nope. She decided she'd been the Bank of Mom for far too long. She suggested he go to Axel for a loan."

"Do you know if Axel loaned Paul any money?" I asked Brooke.

She shrugged. "I only handle the books for Axel's business operation. None of his personal stuff. I guess you'd have to ask Paul that question."

That I would. It occurred to me that if Axel refused to lend his brother the money to fund the Lifestyle Center, Paul's only remaining option might be to force a sale of Apple Tree Farm. A solution that would be far easier with Axel out of the picture.

CHAPTER THIRTY-SIX

Hank yawned. "It's been real nice chatting with you all," he said, "but Brooke and I have, um, work to do."

Was that a four-letter euphemism for a three-letter act? And did I really want to know the answer? Besides Hank was right. I needed to get my children home and feed them. Ben grabbed his fishing gear and scampered off to our car. Jenna plodded behind him as if she carried the weight of the world, or Tony's arrest, on her shoulders.

Mother and I followed the kids. I could tell by her demeanor that something was bothering her. I threw a comforting arm around her waist as we strolled down the sidewalk. "You seem unusually upset about Bradford joining Tom on the task force. You know it's only a temporary gig."

"Robert had no business agreeing to participate," she said. "He knew I was dead set against it."

"I thought the two of you discussed it, and he talked you into it."

"He talked and I listened. I never gave him my permission."

I stopped and stared at her. "I doubt he was asking for your permission, just your acceptance. You're still working with your real estate clients. Do you expect him to sit around watching *The Price is Right* and *The View* while you're at the office?"

"There are always chores he can do around the house if he wants to be helpful," she asserted.

Seriously?

"There's a world of difference between chores and community service," I said.

"I know you're right, but wait until you find out what roles Tom and Robert are assuming in their investigation. You're not going to be any happier to hear what they're up to than I was."

"I have faith in whatever Tom takes on, and you need to trust your husband, too."

"Let me know if you still feel that way after you speak with Tom." She hugged me tightly then walked to her SUV.

My kids were already seat-belted in and ready to go, so we followed Mother's car down the street. I looked forward to a quiet family dinner followed by a relaxing bath followed by a phone call from my honey.

In less than a half hour, we were seated at the table finishing our chicken taco dinner. A McKay family favorite—it didn't get more nourishing or easy than that meal. Jenna offered to do the dishes, which I eagerly accepted. Floating in a bathtub full of plumeria-scented bubbles while reading a new mystery by Heather Haven would be my reward for a very long day.

The home phone rang in the bedroom just as I stepped into the water. I grabbed a towel, threw a wistful look at my fragrant bubbles and picked up the receiver.

"You sound out of breath," Tom said. "Am I interrupting anything?"

"Nope, just a big night in my bathtub, bubbles and all," I replied.

"I wish I were there to share the evening with you." He lowered his voice to a sexy baritone. "Bubbles and all."

Be still my beating heart and everything else that was pulsating, including my tingling toes.

"How are…" I squeaked then cleared my throat to deliver a throaty "you?"

"Are you okay? You sound funny."

"That was my sexy voice. I guess I'm out of practice." In all respects.

"Well, I'm looking forward to helping you practice."

My heart sped up even more. "Are you coming home?"

"As a matter of fact, I am, although not for long. I need to pick up one more addition to the task force on Monday."

"I thought Bradford already drove up there today."

"He's here now. Ali Reynolds is joining the team."

"Detective Reynolds?"

"She offered to assist us before, and now that she's finally wrapped up the Thorson case, she's available."

"She arrested Tony Perez again," I said. "And he's innocent."

"Not as far as Ali is concerned."

"Then she hasn't done her homework or procured all the evidence. In fact, she probably arrested him again just so she could close the case and play with you."

"Laurel, don't be ridiculous." Tom's voice held a tinge of anger indicating I may have pushed a button. "Ali is a professional through and through. Besides, that case doesn't concern you. Please stay out of it."

"An innocent young man has been thrown in jail. That would concern any citizen. Plus Tony's grandmother is a good friend of Gran's. If I don't get involved, who knows what trouble Gran and Nina will get into together. They're determined to prove his innocence."

He blew out a forceful sigh. "Your family. Honestly. I can see why Bradford needed a break."

"What?"

"Oh, nothing. Look, I have to go. Can you get away for lunch on Monday? I'll fill you in when I see you in person. Ali is a good detective. If she says the Thorson case is wrapped, then it's wrapped. I want to close my own case as soon as I can, and we can really use her help here. Don't you want me home safe in your arms again?" His voice moved back to seductive mode. "That's where I'd rather be."

Shoot. How could I complain when he made comments like that?

CHAPTER THIRTY-SEVEN

With two weeks of laundry pleading for attention, I decided to skip chauffeur duty on Sunday. Instead, I handed over the car keys to my daughter and settled in for a quiet day of catching up on household tasks.

Jenna arrived home around three p.m. According to her, Sacramento news commentators had arrived in full force with camera crews and broadcasters swarming over every foot of the farm. Jenna grew tired of reporters thrusting microphones in her face, and after one aggressive bozo asked a particularly insensitive question, she had shoved a powdered sugar donut on the reporter's mike.

I didn't blame her. Reporters blindsided Dorie with questions about Tony's parentage, which came as a complete surprise to her. The widow finally decided enough was enough and closed the farm a few hours early.

"When did you learn Axel was Tony's father?" Jenna accused me. "You should have told me."

"Nina brought it up yesterday. But she only recently figured it out herself." I chewed on a hangnail as I contemplated her revelation. "I wonder how the reporters discovered their relationship. Who would have told them?"

Jenna stared at me, the wheels of her agile brain most likely spinning different scenarios.

"Did Tony know he was Axel's son?" Jenna gnawed on her thumb, unknowingly mirroring me. Like mother, like daughter, unfortunately.

"Nina finally told him her suspicions the Friday night before Axel's murder, although I don't think the DNA results were back yet." I shared everything else Nina and I had discussed the previous day.

"You don't believe Tony killed his father, do you?"

"Honey, I barely know Tony, so I can't possibly say for sure. He certainly had every right to be upset with Axel for a variety of reasons. I'm surprised Axel never put two and two together and figured it out for himself."

"Dorie was so shocked when the reporter mentioned it to her that she was speechless." Jenna said. "I feel so sorry for her. One horrible thing after another keeps happening."

"We need to do everything we can to support her. Did Eric mention anything to you about Tony and him being half-brothers?"

"No, but I saw Eric talking to that same reporter about twenty minutes before the guy approached Dorie."

"Do you think Eric found out and shared the information with the reporter?"

"I wouldn't put anything past him."

"Even the murder of his father?" I asked.

She remained silent for a minute. "Hard to tell. Eric is one weird dude. And he seems intent on making sure Tony stays in jail, which means we need to focus on helping Tony get out. So what do we do next?"

"The towels should be dry by now. You could fold them and put them in the linen closet."

She lifted her eyes to the ceiling. "You know that's not what I meant."

I laughed. "Yes, I know. But I can use all the extra help I can get around here if you want me to continue helping Tony."

Jenna gave me a high five then hugged and thanked me.

I was going to keep asking questions, so I might as well stay in my daughter's good graces while I was at it, and help her to stay in mine.

Monday morning arrived with a twenty-degree drop in temperature and a few dribbles of rain. After too many parched winters, Californians welcomed the sprinkles with open arms, buckets and reservoirs.

I arrived at the bank a few minutes early. After depositing my purse and raincoat in my office, my next stop was the break room. I poured a cup of coffee, added cream and sugar, then peeked at the front page of the *Mountain Democrat*. The headlines screamed the news about Tony's arrest for the *alleged* murder of his father.

The poor kid. I was almost relieved he was temporarily incarcerated so he couldn't be pestered by the reporters. Nina must be beside herself with worry. The article made me wonder how the media discovered the relationship between the father and son. Certainly Nina didn't share the information with them. Did Eric do it? And did he also supply the information to the detective to distract her from looking at him as a suspect and focus on Tony instead?

Based on my daughter's behind-the-scenes report of Dorie's response when the news broke, she had not been aware of the relationship. Would Axel have discussed something this personal with his brother? Although they didn't appear to be particularly close, they were siblings. Did Tony's existence impact Axel's estate?

The more questions I asked, the more I came up with. It was long past time for me to have a chat with Paul Thorson. I googled the phone number for his center, and he answered the phone himself. They must not be pulling in enough revenue to afford office help. I mentioned he'd been recommended to me as a life coach, and he offered me a choice of eight different appointment times in the next twenty-four hours. The life coaching business must not be booming yet. We settled on 5:00 p.m. for a one-hour consultation at his office, located directly above Serenity Sweets. Paul informed me the first hour was free, and I told him that was an excellent concept.

I'd barely hung up when my phone rang again. This time the caller was the bank president's secretary.

"Mr. Chandler wants to meet with you at ten," Belle said. "Will that work for you?"

Did it matter if that time worked into my schedule or not? "Of course," I said to her. "I'll see you then."

I attempted to occupy myself with bank business during the next hour, but it was impossible not to worry about my impending meeting. Was Mr. Chandler curious how successful I'd been in bringing in new deposits?

About as successful as I'd been in solving Axel's murder, which was probably not the answer he was shooting for. I made a few phone calls to some apple and pumpkin farms and by 9:50 a.m., I'd managed to fill my Tuesday with business development calls. Hopefully that would satisfy Mr. Chandler's expectations.

I trotted up the stairs to the executive suite, legal pad in hand and a fixed smile plastered on my face. Belle even complimented me on my new teal blue cardigan set. It didn't take much skill to purchase a sleeveless top and long matching cardigan, but I'd take flattery from the executive fashionista any time.

Laughter drifted out of Mr. Chandler's office so I waited for him to finish his conversation. Belle motioned for me to enter. Since she was the official gatekeeper, I obeyed.

Oh, goody. My least favorite marketing person was chatting with the bank president.

"Good morning, Mr. Chandler," I said, sounding far more perky than I felt. I nodded at his visitor. "Adriana."

"Laurel, lovely to see you as always," she chirped.

Since when? But I could play this game, too.

"Same here," I replied, although my tone was a few degrees less chirpy.

"Thank you for joining us," Mr. Chandler said.

Not a problem. I'm always happy to meet with the man who signs my paycheck. But why was my marketing rival here? I smiled at him and took a seat.

Adriana reached into a folder, produced a few sheets of paper and handed them over to Mr. Chandler. He glanced at them and nodded his approval.

"As you can see," she said briskly, "even though my marketing campaign has only been in operation for a few days, we've already brought in ten new business banking relationships plus two high-deposit clients with assets worth several million each."

"Well done, Adriana." Mr. Chandler smiled as if she'd placed a stack of one-hundred-dollar bills in his palm. I didn't even have a donut to sweeten his day much less any million-dollar depositors.

"How is your campaign going, Laurel?" Adriana asked.

"Great. I have another eight meetings scheduled for tomorrow. Once I'm finished, I'll present the results to Mr. Chandler." Hopefully, one of those meetings would bring in some bank revenue.

Otherwise my progress report would consist of a sticky note with a bold black zero written across it.

"Excellent. I look forward to your report," he said. "Now, how are the plans for the Apple Gala going? Any issues with the change of venue to Valley View?"

Adriana and I both rushed to answer his question. I decided to be gracious and let her handle the update.

"Walter was, of course, devastated by what happened to Axel. The two men were very close," she said. "But moving the gala from Apple Tree Farm to Valley View Vineyards has provided him the opportunity to showcase his new event center. We continue to sell tickets online, so I anticipate attendance will be the same as last year. Possibly higher due to the, um..."

"Murder," I said. "At least the foundation will benefit from all the media attention. There certainly hasn't been any shortage of press regarding Axel's death."

"Can you believe his illegitimate son killed him?" Adriana said. "This is playing out like a soap opera. But you know what they say, even bad press sells tickets."

Mr. Chandler frowned. I doubted the president backed her theory, as far as Hangtown Bank's reputation was concerned.

"Tony did not murder his father," I stated emphatically.

"You're such a softy," Adriana scoffed. "Walter has connections with the Sheriff's Office, and he told me the detective said the case was cut and dry as far as she was concerned."

"Well, they're not always right," I said, trying not to get huffy. But it wasn't easy. Adriana looked so smug about—everything.

"Don't underestimate Laurel," Mr. Chandler said to Adriana. "She's full of surprises."

Wow. A compliment from the bank president. I hoped he was right. And I really hoped any surprises I produced would be positive for the bank.

Or else I might surprise myself out of a job.

CHAPTER THIRTY-EIGHT

We concluded our meeting a few minutes later. Mr. Chandler was pleased to hear the gala would proceed smoothly despite the circumstances. Since this was the largest sponsorship event Hangtown Bank offered each year, success was a high priority.

When I returned to my office, I discovered Tom had called in my absence. Could I meet him at Mel's at 11:30 a.m.?

Sure could. Sure would.

I blazed through a small stack of branch requests and walked into the restaurant only a minute late. Tom waved at me from a rear corner booth. If nothing else, we could swap a kiss or two. I weaved my way between diners and slid into the slick leather seat next to him.

We briefly locked lips. His lips were soft, his beard was not. I grimaced and pulled away.

"I sense you don't approve of my new look," he said, resting his right hand on my thigh.

My tingle meter went out of control. I might not care for his scratchy beard, but the touch of his palm on my thigh worked its usual magic.

I tugged on his beard. "It's an interesting look, but I'll be happy when you're back to normal."

He took my palm in his. "Me, too. And I'll be glad to nail these dirt bags and put them away as long as possible."

Our server appeared, and we quickly placed our orders. I was far more interested in my dining companion than my dining options.

"Since you're closing in on these criminals, can you share anything with me? Like why you need Reynolds' help?"

He tweaked my nose. "Jealous?"

"Never." Okay, kind of.

He swirled the straw around his soda before replying.

"Look, I know you can keep a secret, but you have to promise you won't tell anyone, including your mother."

I held up my hand and promised to maintain complete secrecy no matter how much chocolate any member of my family waved under my nose.

"You might have read about Mexican farmers switching from growing marijuana to a more lucrative product—poppies."

"Not the pretty yellow and orange California poppies that cover the hills in the spring, right?" I said.

"Nope, these poppies are responsible for producing opium which is then turned into heroin. Users have discovered easier methods of ingesting heroin other than needles. In the past that kept a lot of squeamish people away from the stuff. Plus there's a ton of supply out there now so the price has come down. Heroin is fast becoming a huge problem everywhere, including high school campuses in this state."

"And your job is to stop these lowlifes from polluting our schools?" I asked.

"That's the long and short of it. I'll do whatever it takes to stop the heroin traffickers."

"And that's why you're my hero."

He ducked his head. "Just doing my job."

He kissed me and this time I didn't even notice his beard.

Our server chose that moment to deliver our entrées. We pulled apart and remained silent while he placed our orders on the table.

I took a bite of my cheeseburger, but I was far more interested in Tom's task force than I was in my lunch. "You still haven't explained why you need Detective Reynolds' help," I said. "And Bradford's, too."

Tom chewed for a while before answering. "You're not going to like my response."

"So what else is new?"

"True." He took one more bite then set his burger down. "Without going into the details I know you'd love for me to share, let's just say that I'm playing a part and so is Bradford."

"I already determined that from your new appearance. C'mon, I won't be upset."

"There's a high-level drug baron who believes that I want into his action. He's invited me to a party at his penthouse apartment in Reno tomorrow night. It's the perfect opportunity to check out his place. Bradford will accompany me as my bodyguard. The only problem is these parties include a few unusual perks."

"Perks?" His statement perked me up. "Anything I'd be interested in?"

"Are you in the market for a female escort?"

I almost spit burger onto my plate but managed to swallow before sputtering, "Say what?"

He sighed. "I knew there was no good way to explain this. Let's just say that Drug Lord A also runs an escort operation which brings in additional revenue. The escorts can be useful in hooking up their clients with drugs of all kinds. He already told me his party will include the crème de la crème of his women. Even offered me the pick of the litter." Tom winced. "So to speak."

"That is yuck on so many levels. What are you going to do?"

"Well, that's where Ali comes in. She did undercover work for a few years in the city before..." Tom hesitated. "Anyway, the reality of it is that the only way I could think of to decline his generous offer was to tell him I was engaged."

"Engaged to Reynolds?" I squeaked.

He rubbed a hand over his face. "Yes. I told him that my hot fiancée would cut off my balls if she found me cheating on her."

For the first time in months, I was speechless.

"With her help, the two of us can infiltrate what could be the headquarters of this operation. And with luck, wrap up our investigation in a couple of days. Isn't that terrific?"

I could think of a zillion adjectives to describe my opinion of his operation and terrific wasn't one of them.

I pushed my plate away as fear for Tom's safety replaced hunger. "It sounds scary and dangerous," I said, thinking of all the ways his operation could go wrong.

"That's the life of a policeman, Laurel. You know that."

"Yes, but…" My voice faltered as I collected my thoughts. For some reason, solving homicide cases had never seemed to present danger to Tom, even though I'd experienced some close calls when I'd stuck my nose where it didn't belong.

But this time, Tom was walking into a potential minefield.

Tom hesitantly smiled at me. "So you're on board with everything?"

"Do I have a choice?"

His response was muted by the arrival of a very attractive woman. One I wouldn't have recognized if she hadn't interrupted our conversation.

I gawked at the gorgeous, curvaceous female who slithered into the curved booth on Tom's left side.

"Hi, partner," said the new arrival. She cozied up to Tom and wrapped her slender arm around his muscular forearm.

"Detective Reynolds?" My eyebrows shot up to my bangs. She certainly cleaned up well.

"In the flesh," she said.

I eyeballed the detective. She certainly hadn't hesitated to display her flesh, particularly in the cleavage and thigh areas.

"I'm so looking forward to working closely with Tom again," she said. Her hand crept onto Tom's thigh. He placed it back in her lap where it belonged.

"Tom and I are both anxious for this task force to complete its mission," I replied. "But I'm surprised you're leaving without determining who killed Axel Thorson."

She rolled a pair of beautifully made-up eyes. Just because I was annoyed with her, didn't mean I couldn't notice carefully applied cosmetics. Liz would be proud of me.

"That case is closed. The last piece of evidence arrived last night."

"But..." I started to say when she interrupted me.

"Closed. *Finis*. Do I need to spell it out for you?"

No, thanks. I could spell it out for myself.

B-I-T-C-H.

CHAPTER THIRTY-NINE

Of course, the hotshot detective wouldn't deign to disclose the last piece of evidence with a lowly amateur sleuth. My appetite died as well as any opportunity to finish my conversation with Tom. The three of us walked out of the restaurant together. Tom kissed me on the cheek and promised to call as soon as he could. Then he and Reynolds left together.

The fake drug baron and his fake fiancée.

I plodded back to Hangtown Bank, my gloomy frame of mind at odds with the sunny day. The rest of the afternoon flew by like an all-day chess tournament. It was difficult to concentrate on anything when my thoughts kept returning to Tom and his sexy task force associate.

By the time five p.m. rolled around, I found myself looking forward to the meeting with Paul Thorson. Between my anxiety over my bank employment and my relationship with Tom, I could use a little advice.

I left the bank five minutes early and hurried up the street to the Lifestyle Center. Serenity Sweets remained open with one customer at the counter. A sign next to the stairwell to the left of the bakery indicated Paul Thorson's office was located on the second level.

The century-old wooden stairs creaked, announcing my arrival. Paul held the frosted glass door to his office open for me.

Paul was a younger, shorter, clean-shaven version of his brother. After we shook hands and introduced ourselves, he led me into his office where I settled into a cushy chair. Framed posters on the walls displayed encouraging or, depending on your point of view, nauseating saccharine sentiments.

Paul's desk contained a photo of Serenity in her wedding dress, a laptop computer and a few scattered papers, which he pushed into a pile off to the side.

"So, Laurel, what can I help you with today? Are you looking to make a career change?"

"It's more like my employer is considering a career change—for me."

"Ah, yes. Corporate downsizing is responsible for much of my client base. Tell me more about your current responsibilities. Are there particular aspects of your position that you enjoy more than others?"

Great question. Paul actually sounded like he knew what he was doing. When I had more time, I might utilize him for some coaching. In the meantime, I needed to find a way to segue from my marketing career to my investigative hobby.

"I handle marketing and promotions for Hangtown Bank," I explained. "But the board is considering eliminating the department and outsourcing it to a Sacramento firm."

He nodded. "I've talked to many people in your situation. Have they determined when they'll make the decision and whether or not to keep you employed?"

"The decision is tied to my ability to bring in some large deposits from new clients. I'm also involved in planning the fall Apple Gala which was moved from Apple Tree Farm to Valley View Vineyards after, um, after your brother died," I mumbled. "I'm so sorry for your loss."

Paul's grip on his pen tightened momentarily before he set it down. "Thank you. It's been a difficult time for the family. Axel's death was a huge loss for all of us."

"Poor Dorie. She has her hands full trying to keep the operation going successfully. My daughter works at the bakery on the weekends, and it's been a complete zoo there lately. I don't know how Dorie can do it all."

"She can't," he said flatly. "Axel never saw the need to teach Dorie anything about the operation. He assumed his son would take over the reins when he retired. My nephew is both spoiled and lazy. The most practical decision is for Dorie to sell the farm before she runs it into the ground, and we all lose out."

"Is it easy to sell an apple farm operation? I would think a commercial enterprise could take a while."

"It depends. In our case, we already have a purchaser who's willing to buy it lock, stock and barrels. Of apples." He chuckled at his lame joke.

"How fortunate for you. Someone local?"

He drummed his fingers on the desk before replying. "It's not public knowledge yet, and I still need to convince my sister-in-law it's the only option right now. Since you know Dorie, maybe you can persuade her. It's by far the best decision for everyone. I hope to sign the deal and announce it at the gala this weekend since it's the most appropriate venue."

"At Valley View Vineyards? Why there?"

"Because Walter Eastwood wants to buy the place in order to expand his winery. Apple Tree Farm has an asset some people consider even more valuable than wine."

I must have looked confused because he pointed to a plastic bottle on his desk.

"An unlimited water supply."

CHAPTER FORTY

After four straight years of drought, water rights were considered liquid gold in California.

"So Apple Tree Farm has pre-1903 water rights?" I asked.

"Yep. According to the law, the State can't mess with those rights."

From my years as a mortgage loan underwriter, I was somewhat familiar with the different types of water rights ownership in the state. The governor had recently announced that the primary water rights agency would assume control over some of the pre-1914 water rights, a move that had occurred only once before during the drought in the late seventies. But as far as I knew, no one, not even the State, could mess with the pre-1903 water rights. Although if El Nino didn't arrive to save the day this winter, all bets could be off.

"Is Walter hurting for water? How thirsty are those grapes?"

He laughed. "Grapevines aren't as thirsty as a lot of crops. It only takes thirty-two gallons of water to produce a glass of wine."

Hmmm. Maybe I should cut my showers even shorter. It was bad enough having a water shortage. A chardonnay shortage wouldn't do at all.

"Apples use a similar amount of water. In comparison," he said, "almonds are really thirsty and need over a gallon per nut."

I leaned closer. "I think I misunderstood you. Did you say one dinky almond needs one gallon of water?"

"You heard right. It takes a lot of water to produce a pound of almonds. Central Valley farmers were forced to fallow a number of their almond orchards this past summer. So you'll see a shortage of nuts next year."

That all depended on your definition of "nuts." The human variety seemed to be on the increase lately.

"Fascinating stuff," I said to him. And it really was. But I wasn't here for an agriculture lesson. "Those water rights should make the farm especially valuable, shouldn't they?"

He shrugged. "The main reason it's valuable is because Walter's vineyard is adjacent to ours. After he expanded his operation, he realized his own water supply might not be sufficient if the drought continues, so he tried to purchase our farm. Despite my pleas, Axel refused to sell to him."

"So Axel's death could have some positive consequences."

Paul's eyes changed from the pale silver of a rainy sky to thundercloud gray. "I think we've discussed my family's issues long enough. Let's focus back on you."

I glanced at my watch. In less than ten minutes, he'd provided exactly the information I sought. Now all I needed to do was come up with enough dysfunction in my professional and personal life to fill the next fifty minutes of our one-hour session.

No problemo.

Our session ended a few minutes earlier than anticipated. Paul received a call he needed to take and not with me sitting across from him. He offered a free half-hour consultation later in the week, which I promptly accepted. As I closed the door behind me, I heard him greet his caller.

Walter. Although it might not be Walter of Valley View Vineyards. But if I were taking bets, that's who I would put in first place.

I practically bounced down the sidewalk to the parking lot. Paul's information regarding Apple Tree Farm's value to its next-door neighbor provided a useful piece of evidence. It meant that several people had a reason to off Axel, notably Walter Eastwood. Although Paul, who was definitely in favor of selling the farm, and Dorie would also benefit from the sale. I gave Dorie long odds. I couldn't imagine her killing her husband just so she could sell the property.

Unless she needed cash to purchase more designer pillows for her new home.

As for Walter and Paul, they were both odds-on favorites in my race to find the killer, with Walter leading by a nose. They both had wanted Axel to sell the farm, something he repeatedly refused to do.

I was surprised how helpful Paul had been regarding my own situation. The man might not know anything about running a huge apple operation, but he was a terrific listener. In fact, he was so easy to talk to that once the conversation moved on to my romantic life, I'd almost disclosed all the details of Tom's current undercover job to him.

Now that I thought about it, I might have shared too much information with the life coach. Was this one meeting I would soon regret?

CHAPTER FORTY-ONE

On Tuesday morning, I stopped at the bank to pick up extra brochures and flyers that detailed all the awesome services Hangtown Bank provides its customers. I also grabbed additional flyers for the gala. I was determined to be a multitasking maven today.

I told our receptionist I would be making client calls most of the day but promised to check my voicemail periodically. My cell rang just as I reached my car. I juggled the flyers in one hand while I attempted to locate my phone in my purse.

With no more hands to spare, I dumped the flyers onto the backseat and hit the green button on my iPhone before Liz's call could land in voicemail.

"Hi," I eked out as I slid into the driver's seat.

"Good morning, luv, did I catch you at an inconvenient time?" She chuckled. "Nothing naughty going on is there?"

"The only thing naughty in my life lately is my donut consumption."

"You poor dear. When is your honey coming home?"

"He hopes to wrap things up fairly quickly. I just wish this case wasn't so dangerous. He's going undercover with..." I bit my lip before I disclosed too much to my friend.

"Did you say undercover or under the covers?"

Liz had no idea how close she came to hitting the nail on its head. I wouldn't put it past Detective Reynolds to attempt both options. I trusted my boyfriend, but how far would Tom have to go to maintain his cover?

"The first scenario only, I hope. I'm making sales calls. Did you need something?" I didn't want to be rude, but I had clients to visit and suspects to interrogate.

"Perfect timing. Can you please pick up my beauty supplies while you're in the neighborhood?" she begged. "Brian and I drove up to Apple Tree Farm on Sunday. Camera crews were all over the place, so we turned around and came home. I'm really concerned those boxes will get tossed. I promise to throw in a free facial for you."

Far be it from me to refuse a facial. Detecting was not a wrinkle-free hobby. I agreed to visit the warehouse and we hung up. I added Apple Tree Farm to my lengthy list of stops and began my circuit.

All the farms I visited bustled with customers. The lurid murder tableau appeared to be driving in people by the busload. Cheerful orchard owners, whose registers were loaded with cash and credit card receipts, seemed pleased to see me. Especially after I passed out the autumn pricing specials offered by Hangtown Bank, specifically geared to the farm owners.

Most of the owners planned to attend the Apple Gala, the kickoff event for the Apple Tree twenty-five mile bicycle race the following day. That would be one very long weekend for me since the bank sponsored both events.

By two p.m., I'd met with six different apple farm owners and managed to refrain from sampling any of the enticing treats sold in their various bakeries. I grabbed a tuna sandwich at the Camino deli before I drove to Apple Tree Farm in search of Liz's cosmetics. I rubbed my dry face with my palm. I could use that facial and the sooner the better.

My plan was to look so gorgeous the next time Tom saw me that he would completely forget about his fake fiancée. And, if they wrapped up their case before the gala, I could frolic the night away with my honey.

Which reminded me, we were out of honey at our house. Some of the locals swore that eating locally produced honey helped reduce allergies, and I was all for that. Especially this time of year. I sneezed twice in affirmation of my quest.

I found a parking spot close to the bakery and produce barn. Once inside I strolled down the aisles, filling my arms with a container of honey, a pound of garlic-flavored pistachios and an apple-walnut salad dressing, all produced by local vendors. I turned a corner and bumped into Dorie and Walter chatting in low voices.

"Sorry." I displayed my wares. "I'm doing my weekly shopping here."

"Nothing we love more than that." Dorie smiled then introduced me to Walter. "Laurel's daughter works at the bakery on the weekends. Jenna has been a huge asset during these trying times."

He nodded. "Ms. McKay and I are working on the Apple Gala together. Everything coming along okay?"

"Yes, I think you'll be satisfied with the entertainment and the cuisine. Serenity Thorson and I discussed the menu, and it looks quite appetizing."

Dorie wrinkled her nose at the mention of Serenity's name. "Remind me to eat before the gala. My sister-in-law's food is better fit for rabbits than for people."

Walter's eyes grew round, but I reassured him everyone would be awed by her food selections.

"Can I help you with something?" Dorie asked me.

"Would you happen to know where Liz Daley's cosmetic supplies are stored? Your husband offered to give her the Weather Vainery vendor space. Liz left her products with Axel the Friday before he was…" I paused, figuring she would catch my drift.

"I can help you find that stuff," a gruff voice said from behind me. I turned around to find Brent.

"What time is your meeting?" he asked Walter who looked at his watch and replied, "At three o'clock. We're waiting for Paul and Brooke."

Dorie sighed. "So many difficult decisions to make."

"Listen, I got to finish something first," Brent said to me. "Meet me in front of the warehouse in fifteen minutes or so."

"Thanks. I need to purchase these items anyway," I said.

Dorie waved goodbye and walked away with Walter at her side. Brent took off in the opposite direction, and I ambled over to the registers, hoping I wouldn't drop anything and maim any customers on the way. While I waited in line behind several people equally encumbered with groceries, I mulled over a meeting that would include the owners and manager of Apple Tree Farm, the owner of the vineyard next door, who'd been trying to purchase the property for years, and the farm's accountant.

Walter must have finally talked Dorie into selling. I wondered how Eric felt about losing the family farm—his heritage. But if the Thorson family's financial condition was as dire as their CPA had indicated, it was probably for the best.

I grabbed my bagged items and hoofed it to my car. A tiny Miata squeezed into a compact spot a few spaces down. Brooke stepped out of the dust-spotted convertible and reached into the trunk. She pulled out a briefcase, slammed the lid shut and walked in my direction.

"Hi, Laurel," she said. "Are you here for the meeting?"

"Nope, just picking up a few items. Looks like Walter Eastwood may be acquiring this property from the Thorson family."

"I really can't say," she demurred. "That decision will be made by Dorie and Paul. I'm just the bookkeeper."

"They're lucky to have you."

"I hope they agree. My goal is to help my clients to the best of my ability, but I'm not a magician."

"Maybe Walter can work some magic."

"Axel is probably rolling in his urn. Such a shame that young man killed him. And to think he'd recently learned Axel was his father. What a waste of two men's lives."

"I'm still positive they've arrested the wrong person."

"Hank said you were stub—er, I mean tenacious," she said. "Listen, if I think of anything worthwhile I'll let you know. Will you be here much longer?"

"Just a few more minutes. I'm supposed to meet Brent at the warehouse." I stuck my hand in my purse, waded through some receipts and coupons and eventually found one of my business cards. "This has my work phone and my email address. I know Nina will appreciate anything you can find out."

Brooke took the card and walked off, the briefcase swinging in her hand. At the rate I was asking people for help, Gran would have to name her new concern, A DOZEN GALS DETECTIVE AGENCY.

I decided there was enough time to stop and say hi to Nina before I met with Brent. I hadn't talked to her since the detectives re-arrested her grandson.

I asked the girl at the bakery counter if Nina was available. She appeared a few minutes later, indicating I should come around back.

Lately I'd spent more time in the Apple Tree Farm kitchen than my own. I entered through the door leading into the kitchen. The smell of fried apple fritters and donuts permeated the air. I went to give Nina a hug, but she held back, the front of her apron as well as her hands dusted with flour.

Her eyes searched my face. "Do you have any news?"

"Nothing specific to report. Just a few unproven possibilities."

Nina slumped against the long counter. "This is a never-ending nightmare. Tony's defense attorney said the additional evidence cemented the case as far as the judge was concerned. "

"Do you know what they found?" I asked.

"Tony's fingerprints were on that fifty-pound bag of sugar that killed Axel, although that doesn't really mean anything since he handled supplies. A witness says he saw Tony's car leaving the farm close to the time Axel was killed. The authorities claim that sighting, plus the Friday arrival of the positive DNA results, and Tony's argument with Axel put the last nail in my poor grandson's coffin."

"Oh, dear. How high is his bail?"

"No bail. My baby is locked up with all of those lowlife criminals. I don't think I can bear it."

I went and hugged her, flour and all. "I'm so sorry, Nina, but Gran and I are on the case. By the way, did Dorie tell you she's selling the farm to Walter?"

Nina reared back. "What? She wouldn't. Carolyn Thorson will be beside herself. The Thorson family has owned this farm since their ancestors settled here after the Civil War ended."

"Apparently Walter's been trying to buy the property for years, but Axel kept refusing."

"So once Axel was out of the picture, the picture changed all of a sudden?" she asked me. "Doesn't that seem suspicious to you?"

CHAPTER FORTY-TWO

I left the bakery rarin' to go find me a killer. Since I was only armed with a bagful of apple fritters, it was unlikely I'd nab anyone other than a bear with a sweet tooth.

I glanced at my watch. More than fifteen minutes had passed since Brent and I last spoke so I'd better move along.

As I walked toward the warehouse, I noticed Paul Thorson standing next to a short, stocky, silver-haired man dressed in a well-tailored suit. Not exactly caramel-apple-eating attire. The man carried a stylish briefcase in his right hand. Another accountant?

Why wonder when I could mosey up to the two of them and find out.

"Hi, Paul," I said, nodding at the other man.

"Nice to see you, um..." Paul seemed at a loss for my name. I couldn't decide whether to be insulted that he didn't remember our fifty-minute life coaching session less than twenty-four hours earlier, or pleased that I was so unremarkable in appearance I could blend in anywhere.

"Laurel McKay," I reminded him. "We had a session yesterday."

"Of course. I apologize. I have a lot on my mind right now."

"I ran into Dorie and Walter earlier. Looks like things are finally going your way." I turned to the stranger and put out my hand. "Nice to meet you."

He shook my hand. His palm felt clammier than the fish chowder I'd eaten yesterday, and it took all my self-control not to wipe my hand on my slacks. He chose not to introduce himself, so I decided to help him out.

"Are you Paul's CPA?"

"No, he's Axel's banker," Paul answered for him.

The stranger smoothed his silver pompadour. "I prefer to think of myself as a financial strategist."

And I prefer to think of myself as skinny. The stranger gave off a peculiar vibe, but I couldn't put my finger on it. Maybe I just wasn't used to Armani-clad lenders.

"I'm looking forward to our next session," I said to Paul.

"Yeah, right," he replied, although his gaze was fixed elsewhere. "Sorry, yes, I'm sure we can resolve some of your personal issues."

I sighed. "Hopefully, my boyfriend will be back soon and that will eliminate one of my primary issues."

"It must be difficult being in a relationship with a cop." Paul placed a solicitous palm on my forearm. The financial strategist stared at me as if he was memorizing my face but said nothing.

The guy was creeping me out.

"I need to get going," I said. "I'm meeting Brent at the warehouse."

Paul nodded and the two men walked away, their voices low and undecipherable although the "financial strategist" turned back once to stare at me.

Yuck. That guy was creepy with a capital C. I dug into my apple fritter stash for comfort and smiled in delight. Who needed a life coach when a pastry could provide so much more satisfaction?

I reached the warehouse and found both sliding wooden doors wide open. I stood out front waiting for Brent, face raised to the sky, hoping the September sun would burnish my pale cheeks.

After a few minutes of quiet meditation, I decided he must be waiting inside somewhere. The interior of the building felt chilly after the pleasant outdoor temperature. They probably needed to keep it cool to ensure their supplies stayed fresh.

I called out Brent's name but heard nothing in response. The warehouse was dimly lit by sunlight pouring in from only one window near the back of the expansive building. I tried a couple of wall switches near the doors, but they provided minimal lighting. I shivered as I remembered my last visit inside the warehouse. I hoped Brent would appear soon. I didn't want to spend any more time inside than necessary.

While I waited, I decided to cruise up and down the aisles. Liz's products bore a distinctive blue and silver logo, easy enough to spot, unless the boxes were stored way up on the top shelves. I gazed with dismay at the metal shelving, which rose ten feet or more. How the heck did they find anything around here? On the next aisle over, I noticed a very tall ladder with wheels at the bottom. That must come in handy for sliding from one spot to the other.

I chose to search the lower shelves on each aisle first. With luck, I would find her items within a few minutes.

Today was not my lucky day. I saw boxes and bags filled with a variety of staples for the bakery—sugar, flour, salt, and spices. Plus packaging materials. Plastic jugs, paper plates and utensils. Numerous retail supplies they must store for their vendors, but none of the pricey cosmetic variety.

It would be easier to look for a needle in the Trump Tower than to find Liz's supplies in this warehouse.

Twenty minutes elapsed and Brent still hadn't appeared. Walter and Dorie must have asked him to attend their meeting after all. I gritted my teeth and approached the mobile ladder with uncertainty. Between my fear of heights and my inherent klutziness, I wasn't keen on ascending a wheeled piece of equipment. But I hated to be a wuss, and I hated even more to fail my friend, so I tried to convince myself it might be fun.

Like a sweet ride at Disneyland—the ones for ages six and under.

I tentatively lifted my right sandal onto the first rung. It felt secure so I climbed one level higher. So far, so good. I could now view boxes on the second shelf from the top and glimpse the handwriting on some of the cartons on the top tier. I scanned items to the left and to the right of me. No bold blue font with the silver Beautiful Image logo plastered across the face of any boxes.

I climbed down the ladder. Once back on the ground, I slid the contraption over to the middle set of shelving. By now, I felt comfortable using the equipment so I clambered up the rungs with alacrity.

Aha! At last, I'd found Liz's supplies. I positioned myself directly beneath them and reached up. The sound of a motor caught my attention. I glanced toward the open doors to see if someone had driven up to the warehouse. Maybe I could enlist their help in retrieving her stuff.

No vehicles outside. Yet the noise continued to grow louder and louder. Where on earth was it coming from? I tried to peek through the boxes on the shelf facing me, but I couldn't see anything.

I lowered my left shoe onto the next rung of the ladder. My right sandal dangled from my foot as I reached for the next tread down. The shelving began to shake violently. My damp palms gripped the ladder as I struggled to maintain my precarious balance.

Wham! The ladder bounced away from the shelves before it slammed back into them. My forehead smacked against the metal rung, and for a few seconds I was afraid I would black out. An earthquake must have occurred somewhere in the Sierras. I needed to get off this contraption at once.

I looked down, prepared to leap to my safety, when another tremor occurred. Bags of sugar and flour crashed down below, their contents splayed onto the floor. A box nearly grazed my right ear. I held on tight, but it wasn't enough. The metal shelves screamed as they tipped, propelling me backward onto the hard cement floor.

The lights went out. Then it was silent.

CHAPTER FORTY-THREE

I dreamt of apple pie, sugar and spice, and everything nice. In my dream, I was eating a piece of pie. No, that wasn't right. I was stuffed into the pie. Mashed in with all the other ingredients. Someone pushed me into the crust and beat me with a rolling pin. Over and over and over.

I tried to protect my face with my arms, but something was restraining them. "Help me," I screamed.

An angelic voice whispered in my ear. "Laurel, everything is okay now."

I opened my eyes then shrank back from the bright light. An alien covered in white hovered over me.

I blinked and my contact lens settled on my corneas where they belonged. Not an alien—a doctor. And my mother and grandmother seated next to me.

"Mom?" I squeaked, feeling like a kid who'd just scraped her knees and yearned for her mother's sympathy. Based on the pain throbbing in my head, there was more damage than an injured knee.

"How do you feel?" asked the doctor whose youthful face bore a strong resemblance to Doogie Hauser's.

"Like I was run over by a train." I paused for a few seconds trying to recollect. "What happened?"

"We don't know," said Mother. "Rose Margolis, one of the Apple Tree Farm bakers, found you unconscious in the warehouse. The bakery had run out of sugar, and Rose, couldn't find Nina anywhere, so she went to the warehouse to get some supplies. She discovered you lying on the ground, covered with flour and spices."

"We almost lost you," sniffed Gran. "I guess there was a real heavy carton lying just a few inches from your cute little head."

I shivered, which made my cute little head hurt even more. "Based on the way my head feels, something collided with it."

"You have a large contusion on the back of your head and a smaller bruise on your forehead. And a concussion. Two of your ribs are cracked but not broken," the doctor informed me. "I'd say you were very lucky."

"Do you remember what happened?" Mother asked.

I started to shake my head but thought better of it. Now why had I gone into the warehouse?

"It's all kind of fuzzy right now," I said. "I think I was supposed to meet someone there."

"Axel's killer?" Gran asked.

"Maybe. I don't know. You said the shelving landed on me. How did that happen?"

"We were hoping you could answer that question," Mother replied, taking one of my hands in hers. "I called both Bradford and Tom to tell them about your accident, but both calls went straight to voicemail."

Tom. My heart rate sped up, which was apparent to everyone by the sudden spike on my heart monitor.

"They probably can't access their phones right now since they're undercov..." My voice trailed off when I saw the doctor's puzzled expression. "You know on the job."

"We need to report this to someone," Mother insisted. "Those shelves didn't fall down by themselves."

I relaxed against the pillows. Shoot. That hurt, too. The next time I entered the Apple Tree Farm warehouse I would don a helmet first.

Liz and her husband, Brian, burst through the door.

"Are you okay?" She bustled over to my bedside. Her brow puckered as she examined me. "I hope you won't take this the wrong way, but you look like bloody hell."

Liz reached into her capacious Marc Jacobs purse and pulled out a small tube. She quickly uncapped it and started smoothing the lotion on my face.

I pushed her away. "Stop it. I don't need bronzing right now. Besides, it's all your fault I was in the warehouse to begin with."

"My fault?" She placed a manicured hand on her chest, a look of dismay shooting across her face.

"Yes. I just remembered that Brent and I arranged to meet so he could give me your products. I waited and waited for him to show up. It was growing late, so I finally decided to climb on their rolling ladder and look for your supplies myself."

"Did you pull the shelves down, dear?" asked Mother.

I frowned at her. "No, it wasn't my klutz factor at work. Right before everything crashed down, I heard the low sound of an engine on the other side of the shelves. And that's when everything rained down on me."

"See. What did I tell ya," Gran said. "The killer tried to off Laurel."

"I think I'll leave you alone for now," the doctor said, his expression a mixture of confusion and concern. "It looks like you have some things to work out. I'm keeping you in the hospital overnight though." He made some notes on a clipboard then walked out of the room mumbling to himself.

"Do you think Brent was responsible for your accident?" Liz asked.

I reflected back on my visit to the farm. "Several people could have done it. Dorie, Walter Eastwood, Brent. Even Paul Thorson."

Brian interrupted me. "If you're discussing the Thorson murder, then I need to recuse myself from this discussion. That case file was handed over to me this morning."

"Recuse away, dear," said Liz. "But we need to get the police involved. This does not sound like an accident to me. Someone intentionally tried to hurt Laurel. What are you going to do about it since Detective Reynolds is on duty elsewhere?"

"I'll contact the Sheriff and make sure the warehouse is treated as a crime scene," he said. "Unfortunately, several hours have passed so any useful evidence may have been removed by now."

"Did Rose notice anyone else in the warehouse?" I asked.

Mother shrugged. "All they told me was that she found you and immediately rushed back to the bakery to call 911. Nina had returned by then so she contacted Gran who then called me. We rushed to the hospital as soon as we found out."

"I suppose if there was any evidence, it was destroyed by the culprit," I said. "Does this mean I'm making the killer nervous?"

"Or maybe just irritating him," Gran suggested.

My family is always so supportive.

I threw back the thin hospital blanket and started to get up from the bed. "Ouch." I looked down and realized I'd almost yanked the IV out of my arm. I wasn't going anywhere for now.

Liz pushed me back and placed the blanket over me. "Stay," she ordered. "You're not leaving with that concussed head."

"What if the killer comes after me in the hospital? I'm a sitting duck." I pleaded with Brian. "Can you arrange for a deputy to guard my door?"

He shook his head. "There isn't enough proof that your accident wasn't just that. Plus they're short officers right now. I'll do what I can."

"No one's coming after my granddaughter while I'm around." Gran dug inside her huge black vinyl purse and pulled out the scariest weapon I'd ever laid eyes on.

"Is that a missile?" I asked her.

She snorted. "Don't be silly. It's an extra-large wasp spray. I can get an attacker at twenty-five feet."

I didn't want to tell Gran that the odds of her seeing someone twenty-five feet away were zero.

"Okay, then. Are you leaving it with me?"

Mom reached over and grabbed the spray can from Gran. "You're more likely to maim a doctor than anyone else. I would stay with you, Laurel, but I already told Jenna I'd spend the night with her and Ben. She wanted to come to the hospital, but I didn't know whether you were in any shape to see them."

"I'll stay with Laurel," Liz said. "It is 'partially' my fault she's in here."

"Look, everyone, I appreciate your efforts, but I'll be fine. Just tell the staff no one is allowed to visit except family members. That should keep our mysterious attacker out."

Or so I hoped. The bad guys always managed to sneak into hospitals on my favorite crime shows, but I'd never get any rest if Liz or Gran spent the night with me. And now that my brain felt less foggy, I had some serious thinking to do.

Like figuring out who wanted to kill me.

CHAPTER FORTY-FOUR

I awoke at eight the next morning. The nurses had roused me every hour during the night, so I felt even worse than the previous evening. My head still throbbed, even after chugging a glass of water with a Vicodin chaser. The Vicodin made me nauseous, so I decided that future painkillers would come out of my Ibuprofen bottle.

The hospital refused to release me until the doctor approved it. They expected him to make his rounds about noon.

I played with the remote and switched between the various morning shows. Once they moved to cooking tips, it was time to focus on crime tips. I clicked on the Hallmark Channel and landed on one of my favorite crime shows—*Diagnosis Murder*.

It always amazed me how Dick Van Dyke, alias Dr. Mark Sloan, managed to multitask between medicine and murder. On a daily basis, no less. He'd just nailed the wife as the killer when Dorie Thorson walked into my room. She shut the door behind her and reached into a floral tote.

I screamed and hurled the remote at her. Dorie shrieked and the contents of her purse scattered across the room. Seconds later, a nurse flung open the door and slid across the threshold Kramer style.

"What's wrong?" asked the flushed-faced nurse.

"She tried to maim me with the remote," Dorie responded in a shaky voice.

"Sorry. You surprised me." I frowned at the nurse. "I didn't think they allowed visitors other than family members."

"Shall I usher your visitor out?" the nurse asked. Her face bore an "I've got better things to do with my time than act as your personal concierge" expression.

"No, it's fine," I said. Dorie still looked flustered, but she grabbed her handbag and began replacing the contents. The nurse assisted her, then picked up the remote and handed it to me.

"You'll be okay." She phrased it more as a statement than a question. I nodded and fluttered my fingers goodbye.

Dorie dropped into the chair closest to my bed. She scrutinized my face before speaking. "How do you feel? You look terrible."

I shrugged. "That's about how I feel."

"Whatever were you doing climbing around the warehouse all by yourself?" Her face was pinched, and I wondered if she was worried about any potential liability. "You could have been killed."

Evidently.

"Don't you remember Brent telling me to meet him there?" I asked her. "I waited, but he never showed, so I decided to look for my friend's supplies myself."

Her eyes widened, emphasizing the advent of recent crow's feet on her otherwise youthful visage. If I ever located Liz's products, I would give Dorie a sample of the eye cream.

"Axel told me he was concerned about Brent stealing inventory," she said. "Do you think Brent tried to stop you from discovering what he's been up to?"

"I do. I also think he might have killed your husband," I reminded her, since Dorie seemed to have forgotten one significant piece of the puzzle.

"Oh, I can't imagine that, although..." Her voice trailed off as she examined my bruises, which presented a palette of every color in the rainbow. "What should I do?"

194

I thought about her situation for a few seconds. "We don't really have proof of anything. Just suspicions. Do you know Brent's whereabouts at the time of my accident?"

"He could have been anywhere on the premises, including the warehouse. I don't know how I would run the place without Brent's help though." A flash of chagrin crossed her face. "Of course, everything will change in a few weeks."

"Did you decide to sell?" That would alter everything for Dorie, hopefully for the better.

She nodded. "We met with Axel's banker buddy yesterday. Walter agreed to assume the note. I had no idea that Axel mortgaged the farm to pay for the cost overruns on our new house." She sniffed then burst into tears.

I reached over and grabbed some tissues from the box next to the nightstand. Might as well use them since they would probably show up on my hospital bill.

Dorie snatched them from me and honked twice. She wiped the trails of mascara that had formed Fu Manchu lines down her face then discarded the tissues in the wastebasket.

"I don't understand why my husband didn't confide in me," she blubbered. "We could have cut back on the size of our house. Axel never wanted to worry me about financial problems. Now look at all the trouble he left behind."

I grabbed an additional wad of tissues and handed them to her along with another question. "What about life insurance? Did Axel have a decent policy?"

"Yes, and no," she wailed. "I knew he held a million-dollar policy with Eric and me as beneficiaries. What I didn't know was that he stopped making payments because we couldn't afford them."

Poor woman. She was in a world of hurt.

"Dorie, I know it's tough selling a business that's been in the family for so many years. But I'm sure you're making the right decision for you and your son. And for Paul as well. He seems in favor of unloading the place."

"Paul had been bugging Axel to sell for ages, but he had no idea Axel took out that huge loan on the farm. Since my husband held a majority ownership, he had the authority to make those kinds of financial decisions on his own." Dorie scrunched her nose. "I sure didn't care for that banker Axel got the loan from. He seemed—"

"Icky," I said, unable to think of anything more descriptive.

"Yeah. Kind of slimy. I don't know how Axel found him."

"I wasn't officially introduced. Do you remember his name or his firm's name?"

"I don't remember his name, but the company is called Aces Financial Group. Like the hardware store except plural like in a deck of cards."

That didn't sound like the name of a top-rated financial institution. Odd that Axel sought a loan from a finance company. Maybe he'd been rejected by all the regular lenders such as Sierra Mountain Lenders. It was probably a last ditch effort to keep Apple Tree Farm operating. The interest rate would have been well above the norm, which wouldn't help his financial situation.

"In the meantime," Dorie said, "I need to keep the place going somehow. Two more employees quit because of your incident yesterday." She glared at me as if it was my fault I'd been buried under the rubble in the warehouse. I supposed it was partially my responsibility, since I'd been rummaging around the shelves by myself. At least, we knew someone was concerned about what I knew.

I just wish I knew what that was.

"Sorry about your staff leaving," I said. "Did you remember Jenna has her SAT this Saturday?"

Tears gathered in Dorie's eyes once again. I grabbed the few remaining tissues and handed them to her. They had better suffice because I was not letting the hospital staff put another overpriced box on my bill.

She raised her tear-stained face to me. "Do you know anyone who could work there this weekend?"

I sighed. "Maybe Gran or I could help in the bakery. Nina could show us the ropes."

"Laurel, you're a lifesaver." Dorie stood and wrapped her arms around me, which did nothing to alleviate my headache. Although if I could get her to leave me alone that might help somewhat.

"Let me talk to Gran to see what she says," I replied, although I could easily guess my grandmother's response.

Detecting among donuts? What's not to love?

CHAPTER FORTY-FIVE

Dorie was halfway out the door when she stopped and reached into her bag. This time I retained control of the remote and was pleasantly surprised when she withdrew a small box of fudge.

"It's not much, but hopefully it will speed up your recovery." Dorie handed me the fudge and then took off.

As far as I was concerned, chocolate won hands down over Vicodin any day of the week. I reached inside the box and popped a hunk of the soft fudge into my mouth. Another visitor appeared while I was still working on the oversized chunk of chocolate.

This hospital was turning into Grand Central Station. I stared at my visitor mid-chew.

"Cat got your tongue?" Adriana asked, then giggled. "Oh, I guess it's chocolate."

"What are you doing here?" I mumbled through my mouthful of chocolate.

"Walter was concerned your injury might result in a lack of oversight on the gala. He asked me to go over the checklist with you."

Geesh. "I'm fine. Just waiting for the doctor to release me."

"He also said you almost singlehandedly destroyed the Apple Tree warehouse yesterday. He's not too pleased since he agreed to buy the place."

"I wasn't too pleased someone tried to kill me."

"What?"

Since I had nothing better to do while I waited for the doctor than watch television or eat a pound of fudge, I decided to confide in Adriana. She seemed to have a special connection with Walter. Maybe she could provide some insight into the Apple Tree Farm sale.

"Walter led me to believe you brought everything crashing down yourself." She smirked. "You know how klutzy you are."

Thanks, Adriana. Lovely bedside manner you have.

"Anyway, "she continued, "you can imagine Walter's annoyance when minutes earlier he'd signed the contract to purchase the farm."

"He certainly seemed in a rush to buy the place. Kind of makes me wonder if he put this whole thing in motion to begin with."

Adriana's expression morphed from confusion to astonishment.

"Are you on drugs?" she asked.

Technically, yes, but it had been a few hours since the nurse gave me the Vicodin. I was higher on chocolate than anything else.

"Look, someone killed Axel, and they may have tried to take me out as well. How badly did Walter want to buy Apple Tree Farm?"

She fidgeted with her purse strap before inching closer to me. I was becoming increasingly suspicious of everyone lately, so I shrank back into the pillows, wishing Mother had let me keep Gran's wasp spray for protection.

Adriana winced when she took in my assorted bruises. "I'm sure Walter had nothing to do with your accident. His only concern was to wrap up the sale so he could announce it at the gala. He'd already asked me to prepare a press release in advance."

I screwed up my forehead in thought. Either the Vicodin or the fudge had achieved a medicinal effect because it barely hurt.

"When did Walter ask you to prepare the announcement?" I asked her.

"A couple of weeks ago. He told me to keep it quiet until everything was finalized."

I grabbed Adriana's right hand and squeezed it hard. "Think back. Did he ask you to do this before or after Axel was murdered?"

She pulled away from me and rubbed her wrist. "Fine, if it's that important to you." Adriana reached into her purse and grabbed her iPhone. She punched a few buttons and pulled up her calendar. Her dark eyebrows rose.

"We met the day before Axel's murder."

CHAPTER FORTY-SIX

"What should we do?" Adriana asked. "Call the Sheriff? The media?"

The media? The last thing we needed was for her to tweet our discovery in 140 characters or less.

"Calm down. We have to be sensible about this. Walter is an established member of the Placerville and Camino communities, not to mention a Hangtown Bank board member. Just because he asked you to write a press release about the sale prior to Axel's death doesn't mean squat. We can't jump to conclusions and accuse him of murder."

At least, not to his face. Based on past experience that frequently proved to be a bad idea.

"Plus the timing could be coincidental," I said. "Maybe Axel finally agreed to sell to Walter but didn't tell anyone else. Not even his wife or brother."

"That's true." Adriana stood. "I'm sure it's nothing. Do you seriously believe Walter could commit murder?" She eyed me up and down. "Maybe you should stick to marketing. Your so-called detecting doesn't seem to be going so well."

I rolled my eyes. "Fine. But in the meantime, don't say anything about our conversation to anyone. Got it?"

"Mum's the word." She zipped her lip. Considering her PR background, I should probably seize her iPhone and iPad, too.

The nurse arrived with a lunch tray. Adriana took a look at the entrée, said goodbye and wished me well. After surveying the lunch choices provided by the hospital, I reflected that might be easier said than done.

I managed to eat a portion of the bland lunch while I watched the noontime news. Most of the stories centered on local issues, the water shortage in a tiny foothill town, a slight chance of rain this weekend and the Chicago Cubs making it into the playoffs. Wow. That was news.

The "breaking news" banner suddenly scrolled across the screen. Leila Hansen, the KNCA broadcaster from Sacramento, tried to look alarmed, but her Botox-enhanced face seemed stuck in perpetuity with one expression only. Her words, however, chilled me to my bones.

"Our news center just received word that an operation involving members of various federal and state law enforcement agencies has resulted in a shootout. Although participants are as yet unnamed, it appears there is one fatality, possibly of an El Dorado County Sheriff's deputy."

Ignoring my sore ribs, I leapt out of my bed and stood directly beneath the small television provided by the hospital. My breath caught as the screen filled with photos of an office building in Reno.

"Laurel, what are you doing up?" Mother asked as she entered my room. She nudged me toward the bed. "You look as pale as these sterile white walls." She frowned, either at my exertions, or the lack of designer colors in the hospital's neutral decor.

When I didn't budge, Mother's gaze drifted up to the television monitor above our heads. Her frown deepened when she caught the words "Reno" and "task force."

She gasped. "What's going on? Who are they talking about?" Her eyes were now glued to the TV. "Is that Robert?"

I squinted at the small screen, which displayed two EMTs rolling a gurney to a waiting ambulance. The person on the gurney wasn't recognizable to me, although whoever rested on it wore ginormous black wingtips.

I glanced at my mother. Her anguished expression spoke words.

"Mom, there is no way of knowing who that is. There could be a number of gunshot-related crimes going on in Reno. It's a big city. Lots and lots of criminal activity."

I personally knew nothing about Reno's crime rate, but my mother looked like she could use all the comforting words I could come up with, whether fact or fiction.

She pointed at the screen with a shaky hand. "But I know those feet. I mean..." She hesitated, and I wrapped my arm around her trembling shoulders.

"Those could be the shoes of any law officer. Lots of big men in law enforcement. Lots of big feet. Tom has huge feet, too." I stopped because the "big" comparisons could go on forever, and I wanted to concentrate on the activity on the screen.

The report ended and the camera crew switched back to the station. "More updates on the five p.m. news," Leila announced before switching from serious to smiley-face. "Now, let's check on the weather."

I picked up the remote and switched the television off. I led Mother to the chair next to my bed and returned to the rock-hard comfort of my hospital mattress.

"You're here earlier than I expected," I said, hoping to distract not only her, but also myself from my concerns about Tom. "The doctor still hasn't stopped by to sign the release forms."

"I thought you could use some company, and I wanted the diversion. I went into the office, but my heart wasn't in it. Not with Robert out there doing who knows what." Tears formed at the corners of her eyes. "Or having who knows what done to him."

I reached for my tissue box and discovered it was empty due to Dorie's cry fest. My mother fortunately never lacked for supplies. She pulled out a miniature package of tissues with the Centurion Realty logo on it and dabbed at her tears, careful not to mar her makeup.

Great giveaway. So useful, too. And if those great big shoes belonged to my honey, we would need a truck full of tissues.

Usually Mother was the one to boost my spirits, but it was time to reverse our roles.

"Let's talk about something more cheerful," I suggested.

"Like what? Axel's murder? You almost getting killed yesterday?" she spat out at me.

Hmm. Not a great week for anyone in our family. I switched directions.

"Thanks for watching the kids last night. Did Jenna study for her SAT? We'll both be relieved when that's over."

"It may not be over for a while. Jenna told me she's so concerned about Tony being locked up again that she hasn't been able to concentrate. She's even thinking of skipping the test this weekend."

"No way," I protested. "We already paid for it. Besides, she can take it again if she doesn't score as high as she should. It will be good practice for her."

"Jenna seems quite enamored with this Tony. I hope she's not one of those studious girls who for some reason are attracted to bad boy types."

At this point, I couldn't decide which was worse, dating a bad boy or dating someone who spent his life trying to catch bad boys. I only knew I wouldn't be able to fully recover from my injuries until Tom and Bradford were both home safe in the arms of their loving, angst-filled women.

CHAPTER FORTY-SEVEN

The doctor arrived a few minutes later. He proclaimed my injuries to be healing properly but warned me to take it easy for the next few days. I chose not to ask whether his definition of "easy" included chauffeuring children, planning a gala and working at the Apple Tree bakery, all while hunting down a killer.

The nurse stuffed me into a wheelchair and rolled me down the corridor. She seemed to be in a particularly good mood—most likely as thrilled to get rid of her patient as I was to be released from the hospital.

Mother drove me home and announced she would spend the day with me. She placed my teapot on the burner then scoured my pantry looking for something edible. She discovered a blueberry scone mix and decided to whip up a batch. Considering their expiration date was a year earlier, the pastries didn't taste any drier than scones normally did. I enjoyed the pampering and gathered it helped Mother to do something other than fret about her husband.

I was debating who to call for an update on the Reno shooting when my cell rang.

Tom. Thank goodness. I fumbled with the answer button and tried to remain calm. That lasted about two seconds before I shouted into the phone. "Are you okay? What about Bradford?"

The phone was silent for a minute, and I thought we'd lost our connection. Then Tom spoke, his voice still and somber. "I'm fine. But Bradford..." His words disappeared into cell phone ether.

"Tom, are you there?" I repeated to no avail before my phone informed me the call had ended.

"Are they okay?" Mother asked. Her hand shook, and honey-gold liquid sloshed over the rim of the mug she carried and dripped onto my carpet. She dashed back into the kitchen temporarily distracted by a new crisis. A trail of tea droplets scattered across my carpet.

With two kids living in my house, spills occurred on a daily basis, but cleaning up gave Mother something to do while we waited to hear back from Tom. The short wait gradually increased to an hour. I finally switched on the TV hoping for another newsflash. I debated between several talk shows and settled on Dr. Oz's latest tips for losing weight, which seemed to involve all things green: veggies, coffee beans and tea.

If he included green M&Ms, I might even sign up for his program.

My cell rang twice more, each time indicating Tom was on the line, but nothing could be heard other than static. Every time the phone blared, my heart jumpstarted. At this rate, I would suffer a heart attack and land back at Marshall Hospital before long.

The roar of the school bus pulling away interrupted my negative thoughts. Ben entered the house and hurled seventy pounds of solid muscle at me.

"Take it easy, honey. I have a couple of cracked ribs." I tousled his hair and kissed his cheek. "I missed you last night."

"I missed you, too." He examined my forehead. "You don't look so hot. Did the bad guy get you?"

Most likely, but I didn't need to share that with my son.

"Just an accident. How was soccer?"

That question sidetracked any inquiries about me while Ben regaled me with highlights from yesterday's practice. Moments later, Jenna entered the family room.

"Mom, you're back." As she drew closer, her expression went from joy to concern. "You look awful. Grandmother said you're lucky to be alive."

I sent my mother a dirty look.

"You are lucky to have such minor injuries," she replied. "This is why detecting should be left to real detectives." Mother shook her finger at Jenna. "And that means you, too, young lady."

Jenna shrugged, the silent version of "whatever." "I'm sorry you were hurt, Mom, but I'm glad you're still trying to get Tony out of jail."

I didn't bother to correct her. Technically, I'd been trying to recover Liz's cosmetics when the shelves crashed down on me, but if the killer thought I had information worth killing for, then we'd learned something.

Maybe when the swelling in my brain went down, I'd know what it was.

Both kids went upstairs to work on their homework. The five p.m. news came on so Mother and I settled in my matching plaid wing chairs. Pumpkin jumped into my lap, either sensing I needed something to pet or just wanting to cuddle. Her gentle purr calmed me as I eagerly waited for an update.

Leila opened her broadcast with a few local newsworthy items before finally switching to the Reno crime scene. The Reno reporter, looking hot in a suit and tie, held the mike in one hand while he pointed out items of interest with the other. Curious bystanders crowded behind the yellow barrier tape while law enforcement personnel attempted to clean up the scene.

The newsman stood close to a large sign in front of the three-story building. Bright gold letters against a black background spelled out the words Aces Financial Group. I leapt out of my chair, and Pumpkin tumbled to the floor with a meow of protest.

"Authorities haven't revealed the full extent of their investigation," the newsman announced, "but one source claims a joint task force took down a huge money laundering and drug operation today. Sadly, one El Dorado County Sheriff's Deputy was fatally wounded during a shootout, as was one of the suspects. Two other parties were also injured and transported to a Reno Hospital. Their names have not yet been released."

He droned on for another minute but didn't provide any additional information. I glanced at my mother. She sat ramrod stiff, her hands cemented to the arms of her chair.

"It looks like our honeys will be home soon," I said, "assuming they've rounded up all the members of the money-laundering gang."

"You did hear him mention that one El Dorado County Deputy was killed," she said in a whimper.

"Yes, and I'm very sorry to hear that. But your husband isn't an official deputy anymore. Only a consultant. So that means it can't be him." I wasn't certain my logic was logical, but if it provided her some emotional relief, I would stick with it.

She chewed bright pink lipstick off her lower lip. "I suppose that makes sense." Her shoulders drooped. "What a nightmare."

I tried to think of something to distract her. "Did you notice the sign on that building the newsman stood in front of during his broadcast?" I asked. "Aces Financial Group is the finance company that lent money to Axel Thorson. I met one of their employees at Apple Tree Farm shortly before my warehouse incident."

"Now that's a strange coincidence."

"You're telling me. I wonder if this will impede Walter Eastwood's purchase of the farm. According to Dorie, Walter planned on assuming their loan."

"Why would Axel go to a hard money lender to get a loan?"

"He must have been desperate. Maybe the local banks rejected his application, and Aces Financial was a lender of last resort. They could have a legitimate lending business going outside of the money laundering operation." I paused as I thought it through. "In fact, a finance company is the perfect front for money laundering. What better way to use illegal cash than to make legal loans?"

"True. And if the borrower can't pay off the loan, Aces can foreclose and scoop up some valuable property," Mother added.

"Or, if the foreclosure process took too long, they could use other methods," I said. "Like murder."

CHAPTER FORTY-EIGHT

On that cheery note, Mother and I prepared dinner for the four of us. I kept glancing at my cell, but the screen remained message free. After a few minutes of subdued conversation and quiet chewing, my phone rang.

I jumped up, grabbed my cell and walked upstairs, my heart and ribs both throbbing, but for different reasons.

"What's going on?" I asked Tom. "Your task force has been all over the news."

"So I gather," he replied, his voice hoarse. "I hope they're not scaring the rodents back into their rat holes. We weren't able to round up everyone."

"Before I ask any more questions, is Bradford okay? You were cut off last time you called."

"He'll be fine. A bullet clipped him on the shoulder." I crumpled on my bed in relief. Tom added, "He saved Ali Reynold's life."

"Omigod. What happened?"

"One of our target's bodyguards shot and killed a Tahoe deputy, an undercover cop from their narcotics squad. Then the thug took aim at Ali. Bradford shoved her out of the way. That man can move despite his size. He must be spending his retirement watching *Dirty Harry* movies. He took the shooter out at the same time."

"Wow," I said, in awe of my stepfather's prowess. "Mother will either be proud of him or ready to kill him herself."

"Ali can't stop talking about him. I think she's hoping to persuade him to come back to the department."

"I'm just glad you're safe. I've been worried out of my mind."

"It's the nature of my job," he said. "You know that."

I did, but that didn't make it any easier.

"We managed to catch the kingpin and most of his cronies, but a few of his cohorts were out of town when this came to a head yesterday. At least, we have their names and an accomplice or two willing to provide evidence in exchange for a more lenient sentence."

"Would it surprise you to know I met someone from Aces Financial Group yesterday?"

"Nothing you do surprises me anymore," he said. "Can I ask where and why?"

"I bumped into him at Apple Tree Farm. Axel borrowed a huge sum of money from the finance company. A representative met with the owners yesterday to discuss a sale to Walter Eastwood. When Dorie visited me in the hospital this morning, she said Walter agreed to assume the loan. I wonder what will happen now."

Complete silence greeted me. "Tom. Tom?" I said into the phone. "Are you there?"

"Sorry, I'm trying to process what you said, starting with the word 'hospital.'"

"Oh." I wondered how much to share with him. He'd been through so much in the last few days. What were a few bumps, bruises and cracked ribs in the ultimate scheme of things? "I suffered a fall at Apple Tree Farm trying to retrieve some of Liz's cosmetics from the warehouse. Nothing to worry about, Sweetheart. I'm home where I belong. And, hopefully, you will be back here soon."

"It could take us a few more days to sift through their records. I'm curious about the man you met yesterday. What was his name?"

"I didn't catch it, and Dorie couldn't remember either. We both agreed he was icky."

"That description will certainly help when I send out my bulletin," Tom said drily.

"Sorry. If you had a photo, I could identify him."

"Let me see what I can do. Is there any way you can find out his name without ending up in the hospital again?"

I certainly hoped so.

Tom needed to get back to work, and I knew Mother would be dying to find out how her husband was faring, so we hung up. I'd only reached the top of the staircase when she appeared in the foyer below, a dish in one hand and a towel in the other. Her worried eyes searched my face.

I smiled and her shoulders relaxed. "Bradford's fine. A bullet grazed his shoulder. I guess he's a big hero."

"He's too old to be a hero," she sniffed before dissolving in tears. She dried her eyes with the dishtowel proving that true love could overcome a lifetime fear of germs.

"Where is he?" she asked. "Can I visit him?"

"He's at St. Mary's Hospital in Reno. Why don't you call?"

Mom spun on her designer heels and sped back into the family room to grab her phone. My head pounded, my cracked ribs hurt, and the bruise on my thigh seemed to have expanded since yesterday. I followed her into the family room, eased into the wing chair and considered my next step.

Tom's phone call had me wondering if the sleazy lender had anything to do with Axel's death. How likely was it that a mortgage led to murder?

CHAPTER FORTY-NINE

After nine hours of blissful sleep, I arrived at the bank a few minutes late on Thursday morning. Staffers greeted me with sympathetic looks and curious eyes and ears. The Human Resources Director even stopped to chat with me. Since I'd ostensibly been making sales calls, she wanted to know if I planned to file a workers' compensation claim.

Even if I wanted to file a claim, which I didn't, I wouldn't know who to direct it to: Hangtown Bank, Apple Tree Farm, Liz's Golden Hills Spa, or the anonymous killer? I told the director my injuries were minor and not to worry about the bank's welfare.

She breathed a sigh of relief, patted me on my sore hand and recommended I stay out of trouble.

Hah. As if I could.

Stan also stopped by bearing gifts. A jumbo bottle of Ibuprofen and a bright orange hard hat.

"Very funny." I glowered at him.

He reached into his shopping bag and pulled out a small box of candy from the Candy Emporium. "Dr. Stan prescribes two pills followed by two truffles. You'll be up chasing suspects in no time."

He sat in the chair in front of my desk. "Really, Laurel, I think this is one murder you need to sit out."

"You may be right, although it looks like I've made the killer nervous."

Stan frowned. "You've also made me nervous. Promise me you'll be careful."

That I could definitely guarantee. Stan gently hugged me then left my office. Seconds later Liz called to see how I was faring. She informed me we were lunching with Adriana at Serenity's place today. Adriana had requested a sampling of the food Serenity planned to serve Saturday night, and the caterer reluctantly had acquiesced. I couldn't think of a reason to refuse a free lunch so I agreed. Besides, Axel's sister-in-law might know the answers to a few questions of mine.

I walked into the bakery a few minutes after noon. Adriana and Liz were already seated at a small table by the front window.

I slid out a wrought-iron chair and joined them. They both stared at me.

"You're looking, uh…"Adriana stopped and glanced at Liz.

"You still look like a cement truck ran over you." Liz reached into her designer bag. She fumbled a bit and pulled out something that resembled a tube of lipstick.

"I don't think rosy lips will help my appearance," I protested.

"Try it," she insisted. "It's a new product called Magical Erase. It's from the Beautiful Image line. And now that you mention it, did you locate my products before your accident?"

The last thing I'd planned on mentioning was her merchandise until I found out whether they'd been crushed along with me on Tuesday night.

"Not yet." I abruptly switched subjects. "So what's new with the gala, Adriana?"

"Walter's in a tizzy about his Apple Tree Farm purchase and whether he should announce it at the gala or not. Did you know the company who gave Axel his loan was also into money laundering? It's so difficult to believe Axel would do business with people like that."

"Desperate people sometimes do desperate loans," I said.

Three plates of savory smelling food were placed on the table. "I heard what you said about Axel and that lender," Serenity said. "I can't believe he signed his and Paul's inheritance away to that crook."

She grabbed a fourth chair and joined us. "Eat up. I've got a freezer full of ribs for the gala so you better like it." The "or else" was implied in her tone of voice. I couldn't blame Serenity. It was a little late to be sampling the gala menu.

Anything would be an improvement over the hospital food I'd recently consumed, however Serenity's fare deserved four stars at a minimum. All three of us cleaned our plates with contented smiles.

"Excellent meal," I said to her. "And amazing you can pull it off with all of the stress you two have been under."

"If Axel had sold the property when Paul first begged him to unload it, none of this would have happened," she complained.

I was about to ask her to elaborate when she addressed Adriana. "Are you satisfied with the cuisine, Ms. Menzinger?"

"It will do," Adriana replied in a cool tone. "Please have your staff at Valley View Vineyards no later than four p.m. on Saturday."

Serenity nodded and stood. She retrieved our empty plates although I could swear she muttered "up yours" as she walked away. The sound of earthenware clattering against a metal counter assaulted our ears.

"That's one task out of the way," Liz said as she placed her napkin on the table. "Laurel, what's left on your list?"

Twenty items remained on my list, the first being the most critical—to identify the killer before I wound up as prime-time viewing at Fullers Mortuary and Chapel.

Liz and Adriana both had meetings, so they grabbed their handbags and walked out of the restaurant. I stayed behind, wanting to grill Serenity without an audience. She began clearing the rest of the dishes, and I approached her with my question.

"I'm sorry for what you're going through," I said. "What a shame Axel felt he had to conceal his financial difficulties from his brother and mother."

215

"I still can't believe he got a loan from that crook. You wouldn't believe the interest rate the guy charges."

Yes, I would. Probably four to five times the going rate for a standard bank loan.

"Do you know who recommended Aces Financial Group to him?" I asked her. Before she could answer, her husband walked through the door. She repeated my question to him.

"Haven't a clue," Paul said. "For all I know, Axel picked up the phone book and threw a dart at the yellow pages. Now that the feds are involved, we're totally screwed."

"Their investigation could take months, even years," I said.

Paul grimaced. "Yeah, even if Walter wanted to assume the loan, there's no way to do it now."

"The bright note is that his CPA thinks we can hold off on making the loan payments," Serenity added. "Not that we want to be delinquent, but who would we send them to now?"

CHAPTER FIFTY

By Saturday, my head hurt less but looked worse since my blue eyes and reddish hair clashed with my chartreuse forehead. I tried some of Liz's magic erase product, but it seemed to lose its magical properties once it landed on my skin.

Jenna was a nervous wreck. I feared by the time she finished her exam she'd have bitten off her toenails as well as her fingernails. After barely eating her oatmeal, she started crying, lamenting that she couldn't possibly concentrate while Tony languished in jail. Her crying jag finally ended when I assured her I was still on the case. After dropping her off at the high school, Ben and I continued on to our next stop at one of the local soccer fields.

My soccer mom duty had excused me from helping at Apple Tree Farm today. I hoped Gran would prove to be an asset. There was always the risk she would eat up all their profits.

My son possesses nerves of steel, an excellent trait for a halfback, so he's usually far calmer during his games than I am. Tom's daughter, Kristy, is also fearless, possibly because she stands a foot taller than the other third graders. She's determined to make the US Women's National Soccer Team and play in the World Cup. No doubt she'll do it.

Much as I tried to focus on Ben's game, my thoughts kept returning to Axel's murder. Would the killer attend tonight's gala? And if so, did that mean I could be in danger? No one had fessed up, so Dorie insisted my injuries must be due to my own negligence. Or klutziness. I was the only person who believed my fall was intentional.

Other than the perpetrator. Could Brent have done it to keep me away from the warehouse? Or was Axel's killer warning me to stop investigating?

Ben and Kristy won their game, so we celebrated with the rest of the team at Papa's Pizza Parlor. We zipped through lunch and arrived at the high school in time to pick up my dejected daughter.

"I blew it," she said, slamming the car door shut.

"You always say that after a test. Then you end up with an A." I reached over and patted her knee as she strapped herself in.

"My answers sucked. I sucked. Life sucks."

"Jenna sucks, sucks, sucks," Ben sang out from the back seat. Kristy chimed in.

"Pipe down," I said. "Jenna's had a tough day. "

"Tough month," she elaborated. "Can we stop at the jail to visit Tony?"

"Yeah, yeah, can we?" the backseat duo asked.

"Not today," I said to Jenna, before looking over my shoulder and glaring at the eight-year-olds. "And not ever for you two. Let me get through the gala and Apple Tree Race this weekend, and then we'll plan a visit to Tony."

Jenna nodded before closing her eyes and escaping into teenage daydream land. We dropped Kristy off at her grandparents' house then returned to our own home. Once inside, Ben snatched the portable kitchen phone so he could call his cronies and compare notes about their respective soccer games. Jenna grabbed an apple and slowly ascended the stairs. I wanted to offer a comforting shoulder, but she looked like she wanted to be alone. After the last couple of days, I wouldn't have minded curling up under a blanket and nursing my wounds, but the show must go on. To the Apple Gala I would go.

Liz and Brian picked me up at my house a few minutes before four. Since Liz was performing, she'd dressed in her saloon gal costume. Despite the formal title of the event, galas in our county tend to be casual. I'd chosen a pink plaid shirt and a short denim skirt, along with a new pair of heeled boots. We arrived a half hour before the event officially opened. The volunteers were already seated at the welcome table, placed in front of the cream stucco Mediterranean-style tasting room. Two portable bars at each corner of the huge flagstone patio offered an array of Valley View Vineyards wine, along with local brews. The bartenders sported buzz cuts and burgundy logo-trimmed shirts.

If Walter ended up purchasing Apple Tree Farm, I wondered if he would merge the two operations or run them separately. Or was that a moot question at this point? Time to track down our host and find out.

Walter was dressed to kill in Wyatt Earp-styled evening attire. I hoped the two silver-handled Colt pistols stuffed into his holster were empty. Despite the western theme, Adriana and I had not arranged for a shootout at the vineyard tonight.

"You gals have done all right," Walter said.

"We aim to please." I performed a mini curtsey, not an easy task when wearing a tight denim skirt. "We're expecting a bigger turnout than last year."

"Good, good. I hope Valley View can host the gala from now on. If we hadn't had so many interruptions, we could have put on an even bigger shindig."

I wondered if Walter included Axel's murder as one of the interruptions. When I glanced toward the entrance, I noticed a few early arrivals. I'd better pester Walter before he became too popular.

"Will your purchase of Apple Tree Farm still go through?" I asked, curious to know if the status of Aces Financial would impact the sale.

Walter scowled. "That loan guy, Lionel Nelson, called me yesterday. He claims his operation is legit. That the feds were only interested in the head honchos running the drugs and doing money laundering. All of his loans are supposedly on the up and up."

"Do you believe him?"

"Well, they sure don't run a tight operation like Chandler does at Hangtown Bank," Walter sniped. I couldn't help chuckling at his remark. I bet Mr. Chandler knew where every penny of the bank's money went.

"I'm supposed to meet Lionel tomorrow morning and talk things over," he said. "You used to underwrite loans. Would you trust this fellow?"

"I didn't talk to him long enough to form an opinion," I replied, hesitant to admit that the lender creeped me out. I wasn't certain that was sufficient basis for a business decision.

"Well, I need this deal to go through, so I'll see what I can squeeze out of him." Walter squinted at me. "Looks like you're still all banged up from your fall the other day. Probably be best if you don't climb around any of my warehouses, okay?" Walter tipped his hat to me and strode off, his expensive black jeans so new and stiff they looked like they could walk by themselves.

I continued to stare at Walter's retreating back. What did he mean by that comment? Was he merely being solicitous? Or was that some sort of threat?

I needed to stop turning everyone into a suspect. I scanned the activity around me trying to decide where I could most be of use. The patrons standing in line at the bar seemed in a convivial mood despite a wait for the vineyard's award-winning wines. The buffet line moved quickly thanks to Serenity's efficient staff. Volunteers were busy selling raffle tickets to the guests.

Hank and Brooke strolled in my direction, his arm tight around her slender waist. Hank sported faded jeans, a blue plaid shirt and scruffy work boots. A straw cowboy hat covered his receding hairline. Brooke's attire fit her personality, conservative yet tasteful.

I eyed her long, designer-jeans-clad legs, cream shirt and colorful vest from a short-legged somewhat envious perspective. Hank wore a hungry look as he gazed at Brooke, but I couldn't tell if he directed it at his girlfriend or the barbeque buffet beyond. I was pleased Hank finally had someone in his life.

Mostly. I doubted my children were prepared to add a stepmother into their family circle, but I could be wrong. Maybe it was just me not accepting that Hank had finally moved on.

Those thoughts were too morbid to contemplate during the gala. Time to switch to a lighter subject, such as murder.

"It looks like Walter may be purchasing Apple Tree Farm after all," I said to Brooke as the couple joined me. "He's meeting with that loan officer, Lionel something or other, tomorrow."

She looked startled. "That's a surprise. I thought the deal was off the table after the feds raided the parent company."

"Walter says he's willing to talk to him. He really wants that farm."

"Tom Hunter's quite the hotshot now, isn't he?" Hank said. "Are you and he still an item?"

"Of course." I bristled at his suggestion. "We're as item-y as ever." I pointed to the buffet. "Aren't you hungry?"

It's good to know some things never change, and the way to distract my ex-husband was still through his stomach. Hank latched on to Brooke's hand and off they went in pursuit of food. She waved goodbye as she tried to keep up with Hank's hungry strides.

I stared after them brooding over how quickly their relationship had progressed. At the rate my romance with Tom continued to bloom, it would be our titanium hips, not our lips that someday became joined in holy matrimony.

With my mind preoccupied with thoughts of Tom 120 miles away, I didn't notice anyone approaching until I was grabbed from behind. I tried breaking away, but the iron-fisted grip was too strong.

Was the killer about to finish me off?

CHAPTER FIFTY-ONE

I stomped on my assailant's foot with my high-heeled boot. The man cursed and released me. I whirled around to discover the top suspect on my list. Brent. The farm manager exuded beer breath potent enough to knock someone unconscious. I hoped that wasn't his intent. One concussion a week was sufficient for me.

"What do you want?" I asked, as I moved out of reach of his strong arms and even stronger breath.

He narrowed red-rimmed eyes at me but maintained a proper distance. "Just wanted to chat with you. You're still lookin' a mite beat up," he said. "Think you can manage to stay out of trouble tonight?"

I fisted my hands and placed them on my hips. "Is that a threat? Are you the one who knocked the shelving on me?'

"I warned you the warehouse was dangerous. Maybe next time you'll heed my warning." He shifted gears suddenly and said. "I found your friend's lotions and stuff."

"You did? Were they shattered from the fall?"

"A couple of jars cracked, but most of it looked okay to me. They packed them pretty well."

"Where did you put them?"

"In a safe place. Nina said you're helping at the bakery tomorrow morning. How about we meet at the warehouse before anyone else arrives?"

Was he serious? Any reader of cozy mysteries knows better than to meet a suspect all by herself.

"That won't work for me, but I'll stop by after my shift is done. With Liz, and her husband, a deputy district attorney," I clarified, so he knew I would have backup in case he tried something.

"Hope nothing happens to that stuff before then." He shot me a dark look. "Or to you." He wheeled around and took off leaving me more perplexed than before. These Apple Tree employees were starting to get on my nerves. If not for Jenna's conviction that Tony was innocent, and my fear she'd try to solve this case if I didn't, I'd leave this area and not come back until all the rotten apples had disappeared.

I decided it was time for a drink so I headed to the bar. I chatted with a couple of acquaintances, snagged a glass of viognier, the vineyard's white wine that most resembled my favorite chardonnay, and went in search of Liz and Brian. I wanted to share the news that her products were secure and intact. For the most part. Although based on Brent's elusive comment, I wasn't certain for how long.

The sound of the band Liz hired for tonight's event caught my attention. The Sassy Saloon Gals should be performing shortly, followed by a dance medley from *West Side Story*. The El Dorado Musical Company would begin performances the following week, so their preview tonight was an attempt to boost ticket sales. I hoped Stan had learned the steps by now. If not, this could be the first ever *West Side Story* production deemed a musical comedy.

The Sassy gals, dressed in low-cut red sequined tops and black satin skirts, paraded around the stage, strutting their assets and high kicking their way into a round of loud applause. The music switched from country rock to fifties rock n' roll as several young men and several not-so-young men took to the stage.

After years of viewing *Dancing with the Stars*, Stan had quickly picked up ballroom dancing nine months earlier. It would be interesting to see if he could morph into a swivel-hipped dancing hoodlum as readily.

The male dancers, representing both Sharks and Jets, were dressed in black tee shirts, tight jeans and leather jackets. Their slick ducktails evoked believable gang members, as long as you overlooked the receding hairlines and pot bellies of a few of the middle-aged cast members. Stan managed to keep up with the dance crew, although one of his pasted-on sideburns flew off during a spin. It landed on the cheek of a spectator standing in the front row.

An Instagram moment for sure.

The dancers bowed amid hooting, hollering and clapping. The man next to me let loose with an ear-splitting whistle so I shifted a few steps away. As I looked off in the distance, a ray of waning sunlight highlighted the shiny silver pompadour of a male I recognized, conversing with someone in the shadows of the tasting room.

Now why was Lionel-the-lender hanging out at the gala? And who was his companion?

CHAPTER FIFTY-TWO

I sidled away from the crowd to catch a better glimpse of Lionel's acquaintance. It was Nina. She walked away, her long braid bouncing against her back. I was about to chase after her to find out what she and Lionel were discussing when Stan unexpectedly appeared. He grabbed my right hand, twirled me in a circle then proceeded to dip me.

"How did I do?" he asked. He continued without waiting for my answer. "That was the most fun I've had since the ballroom competition last New Year's Eve."

If Stan retained fond memories of the competition then he apparently didn't remember that one of us was almost killed that night.

"You did great," I replied, looking off to the left for my quarry. Lionel was now talking to another woman who looked vaguely familiar. I was surprised he knew so many people at the event.

A hand tapped me on my shoulder, and I turned to discover Hank.

He greeted Stan then asked, "Have you seen Brooke?"

"Not recently," I said.

Hank shoved his hands in his pockets. "Several of her clients are here, so she probably stopped to chat with them."

"Everything okay between you two?" I asked.

Hank's murky green eyes lit up into two shining emeralds. "It's going great. In fact..." He stole a glance at me. "I'm thinking of popping the question."

"What question?" I asked.

Stan punched me on my arm. "*The* question, you ninny. A proposal."

"Of marriage? But you haven't dated that long."

Hank's smile was wider than the buffet table. "When you know, you know."

Well, that was plain idiotic. I knew that for a fact. You don't propose to someone after only dating them a few months. Tom and I were still fine-tuning our relationship after a year.

Hank ambled off in search of his prospective fiancée. Stan began whistling "Here Comes the Bride."

"Cut it out," I scowled at him. "Can you believe Hank wants to propose already?"

"Hey, Brooke is smart and beautiful. What's not to like?" Stan asked. "You're not jealous, are you?"

"*Moi*? Don't be silly." But his comment bothered me. Was I jealous? The loudspeakers distracted me, and I shrugged off my unpleasant thoughts. I transferred my attention to the stage where Walter Eastwood stood, microphone in hand. He called on Dorie and Eric Thorson to join him. Applause burst from the onlookers as Dorie and her son climbed the makeshift staircase to the stage. She looked petrified to be in the public eye but remained composed while Walter regaled the crowd with stories of the Thorson family's accomplishments, Axel's in particular. Eric looked bored with the entire proceeding. Until he glanced into the audience. Then his expression turned fierce.

That was weird. I craned my neck in the direction Eric had glanced at but only recognized one person—his Uncle Paul. Was there more Thorson family drama in the works?

I turned my attention back to the proceedings as Walter handed Dorie a plaque. They all left the stage amid applause. Behind me someone muttered "asshole."

I turned around to find Weather Vainery Vanna standing there, her face a deep and angry red.

"Hi, Vanna," I said. "Guess you're not too happy with Walter? Or still mad at Axel for giving away your space?"

"Huh?" she said. Her face looked puzzled before recognition set in. "Oh, you're Virginia's granddaughter, the banker detective. How's that going for you?"

So far, the most positive result of my investigation was a concussion and two cracked ribs. Not much to brag about.

Then it dawned on me that Vanna was the second woman I'd noticed conversing with Lionel. "Are you getting a loan from Lionel Nelson at Aces Financial Group?" I asked.

"Who?"

"That man with the silver pompadour." I pointed toward the tasting room where I'd seen them talking earlier.

"Oh, him. He's a lender?"

I nodded and she muttered an oath. "Shoot, wish I'd known that. I got rejected by Sierra Mountain Lending, so I could've hit him up for a loan. He stopped me to ask if I knew of a decent motel in town."

Interesting. Vanna gave me the names of the two motels she'd mentioned to him, and I promised her that if I tracked him down I'd have him call her about a loan. She seemed satisfied with my assistance and walked off smiling. I decided not to tell her that with the information she'd shared with me, my goal was to secure him overnight accommodations in the county jail. I left a message on Tom's cell that one of his "rats" was in the hood and to call me back ASAP.

With the entertainment and commemoration ceremony over, most of the attendees began to depart. Liz and Adriana stood with Serenity by the buffet table. I strolled over to see if there was anything further I could do. Since Liz and Brian drove me here, I couldn't go home until they were ready to leave.

I complimented Serenity on the cuisine. She smiled with relief and mumbled a weary thanks.

"Can I help with the cleanup?" I asked Liz, praying the answer would be a negative.

She yawned. "I am absolutely knackered, but we should be able to leave in a bit."

"Great. I'll make a pit stop first."

"I'll come with. I've been too busy all night to use the loo."

A line of attendees stood in front of the three Porta Potties, so we joined them. Traffic in and out of the first two units moved at a speedy pace, but the third one remained shut.

"Do you think someone accidentally locked the door before they exited?" I asked Liz.

"That would be bloody stupid, but let's go check. My bladder is about to explode."

We approached the last unit. I knocked on the door but heard nothing in response.

"Yoo-hoo," Liz called out, "Anyone on the pot in there?"

No one replied so I assumed the door must be stuck. I yanked on the handle, and the door flew open.

I stared into the wide open eyes of Lionel-the-lender. He looked surprised. Almost as stunned as I was to find him in there. It was so dark inside the portable toilet that it took me a second to register one additional surprise.

A bullet hole between his eyes.

CHAPTER FIFTY-THREE

I jumped back and landed squarely on Liz's beaded flip flop.

"Ouch," she cried out. "Watch what you're…" Her words trailed off as I moved to the side giving her a ringside view.

"Crap," she said.

A line formed behind us.

"What's the holdup?" yelled someone.

"Hurry up," a male beer-infused voice jumped in. "Either shit or get off the pot."

"Sshh," admonished a softer feminine voice, "maybe he's constipated."

I reached for the door, slammed it shut and faced the small crowd. "Sorry, everyone. Party's over. Please head to your cars."

"And drive safely," Liz amended. She whispered in my ear, "What should we do?"

"Get Brian and Walter. I'll call 911."

I reached into my purse, and it rang just as I grabbed hold of it. Perfect timing.

"Hon, I got your message," Tom's deep voice rang out, although I could sense an undercurrent of fatigue. "So you know where this Lionel is right now?"

I nodded then realized we weren't on face time. "Yep. I sure do."

"Do you think you can keep him occupied until I can get a deputy there?"

I peered over my shoulder at the Porta Potty. "Shouldn't be a problem."

"That's my girl." He chuckled. "Now, the only hitch we have is that no one recognizes the name Lionel Nelson. We think he's using an alias for his finance company work. Any way you can snap a picture of him when he's not looking and send it on to me?"

Ick and double ick.

"There's something I need to mention about, um, Lionel." I blurted out the loan officer's current status in all of its disgusting detail.

It took Tom so long to respond I thought we'd lost our connection. He cleared his throat. "I suppose that will make him less likely to object to you taking a photo."

"Fine," I snapped. "Hold on." I held my breath, opened the door and aimed my iPhone at Lionel. His head listed to the left, but we weren't going for any prizes at this point. I swatted at a few bottlenose flies swirling above his still luxuriant pompadour.

I slammed the door shut and texted the photos to Tom.

"Thanks," he said. "I owe you."

"Yes, you do." I was interrupted when Brian, Walter and Liz walked up. I told Brian that Tom was on the phone and handed it over to him.

"We got a dead guy in the john?" Walter huffed and puffed. "What happened?"

At first, I was startled by his question then I realized Liz had no idea who occupied the portable toilet. Walter took matters into his own hands and threw open the door. The stench, which had not improved in the last five minutes, almost blew me away.

"Hell's bells," Walter swore. "Now why did Lionel have to go and get himself shot?"

Wasn't that the question of the hour?

CHAPTER FIFTY-FOUR

By the time the detectives cordoned off the crime scene, most of the gala attendees had vanished, with the exception of the weary party planners, catering company staff and the owner of Valley View Vineyard and Orchard.

"If you two hadn't forced your way into that Porta Potty, we'd be home by now." Adriana grumbled.

Liz and I sent shocked looks to her.

"Hey, my job is to plan parties, not solve mysteries." Adriana frowned at her feet where two noticeable blisters stared back at her. "I could have been soaking these babies in my Jacuzzi."

"A man has been murdered, Adriana," I said.

She shrugged. "You said he was a lowlife money launderer. He probably had it coming."

"Even a low life deserves his day in court," said Brian as he joined us at the table. "It's my job to put him away."

Liz leaned over and nibbled on Brian's ear. "Can we go, Sweetcakes?"

If it would get me home quicker, I'd be happy to nibble on Sweetcakes other ear.

"Soon," he said. "Since most folks had already left by the time you found him, the detectives want a list of attendees. I assume one of you has that information?"

"You've got to be kidding," Adriana said. "They think one of the people attending the gala offed this creep? Isn't it obvious it was a mob hit?"

"I didn't realize you were an expert on crime families," I said to her.

"I watch television now and then," she said defensively. "You learn stuff."

From what I'd gathered from Tom, the stuff on TV was usually wrong. But she had a point.

"Adriana is right. The shooter could have entered from anywhere on the property. They didn't need to check in at the entrance."

Brian swiped a hand over his brow. "That's why two members of the task force are driving here later tonight."

My heart soared at his words. "Anyone I know?"

He winked. "I guess you'll just have to wait to find out."

I was still waiting to find out if Tom was on his way when my alarm rang at 4:30 a.m. I hit the snooze button wondering why my clock radio went off when it was dark outside.

Then I remembered. Today was the bicycle race. Gran and I had both agreed to help at the Apple Tree Farm bakery this morning. Between worrying about Tony's incarceration and her exam, Jenna had become sniffly and sick yesterday. Her germs didn't need to be shared with the hundreds of people participating in today's race.

Because the participants in the annual bicycle race needed to sign in before the nine a.m. start time, Dorie and Nina expected hordes of donut-eating cyclists before and after the race.

I was so exhausted from helping with the gala that I was afraid I'd fall asleep on my feet and land headfirst in the fryer, turning into a gigantic Laurel fritter.

My shower helped, especially after I turned on the wrong faucet. Nothing like a cold blast of water to get the gray cells percolating. I downed two cups of coffee while blow-drying my hair and contemplated the mystery of last night's shooting.

Despite the fact the man was shot "execution style," and that some of his criminal accomplices may have wanted him out of the picture, a number of local attendees were acquainted with Lionel. Would any of them benefit from his death?

Walter was anxious to purchase Apple Tree Farm. Dorie and Paul were equally enthusiastic about selling the property to him. But the financial brouhaha that ensued after the task force took down the money laundering drug dealers might have put a crimp in their plans. If Lionel disappeared, would the loan also vanish from the books?

Serenity could have stepped away from the buffet and shot him. Brooke and Brent were also present at the gala, but they had no motives for killing him other than he was icky. I'd seen Nina speaking with him, but they most likely were discussing her bakery operation.

Maybe Vanna tracked him down, and he rejected her loan request. I couldn't see Vanna shooting Lionel though. She was far more likely to whack him with one of her metal weather vanes.

With my head reeling from too little sleep and too much caffeine, I started the car and backed it out of the garage, thinking how glad I'd be when this day was over.

Truer words were never spoken.

CHAPTER FIFTY-FIVE

Despite eating my weight in donuts over the years, I'd never attempted to make any myself. Now I knew the secret, which I planned to take to my grave.

I discovered donut making was not for the weak of heart or biceps. Gran, however, excelled at kneading dough, Nina could flip donuts in and out of the fryer in a blink of an eye, and Dorie frosted like Betty Crocker's twin sister.

After flunking all the culinary tasks assigned to me, we discovered that I possessed one useful skillset. I could compute change without the help of the register, and when I occasionally ran out of dollar bills, could talk customers into buying more donuts.

Counter duty provided one positive aspect: the opportunity to view male customers in their cute bicycle shorts. Contrary to Brian's optimistic remark the previous evening, Tom did not appear on my doorstep or anywhere else this morning. I could gawk away at muscled cyclists until he did.

While I considered myself a discreet ogler, several men openly checked out a newcomer as she walked in. Brooke's turquoise shorts exposed firm, shapely legs and muscular calves. Her sleeveless top displayed well-defined biceps.

Hank, by comparison, looked a tad out of shape in a too small tee shirt and bike shorts. I doubted any female gawkers would be ogling him anytime soon.

"What are you doing behind the counter?" Hank asked me. "Isn't Jenna here today? How did her test go?"

"She's feeling under the weather, so Nina talked Gran and me into helping out," I said. "I didn't realize you two were registered for the race."

"Brooke's quite the athlete." Hank shot an admiring look at his girlfriend. "She used to be a dancer, so she's very limber."

Brooke elbowed Hank. "You look tired, Laurel. Did you have to stay late cleaning up after the gala?" she asked.

I was about to disclose the exact details of my horrid clean up duty when I remembered the public might not be aware of what occurred at Valley View late last night. The Sheriff's Office had ordered Walter to close the winery today, but they'd only taped off the immediate area around the Porta Potties. Since the discovery occurred so late Saturday night, the murder didn't make it into any of the morning papers.

"Late night, early morning. What can I get you two?"

"Just a water bottle for me," Brooke replied.

"A fritter to go," Hank said. "A little energy boost for the road."

I handed Brooke her water and gave Hank his sugary breakfast. While he reached for his wallet, Brooke told him she needed to stow her purse in the car. My eyes moved over to the black leather shoulder bag she wore hooked over her right shoulder.

"Did you buy that purse from Glenda?" I chuckled, remembering my conversation with the vivacious saleswoman. "I bet she asked you the size and caliber of your gun before she sold it to you."

Brooke looked taken aback by my question. She mumbled something to Hank and then disappeared.

"Did I offend her?" I asked Hank. Not everyone gets my sense of humor.

He shrugged. "Women. Can't live without them. Can't understand them. See you after the race. I'll need to restock by then."

Hank took off after Brooke, and for the next few minutes I stuffed pastries in bags and dollar bills in the register.

At ten minutes to eight, a bullhorn sounded. The few remaining customers left for their two-wheeled vehicles, leaving the bakery gloriously empty. Nina came over and hugged me.

"Laurel, we couldn't have handled that mob without you."

"Thanks," I said. "I was so busy I didn't even have time to pee."

She laughed and told me to attend to business. After last night's misadventure, I decided to stay away from the temporary facilities they'd brought in for the event and use the regular restrooms.

On my way, I walked past Glenda's booth. Despite my frazzled appearance and flour-coated apparel, she recognized me.

"Hey, it's Laurel, right?" she asked. "Did you bring your gun today?"

"Sorry. I left my artillery at home."

She shook her head, her golden pageboy swinging back and forth. "These days, it's not safe to walk around without protection. You never know who could be lurking behind a bush or apple tree."

Or in a Porta Potty.

I reached for the purse I'd admired during my last visit, an exact duplicate of the one Brooke carried this morning. "Is this a popular model? A friend of mine, Brooke Martin, has one just like it."

"You know Brooke? She's my CPA." Glenda smiled. "She lets me pay her bill in leather goods."

So that explained it. Just because she owned a pistol-packing purse didn't mean Brooke carried a gun with her.

"That girl could shoot a sequin off my tee shirt from fifty yards using that Glock of hers," Glenda said. "You been out to the range with her yet?"

Nope. I stayed away from them whenever possible, shooting ranges as well as kitchen ranges.

I promised Glenda I'd return next time with my weapon in hand. She'd given me much to think about. Hank planned on proposing to Brooke in the near future. Was he aware of her sharpshooting ability? Did I want a Glock-toting CPA as my kids' stepmother? No, I did not, but how much input would I have in that decision? My stomach clenched as I worried about my children's future.

My own purse beeped. I reached in and snagged my cell. Tom, finally.

"Are you on your way here?" I asked.

"Shortly. It took longer than anticipated to get a search warrant for all of the Aces Financial Group's records. I've been going through Lionel's loan files," he said. "When I finally found the Apple Tree file, I discovered a small manila envelope tucked into the back. It was filled with nude photos of a woman, probably taken a decade ago or longer."

"I underwrote loans for a living. Nude photos are not standard loan documentation. Do you have any idea who the woman is?"

"That's where I was hoping you could help since you're familiar with the Thorson family. Can I shoot a couple of them to you?"

Ew. Well, looking at photos of a naked woman certainly wasn't as bad as snapping photos of the dead lender last night.

"Sure. Send them over," I agreed, wondering if the photos were of Dorie Thorson. Who else's photos would be stuck in the Apple Tree loan file?

A second later my phone pinged answering that question.

CHAPTER FIFTY-SIX

"Good grief," I said to Tom. "That looks like a young Brooke Martin, Hank's future fiancé."

"There's another photo of the same woman dressed provocatively, standing next to the head of the drug ring we just took down. I think there's a strong possibility that Hank's future fiancée was a former escort."

"Brooke is, I mean was, Axel's CPA. Lionel could have recognized her name on the financial statements, or seen her photo on her website," I said. "I wonder if he was blackmailing her."

"Anything is possible with these scumbags."

"I doubt if Brooke's more conservative clients would approve of her earlier job experience."

"They'd be even less likely to approve of nude photos of their CPA posted online," Tom added. "I need to interview her. I'm leaving right now."

"Is there anything I can do?"

"Stay out of trouble."

"Besides that."

"Do you know where I can find her?"

"I saw both her and Hank this morning. They signed up for the race, so they're somewhere on the streets of Camino. They should return to Apple Tree Farm within the next hour or so."

"Great. Now promise me you won't attempt to interrogate her first."

The image of the dead lender popped into my head making my reply a no-brainer.

"Promise."

We signed off, and I finally completed my pit stop. Tom could stop me from investigating, but he couldn't keep my brain from asking questions. Many people hide dark secrets from their past, myself included. I still hadn't told my mother that I was the one to devour the box of chocolates my father gave her one Valentine's Day. I let my older brother take the blame for me. One of these days I needed to fess up.

Although by now, she'd most likely figured out that her little chocoholic had committed the crime.

Stealing chocolates was a far cry from blackmail though. Hank had seemed proud that Brooke used to be a dancer. Was he also aware of her additional skills? Did it really matter to him? Or to me for that matter?

Yes, it did.

Especially if revealing photos from Brooke's racy and possibly criminal past had led to more lethal crimes like murder. Would Brooke kill to protect her reputation?

My theories were flying faster than the speedy cyclists who were zooming down Apple Tree's long driveway leaving a funnel cloud of dust in their wake. They looked hungry so I sped up my own pace back to the bakery counter. Any detecting would wait until an official detective was on the premises.

The next hour whizzed by as I served hungry and thirsty men and women of all ages. I didn't see Hank or Brooke, although a weary Stan, dressed in a shiny lime-green and black spandex outfit, stopped by for a sugar infusion. The traffic at the counter eventually slowed, and Nina told me to take a break.

Between the hot October weather and the temperature in the bakery, my body, hair and spirit felt wilted. Not to mention that my brain felt fried from all of the various criminal scenarios I'd been pondering. I finally decided that Hank and Brooke must have left without saying goodbye. That was a relief since I hadn't been certain I could maintain a poker face if I saw her again.

I grabbed my purse and walked toward the ladies room hoping a splash of cold water on my face, a touch of fresh lipstick on my dry lips, and a brush through my unruly curls might perk me up.

I walked out of the stall at the same instant that Brooke entered the ladies room. Despite riding twenty-five miles on a ninety-degree day, she appeared as fresh and lovely as ever.

"Hi, Laurel." She smiled. "You look even more fatigued than I do."

My tongue tied itself into a few knots as I tried to maintain my composure, not an easy task after viewing photos of a naked Brooke earlier in the day. Photos that were still on my iPhone. And how could I encourage Brooke to stick around long enough for Tom to interview her without making her suspicious of me?

"Tough work selling pastries." I offered a nervous smile. "You and Hank should stop at the bakery. You must need a carb infusion after your workout."

"I'll pass on the sweets." She patted her flat stomach then shot me a conspiratorial smile. "But you know Hank. I'm sure he'll be panting for something before we take off."

"Do you have plans for the rest of the day?" I asked in as casual of a manner as I could muster. I didn't want to blow it for Tom. Not after all of his hard work.

I reminded myself that I'd been in similar situations before. There was no need to freak out just because I could be facing a potential murderer. Beads of sweat dotted my forehead. I dampened a paper towel and dabbed at my face.

"You look odd." Brooke glanced at me in the mirror as she washed her hands. Her black purse rested on the counter next to the basin. "Are you okay?"

"I feel hotter than a vat of caramel sauce right now." I fanned myself as I attempted to sound normal. "I never realized how tough it is to work in an apple farm bakery."

"It's a more challenging business than most people realize," Brooke said as she grabbed a paper towel from the holder.

"I guess Dorie is learning firsthand how difficult it can be," I said. "I hope she'll be able to keep the farm going now that she doesn't have to worry about their lender."

Brooke crumpled the paper towel and aimed it at the garbage can. As it deflected off the rim she asked, "How did you know Lionel was dead?"

I froze in place. The better question was how did Brooke know Lionel was dead?

Unless she was the killer.

I stepped back and my left arm knocked Brooke's purse off the counter. The contents scattered. A lipstick and compact bounced off my shoes.

And a black gun slid across the floor, landing at Brooke's feet. She reached down and calmly picked it up.

Crap.

CHAPTER FIFTY-SEVEN

I tried to push past Brooke to exit the ladies room. She shoved me aside, slammed the door shut and locked it. She aimed the gun straight at my chest.

"I need to get back to the bakery," I said. "Nina will be pounding on the door if I don't show up soon."

"Nice try." Brooke smirked at me. "I could tell you caught my slip."

I widened my blue eyes. "I didn't catch anything. Nada. Truly."

"Right. Hank told me you're smarter than you look."

Thanks for nothing, Hank.

She unlocked the door before motioning at me to walk ahead of her. Just as I contemplated making a break for it she warned me, "Don't do anything silly. This purse is designed for shooting right through this hole and, trust me, I know how to shoot."

I didn't doubt Brooke's shooting ability, not after my conversation with Glenda. Darn that Glenda and her pistol-toting purses.

"And, if I miss you," Brooke continued, "there are other women on the premises I won't hesitate to take care of. Like Hank's roomie."

Gran.

Despite the heat, a chill enveloped me as we moved forward down a deserted gravel trail that circled the perimeter of the property. Eventually it would lead to the parking lot. What was her intent? To temporarily get rid of me so she could make an escape?

Or did she have something more permanent in mind.

I slowed my pace hoping Tom would arrive before anything nasty happened. Like my body becoming riddled with bullets.

"Did Lionel threaten to reveal you were once an escort working for a drug lord?" I asked.

Brooke grabbed my shoulder and spun me around.

"Who told you that?"

"My boyfriend, the detective." I peeked at my watch. "He should arrive here any minute now."

Her brows drew together. "How did he find out about my past?"

"The task force that took down the money laundering operation found the Aces Financial Group's loan files, including Axel's loan on Apple Tree Farm. It contained revealing photos and information about you and your, um, former profession."

Anger flared and her hand shook briefly. "I was just a dumb college student trying to make ends meet when Hector recruited me. Lionel worked for him in another capacity before they established the finance company. I finally escaped and made a new life for myself, but then…"

"But the past is never far behind you," I finished for her. "Axel learned your secret, didn't he?"

She nodded. "Axel submitted his business financials, which I'd prepared, with his Aces loan application. When Lionel saw my name on the reports, he thought it sounded familiar. He looked up my website. Then he remembered me. Too much of me, unfortunately."

Her eyes misted, but that didn't distract her from aiming her gun. "The rat passed the information on to Axel. Axel told me if I didn't 'fix' his profit and loss statement to present to his new lender, he'd tell everyone in the county about my past. He left me no choice. I agreed to meet him in the warehouse that evening. Told him I'd take care of everything."

"So, instead, you took care of Axel," I said.

"He wasn't the good guy everyone thought he was," she said. "So I sweetened him up."

My cell blared Tom's ringtone.

"Don't answer that," Brooke cried.

"It's my boyfriend. He's on his way here to interview you about Aces Financial Group. He'll know something is wrong if I don't pick up."

She tapped the fingers of her left hand against her hip.

"Okay, call him back, but don't do or say anything foolish."

I nodded. She watched as I reached into my purse for the phone. As I hit speed dial she told me to put it on hands free.

It rang three times before Tom answered. "Hi, Sweetheart. I was getting worried about you."

"Busy selling sweets, um, Sweetheart."

"You sound weird. Is everything okay?"

"Just tired, and it's kind of noisy around here." Although the only noise in the vicinity was the sound of my two frightened knees knocking together.

"I should be there in ten minutes," he said. "Is Brooke close by?"

Unfortunately, yes.

Brooke grabbed the phone out of my hand and ended the call.

"Hey," I said. "Why did you do that?"

"Because I have a plan. Now call your honey back and tell him Hank and I left and are on our way to Tahoe. To Harrah's. That will send him in the opposite direction."

She handed the phone to me, and it rang before I could make my call.

"Laurel, what happened?" Tom asked.

"Oh, just klutzy me. Sorry."

"Did you learn anything?" he asked. "I'm anxious to wrap this up so you and I can..." He lowered his voice and started to explain in great physical detail exactly how he planned to entertain me this weekend.

I interrupted before he could get too descriptive. From the look on Brooke's face, she was enjoying his comments far too much.

"Sounds swell," I said. "Brooke and Hank left for Tahoe. They're going to see Bob Dylan tonight. Too bad you weren't able to get tickets for us. You know how much I love…"

Brooke grabbed the phone and slammed her thumb on the red button, ending the call.

"I didn't ask you to elaborate," she said. "What was all that nonsense about Bob Dylan?"

"I was trying to make it more realistic. To give you extra time to get away." And provide a clue to my boyfriend.

Her eyes narrowed as she appraised me. "I don't trust you. Hand over that phone." I reluctantly gave her my cell, wondering if that would be my last contact with any loved ones.

We walked silently for a minute before I spoke up again. "So where is Hank? Won't he be looking for you?"

"Probably. He's a sweetheart. You shouldn't have let him go."

"I didn't let him go. He let me go." I bristled every time I thought back to the day my ex announced he was leaving me for a female client. "Did you know he planned to propose to you?"

Brooke didn't respond so I turned around. Slowly.

"I really messed up." One lone teardrop ran down her face. She swiped at it. "Hank's the most decent guy I've ever met."

My mouth opened and shut. Brooke probably wouldn't appreciate me mentioning she hadn't set the bar very high.

I almost felt sorry for my captor. I wondered how to turn this situation around and make her sympathize with me.

"But life goes on," she continued. "That's what I told myself when I escaped from Hector's grasp and set up my accounting practice. If I could change my life once, I can do it again. I just need to remove any remaining obstacles."

She shoved the gun mere inches from my face. "Now, move it," she said to the one remaining obstacle to her new life.

CHAPTER FIFTY-EIGHT

We continued our lonesome march down the trail. Every time I slowed my pace, Brooke jabbed me with the Glock. I became so annoyed that I almost backhanded her one time but stopped myself since that seemed a surefire way to end up dead. As we drew close to the parking lot, my spirits perked up. Certainly once we were in the vicinity of others, I could make a move.

The parking lot was emptier than earlier this morning, but vehicles in every color and make still dotted the large area. Brooke moved within inches of my left side, the gun presumably aimed at me through the convenient opening in the purse.

"If you promise to stay quiet, I'll let you go once I've left town," she said.

"They'll eventually track you down," I replied. "You can't keep running for the rest of your life. If Lionel recognized you, don't you think the police or FBI will, too?"

"Lionel Nelson was more useless than a boil on my butt. You wouldn't believe the size of his blackmail demands once he guessed I killed Axel. Greedy SOB. I did the world a favor by getting rid of him."

That was one way of looking at murder.

As I tried to think of a diversion, someone called out my name. Then Brooke's. Her head snapped up as she located the source whose voice I'd already recognized. Gran.

"Yoo-hoo," Gran called, waving her hands at us. She stood in front of Brooke's blue Miata parked a few rows away. Standing next to her was Hank. The two of them wore matching black and orange Giants baseball caps. Hank smiled and walked toward us.

"Stop," Brooke cried out.

He halted, a puzzled look on his face before he continued forward.

Brooke was so close I could hear her heart pounding just as fast as mine.

"I mean it, Hank," she shouted. "Don't come any closer."

She obviously hadn't dated Hank long enough to know how he would respond. When he smiled, ignored her request and continued to approach us, she pulled the gun out of her purse and shoved it into my side.

"Whoa, Hank," Gran yelled. "She's got Laurel. And a bad ass gun."

Hank stopped, his eyes as large as the caramel apples he held in both hands. He must have bought one for his girlfriend. How sweet.

Even sweeter was the sound of a siren in the distance. Please God it was Tom and not an accident.

Brooke's eyes raked the parking lot looking for an escape route. An Apple Tree golf cart was parked on the pavement not far from us. Further away, in a small grove of apple trees, Eric Thorson appeared to be sweet-talking a teenage girl. He completely ignored Gran's shouting. And Brooke's and my presence as we moved closer to the vehicle.

Brooke shoved me in the cart and pushed me into the driver's seat. She once again rammed the gun into my side.

"Get us out of here."

"What if I refuse?" I said, comforted by the fact there were numerous people in the vicinity who might come to my rescue.

She leaned forward and aimed her Glock.

The bullet hit the asphalt two inches in front of Gran.

"The next two bullets are dedicated to you and your grandmother. Do you still need more convincing?"

CHAPTER FIFTY-NINE

Since Eric had left the key in the ignition, I merely shifted the lever to forward, and we took off through the parking lot. Multiple sirens screamed in the distance accompanied by cyclists yelling at me as I veered around them. I nicked one bicycle tire. The owner raised his fist and shouted a colorful obscenity. I mouthed "Sorry" as our cart rocketed past him.

A young couple holding hands and munching on donuts drifted in front of us. Their eyes opened wide when they saw the golf cart careening toward them. They split apart just in time. His donut flew out of his hand and landed on my lap. If crazy Brooke got her way that could be the last donut I ever laid eyes on.

My eyes teared, either from despair or the wind in my contacts.

"We need to stop," I cried out. "There's something in my eye. I can't see."

"Forget your eye. You'll have a bullet in your head if you don't shut up."

I blinked and my contact bounced back where it belonged. Just in time for me to realize we were about to enter the corn maze. And not the usual way.

The cart plunged into the stack of hay bales forming the maze. The bales were tossed aside like pillows. I yanked the wheel to the right before we knocked down any of the intrepid maze runners.

The downward slope steepened, and we flew down the hill headed for the thick woods below. The cart hit a large rock, and I bumped into Brooke's shoulder. She rocked to the right but didn't drop the gun.

The terrain was so rough in this section that even a four-wheel drive would have difficulty catching up to us. I could hear voices yelling in the distance, but it wasn't safe to look back. Not that it was all that safe to look forward either.

Brooke glanced over her shoulder. "Can't you get this thing to move faster?"

I started to reply when we ricocheted off another boulder. This time Brooke swayed into me, nearly pushing me out of the cart. My left leg dangled in the air, but I maintained my grip on the steering wheel.

Then a bullet pinged off the back of the cart.

Hey! The good guys were becoming as dangerous as my kidnapper. Someone needed to put a stop to this madness before I ended up in the hospital—or the morgue.

Brooke twisted to the right, using both hands to grip her gun and aim it at whoever tailed us.

I suddenly remembered one time when I spun the wheel of a bumper car too quickly, causing Hank to flip out of his seat. Would that same principle apply to a golf cart?

There was no time like the present to find out.

I jerked the wheel all the way to the left. Brooke bounced upward and smashed her head against the roof. She screamed as she fell out of the cart and tumbled down the hill. The gun flew out of her hand and tumbled along with her. She rolled and rolled and rolled until she finally stopped.

Then she remained still.

Now I was moving in the opposite direction—uphill. Headed directly in the path of the golf cart that had been hot on our trail. The driver turned his wheel to the left and narrowly missed colliding with me.

I took my foot off the accelerator but instead of stopping, the cart slid backwards.

The cart bumped against rocks and brush. It finally crashed into a small pine tree and shuddered to a stop. I sat in shock, sighing with relief until a large branch whipped across my face leaving me with a mouthful of needles. Ouch, that stung. I pushed the tree limb to the side and cautiously stepped out of the vehicle.

The other golf cart had overturned but the two occupants, Tom and a deputy, stood upright. The deputy hoofed his way down the hill, his gun pointed in Brooke's direction, but she didn't look like she was going anywhere. Tom strode toward me, his arms wide open, his expression grim.

I shaded my eyes and looked uphill in the direction I'd just come. A swarm of bicycles bounced their way down the hill, led by a tandem bike driven by the only duo crazy enough to ride the contraption, Hank and Gran.

Those Tai Chi classes were paying off. Gran remained ramrod straight on the bike. I noticed her feet couldn't reach the pedals, but on this downhill slope, Hank didn't need any help. I expected him to come to a halt to see how I'd survived my brush with death. Instead they churned right past me, stopping when they reached Brooke's side.

Give me a break. Did the man not notice the gun his former, I hoped she was now his former, girlfriend had pointed at his former wife?

Seconds later, my annoyance with my ex disappeared as my boyfriend scooped me up in his arms. Now that was more like it.

CHAPTER SIXTY

Our rapturous kiss ended far sooner than either of us wanted, but Tom had questions to ask, and I had answers for a change.

Brooke remained unconscious. The armed deputy stood over her while Hank sat by her side holding her limp hand in his. Paramedics were carefully working their way down the hill.

Stan had also attempted to come to my rescue, but the steep hill proved his undoing. When the front tire of his bicycle dipped into a rut, Stan somersaulted over the handlebars, his skinny legs flailing in the air. Not wanting to watch him crash, I covered my eyes with my hands. After hearing a few people clap, I peeked through my fingers. All that dance training had paid off. Stan had managed to stick his landing. He grinned, walked toward us and hugged me.

Tom continued to rattle off questions nonstop. I held up my scratched palms in protest.

"Why don't I summarize everything for you," I said. "Brooke killed Axel and Lionel. They both threatened to expose her past. After Axel's death, Lionel also upped his demands since he correctly guessed she'd murdered Axel."

"She admitted everything to you?" Tom asked, his eyebrows raised.

I shrugged. "What can I say? I'm easy to confess to."

"They should give you your own talk show," Stan said. "Killer Confessions."

Tom rolled his eyes, but I thought that show might catch on.

"Anyway, once Brooke learned a detective wanted to interview her, she realized she didn't have many options left other than taking a hostage and escaping." I kissed Tom on the cheek. "Thanks for picking up on my clue."

"I always listen to every word you say." I rolled my eyes and he laughed. "Okay, most of the time. But I remembered you don't properly appreciate Bob Dylan. That clue was enough for me to turn on the siren and race over here."

Tom's cell rang. He excused himself and walked away while Stan and I watched the drama unfold in front of us. The paramedics lifted Brooke on to the stretcher, her neck and head protected by a brace. Hank remained at her side. Even from this distance, we could see tears rolling down his face.

"That is so touching," said Stan. "Just like the final scene of *West Side Story*." He placed his hands over his heart and started screeching off key.

I covered his mouth with my hand. Two weeks of dance rehearsal had not improved Stan's singing. And even though I felt sorry for Hank, I was thankful my ex had dodged a bullet.

And so had I.

CHAPTER SIXTY-ONE

A wise man said, "The show must go on." Despite a few small hiccups on opening night, *West Side Story* opened to a sold-out crowd a week later. Mother and Bradford, Liz and Brian, and Tom and I attended. At the show's finale, we applauded the cast with palm-smacking fervor. Stan delivered a bouquet of flowers to Zac, the director, who bestowed a smack on my friend's blushing cheek.

We met up with Stan after the performance, and he introduced us to Zac. We all shook hands with the director and complimented him on the show.

"It can't be easy casting a bunch of amateurs in a musical like this," I said to Zac.

Even in the dim lighting of the old theater, Zac's teeth gleamed white as he smiled. "I try to showcase everyone to the best of their ability." The director eyed Tom appraisingly. "We're doing Peter Pan for the holiday show, and I'm short one critical character— Captain Hook. You've already got his look. Can you sing?"

Before Tom could decline, I did it for him. "That beard will be history." I smiled at Tom. "Hopefully tonight."

Stan nudged Zac. "Tell them about the cruise," he said in a stage whisper loud enough for the entire theater to hear.

"In January, I'm filling in for the stage director on a Nordic Seas ship cruising the Caribbean. I spent my early musical years aboard ship, sliding from one end of the stage to the other." Zac rocked back and forth illustrating his point.

"And I'm going with." Stan grinned. "I have two weeks' vacation saved up and can't think of a better way to use it."

Neither could I. How wonderful it would be to cruise the high seas, visit exotic locales, to savor balmy breezes and soft sand. Then in the evening, wining and dining to your heart's content. My friend was lucky, and I couldn't be happier for him. I just wished I could go along.

We invited Zac and Stan to join us for dinner. They declined, saying they had work to do, although Stan winked at me as they walked away. The six of us piled into our respective cars and drove to Smith Flat House, the perfect after-theater dining spot.

Once inside the restaurant, we sat at a table for six. The seating was a little tight, so Tom and I squeezed next to each other, thigh to thigh. My body vibrated. I was so content I nearly missed out on his conversation with my stepfather.

Tom pointed at Bradford's left arm, which still rested in a sling. "How's the injury healing?" he asked.

"The doc says I'll be as good as new in another week." Bradford threw a glance at my mother. "Although from now on, I'll stick to investigating from a desk."

"You'd better," said Mother. "Or I'll tie you to the bed."

"I can work with that," he said, causing my mother to blush and the rest of us to laugh.

"I'm just glad to have Tom back where he belongs." I sighed happily.

"I heard through the DA grapevine about that new position you were offered," Brian said to Tom. "Are you going to take it?"

My fork fell out of my hand and landed in Tom's lap, almost injuring something I'd become very fond of. He retrieved it and returned it to me. "Lose something?" he asked.

"I'm not sure. You tell me. What's Brian talking about?"

Tom shook his head. "We can discuss it later. So, Brian, I heard they denied Brooke bail."

I chewed on my lip. If Tom thought he could distract me by referring to the woman who almost killed me, he was right.

"Despite her desperate acts," I said. "I still feel a little sorry for Brooke."

"Even after she held you at gunpoint?" Liz asked.

"I said a little sorry. Hank is devastated. He was ready to propose to her."

"She sure fooled me," said Mother. "I guess you can't always tell a Brooke by its cover."

We laughed, but our revelry was tinged with sadness. Brooke had suffered from the men who took advantage of her over a decade ago and then later persecuted her. But she did not have to resort to killing them. Maybe if she'd shared her past with Hank, none of this would have occurred.

I felt sorry for my ex, but Gran was doing her best to help him recover. As she put it, "A donut a day will keep his depression away."

"What's going to happen to Apple Tree Farm?" Liz asked.

"The feds seized all assets including Aces Financial Group," Tom said. "However, as it turns out, one of Lionel's clerks screwed up. The mortgage was never officially recorded as a lien on the property. It had been signed by Axel and notarized but got stuck in a pile of paperwork. It could remain stuck in paperwork purgatory forever."

"Dorie deserves a break," I said. "I hope the Thorson family can keep the operation going for years to come."

"I hope so, too," Liz said. "Because I still don't have my products, and I know they're trapped in there somewhere."

"Dorie was about to fire Brent when he disappeared off the grid. She's not sure how much he stole from the farm, but she's positive her new inventory manager will get to the bottom of it."

"Anyone we know?" Mother asked.

"A kid who could use a break," I replied. "Dorie thought that after all Tony Perez had been through, he deserved a decent job. Technically, he's a Thorson heir, and now he and Eric can learn the business together. With Dorie and Nina overseeing the two young men, they will, hopefully, learn to work with each other."

Not to mention, Tony should be far too busy to date my daughter.

"Did you ever discover who knocked the shelving over?" asked Liz.

I shrugged. "Tom checked the warehouse equipment, and one of the fork lifts was dented, possibly from smashing into the shelving. Brooke claimed she wasn't responsible, so we'll have to assume it was Brent."

"Don't worry. We'll find him," Tom said, and I smiled at my hero.

Our server arrived with our meals. Conversation halted while we contentedly chewed until a loud soprano voice interrupted us.

I looked up and cringed. Would this woman ever disappear from my life?

"Hi, Adriana," Liz cooed at her customer who was dressed in an expensive little black dress designed to show off her figure. Obviously not purchased at my favorite designer store—BudgetMart. "You look lovely tonight."

"Thank you," she responded. "We're celebrating." She pointed to a table on the opposite side of the restaurant where Walter waved to us. These two were becoming as thick as thieves.

I felt compelled to ask, "What are you celebrating?"

Her smile beamed brighter than the overhead lighting. "I was asked to run the marketing department of Hangtown Bank. Mr. Boxer opted to retire, and Mr. Chandler decided that since you and I work so well together, we should make it permanent. Isn't that fantastic?"

My jaw dropped at Adriana's revelation. Liz took one look at my expression, grabbed the bottle of chardonnay and handed it to me.

"Toodles." Adriana waved to our group. "I'll see you Monday at the office, Laurel. Don't be late."

CHAPTER SIXTY-TWO

The drive back to my house was as quiet as a graveyard shrouded in fog. After Adriana's revelation, my appetite vanished. I barely touched my dinner or my chardonnay. My mother questioned whether I was coming down with something.

I certainly was—a significant case of the banker blues.

Tom remained silent, lost in contemplation of something or other. Was it this new job opportunity? Did it have anything to do with Ali Reynolds? Although the task force had successfully completed its mission, Tom had not shared any intimate details of his partnership with the female detective.

Was that a good thing or not?

Tom parked his car in my driveway and shut off the ignition. I waited for sixty seconds before I decided this was a heck of a way to spend our first evening alone together in over six weeks. Someone needed to get the conversational ball rolling.

"So..." I said, adding a heavy dose of nuance.

"So," he echoed. "Adriana's announcement must have been quite a shock for you."

"I'm still stunned. I can't imagine working for that woman on a full-time basis. Or even an hourly one."

Tom reached over and clasped my left hand. His thumb made gentle circles on the inside of my palm.

Oh, that felt good.

"What about that new position Brian mentioned?" I asked him. "Is it an amazing opportunity?"

He nodded slowly but still didn't elaborate.

Alrighty then.

I yanked on the leather door handle, and the door flew open. The movement finally triggered a response from Tom.

"We need to talk," he said. "Let's go inside where it's more comfortable."

Based on the tone of his voice, there wasn't a room in my house that would welcome whatever news he planned to share. I hurried down the sidewalk, half tempted to slam the door in Tom's face. But relationships demand common sense and decorum, not emotional histrionics.

Tom followed me inside as I turned on a couple of lights. The kids were spending the night with Hank and Gran. Their mission: to cheer up my ex. At the rate this evening was going, I might need my own cheerleading squad by morning.

"Do you want anything to drink?" I asked Tom. He declined so I plunked down on my sofa. Seconds later, Tom sat next to me.

That was a good start, but if we were ever to finish this conversation, I'd better ignite it.

"It was tough worrying about you this past month," I said.

"Fighting criminals can take a toll on any relationship," he replied.

"That it can. So many things to worry over." I fiddled with my watch then finally asked the question I'd fretted over for the past week. "So how was it working with Ali Reynolds again? Just like old times?"

Tom placed his hand on my thigh. Another good sign.

"She's a good cop. Handled herself well... as usual."

I placed my palm on top of his. "You never told me about that incident at SFPD. What was that all about?"

Tom shifted and moved a few inches away from me. Uh oh.

"Ali is a smart and dedicated officer. She thinks fast on her feet. But sometimes she's a little headstrong and makes decisions too quickly."

"Like latching on to the first suspect she comes across?" I felt obligated to add that to the conversation.

He leaned over and kissed my cheek. Nice move, Tom Hunter.

"It happens to the best detectives," he said, "but I don't think she liked being shown up by an amateur."

"At the rate I'm solving cases, maybe Gran and I *should* open up our own agency. It would be better than working for Adriana."

Tom slid closer and wrapped his arm around my shoulder.

"Instead of Two Gals Detective Agency, why don't you open up One Terrific Gal Marketing Agency? I know you'd be a hit."

That did have a nice ring to it. Sweet of Tom to worry about my career and not just his own. Wait a minute. Was he trying to distract me?

"I'll think about it," I said. "But back to you. What's the deal on this job, and why are you so reluctant to tell me about it?"

He blew out a forceful breath. "Homeland Security also participated in our task force, to a limited extent. They're expanding their Sacramento office, and they've offered me a position. It's an exciting opportunity and also means more money."

I tilted my head at him. "Those are two positives. So what exactly is the negative that you're holding back from me?"

"My assignments could involve some travel, maybe a couple of weeks at a time."

My shoulders slumped. "The last six weeks have been tough on our relationship. I even worried that something might be going on between you and Ali."

"Ali?" He laughed. "Not hardly. Besides, no one," he looked deeply into my eyes when he said this, "could take your place."

I shivered, but in all the right places.

"But she's smart, attractive and a fellow officer. What's not to like?" I knew I was displaying a huge lack of self-confidence, but I needed to lay it all on the table. Or in the current situation, my sofa.

"Ali is intelligent, but she has a tendency to make rash decisions. Since you're obviously dying to know what happened to her at SFPD..." I leaned so close I was practically sitting in Tom's lap, not a bad position to be in. "She arrested a politician with a nasty habit of seducing minors, then walked him into the station stark naked."

Oh. And that was a bad thing?

I couldn't help chuckling. Given time, maybe Ali Reynolds and I might form a friendship after all.

"Does that satisfy your curiosity?" Tom asked, nibbling on my ear.

Ping. I almost forgot my original question as I wiggled even closer to him. "So what have you decided about this job offer? I won't stand in your way, but your travel schedule could make seeing each other even more difficult than it has been."

"I realize that." Tom took my hand in his. "And I feel strongly that this career decision should be made by the two of us."

I squeezed his hand. "I'm touched."

"Good. Because I'm in this for the long run." Tom's eyes darkened and his voice grew husky. "I love you and I love your kids. We've gone through a lot together this past year, but we survived. Before we talk about the job, there's an even more critical decision you need to make."

Tom sounded so serious. What decision could possibly be more important than his new job offer?

"You know that Caribbean cruise that Stan and Zac are taking in January?" he asked.

I nodded while wondering what a boat trip could possibly have to do with his career options.

"Wouldn't that be a wonderful place to spend our honeymoon?"

THE END

AUTUMN DESSERT RECIPES

There's nothing my mother loved better than sharing recipes and trying new ones. In her honor, I asked friends and fans to submit their favorite fall dessert recipes. From the numerous entrees that were submitted, the following apple, pear and pumpkin recipes were drawn. And in honor of Laurel McKay, we have one gooey brownie recipe for all the chocolate lovers out there. Enjoy.

APPLE TOFFEE CAKE
(Lavonne Giordano)

1/2 cup butter	1 tsp. cinnamon
2 cups sugar	1 tsp. baking soda
2 eggs	1/2 cup nuts chopped
1/2 tsp. rum flavoring	(optional, but pecans are
4 medium apples	great!)
chopped to make 2 cups	6 oz. bag of butterscotch chips
2 cups flour	(optional)
1 tsp. salt	

Cream butter, sugar until light and fluffy. Add eggs and flavoring, beat well then add apples and blend together.

Sift dry ingredients and add to apple mixture, mix until well blended. Batter will be thick.

Spread in a greased 13" x 9" x 2" pan. Sprinkle chips and nuts and bake at 350 degrees for 50-55 minutes or until toothpick inserted in middle comes out clean.

Rum Sauce

1/2 cup sugar	1/4 cup butter
2 tablespoons cornstarch	1 tablespoon rum flavoring
1 cup water	1/8 tsp. salt

In a 1 quart saucepan combine sugar and cornstarch. Stir in water to blend, and cook at medium heat to thicken. Cook for 2-3 minutes. Remove from heat and add butter, rum flavoring and salt.

Serve warm over warm cake.

IN THE BAG APPLE PIE
(Maureen Rumsey)

1 cup sugar
2 tablespoons flour
1 teaspoon cinnamon
6-8 tart apples (My favorite is Apple Hill Jonathans)

Slice apples into bowl and mix with cinnamon mixture. Dump into single pie crust.

Mix together 1/2 cup sugar, 1/2 cup flour, and 1/2 cup butter

Mush it all together and sprinkle over top

Put uncooked pie into a brown grocery bag, fold over the top and secure with a paper clip. Bake at 425 degrees for 1 hour.

APPLE WALNUT COBBLER
(Patricia Scharrer and Margaret Scharrer)

1/2 cup sugar	1 cup sugar
1/2 teaspoon cinnamon	1 cup flour
3/4 cup coarsely chopped walnuts	1 teaspoon baking powder
	1 egg, beaten
4 cups tart apples, thinly sliced	1/3 cup melted butter

Lightly butter a 9 inch cake pan then line cake pan with apples. Put the mixture of 1/2 cup sugar, cinnamon and half the chopped walnut on top of the apples. Mix the other ingredients and spread on top.

Sprinkle with remaining chopped walnuts.
Bake at 325 degrees for 45-50 minutes.
Garnish with whipped cream.

CARMELIZED UPSIDE-DOWN PEAR TART
(Polly Schack)

4 large firm-ripe Bosc pears	1/2 cup sugar
(2 pounds total)	1/2 teaspoon cinnamon
1/2 stick (1/4 cup)	Pastry dough
unsalted butter	

Peel and halve pears, the core (preferably with a melon-ball cutter). Heat butter in a 9- to 10-inch well-seasoned cast-iron skillet over moderate heat until foam subsides, then stir in sugar (sugar will not be dissolved). Arrange pears, cut sides up, in skillet with wide parts at rim of skillet. Sprinkle pears with cinnamon and cook, undisturbed, until sugar turns a deep golden caramel. (This can take as little as 10 minutes or as much as 25, depending on pears, skillets, and stove.) Cool pears completely in skillet. Put oven rack in middle position and preheat oven to 425°F.

Roll out dough on a lightly floured surface with a floured rolling pin into a 12-inch round and trim to a 9 1/2- to 10 1/2-inch round. Arrange pastry over caramelized pears, tucking edge around pears inside rim of skillet. Bake tart until pastry is golden brown, 30 to 35 minutes. Cook on rack 5 minutes.

Invert a rimmed serving plate (slightly larger than skillet) over skillet and, using pot holders to hold skillet and plate tightly together, invert tart onto plate. Serve tart warm or at room temperature.

Makes 8 servings

PUMPKIN CHEESECAKE SNICKERDOODLES
(Cathy Ann Adkins)

3¾ cups all-purpose flour
1½ tsp. baking powder
½ tsp. salt
½ tsp. ground cinnamon
¼ tsp. freshly-ground ground nutmeg
1 cup unsalted butter, at room temperature
1 cup granulated sugar
½ cup light brown sugar
¾ cup pumpkin puree

1 large egg
2 tsp. vanilla extract
Filling Ingredients:
8 ounces pumpkin spice cream cheese

Cinnamon-sugar coating:
½ cup granulated sugar
1 tsp. ground cinnamon
½ tsp. ground ginger
Dash of allspice

In a medium bowl, whisk the flour, baking powder, salt, cinnamon, and nutmeg together. Set aside.

In a kitchen aid mixer with a paddle attachment, beat together the butter and sugars on medium high speed until fluffy about 2-3 minutes.

Blend in pumpkin puree, beat in egg and then add vanilla. Slowly add dry ingredients on low speed just until combined. Cover and chill dough for an hour.

Preheat oven to 350 and line your baking sheets with parchment paper. In a small bowl, combine the sugar and spices for the coating and set aside.

To make the cookies, take a tablespoon of the cookie batter. Flatten it like a pancake and place a teaspoon of the cream cheese in center. Form another tablespoon of the cookie batter into a flat pancake shape and place on top of the cream cheese. Pinch the edges together sealing in the cream cheese and roll into a ball. Roll in the cinnamon sugar coating and place on the prepared baking sheet 2 inches apart.

Repeat until the dough is gone and flatten the cookie dough balls with a heavy bottomed glass or measuring cup.

Bake the cookies for 10-15 minutes or until the tops start to crack. Let cool on the baking sheet for 5 minutes and transfer to a wire rack. Enjoy!

Note: if you can't find the pumpkin spice cream cheese, make the cream cheese filling, by blending 8 oz. cream cheese, 1/4 cup sugar and 2 teaspoons vanilla together. Chill for an hour.

PUMPKIN ROLL
(Sharon Bitz)

Cake

1/4 cup powdered sugar
   (to sprinkle on a towel)
3/4 cup all-purpose flour
1/2 tsp baking powder
1/2 tsp baking soda
1/2 tsp cinnamon
1/2 tsp ground cloves

1/4 tsp salt
3 large eggs
1 cup granulated sugar
2/3 cup pure pumpkin filling
   (I use canned filling)
1 cup chopped walnuts
   (optional)

Filling

1 pkg cream cheese
   (room temperature)
1 cup sifted powdered sugar
6 tbs softened butter

1 tsp vanilla extract
Powdered sugar as an optional
decoration

For Cake: preheat oven to 375°F. Grease a 15 x 10 inch jellyroll pan and line it with waxed paper. Grease and flour the paper. Sprinkle a thin, cotton kitchen towel with powdered sugar.

COMBINE flour, baking powder, baking soda, cinnamon, cloves and salt in a small bowl. Beat the eggs and granulated sugar in a large mixer bowl until thick. Beat in pumpkin. Stir in flour mixture. Spread evenly into prepared pan. Sprinkle with nuts.

BAKE for 13 to 15 minutes or until the top of the cake springs back when touched. (if using a dark colored pan, begin checking for doneness at 11 minutes.) Immediately loosen and turn cake on to prepared towel. Carefully peel off paper. Roll up cake and towel together, starting with narrow end. Cool on wire rack.

For Filling: beat cream cheese, 1 cup powdered sugar, butter and vanilla extract in small mixer bowl until smooth. Carefully unroll cake. Spread cream cheese mixture over cake, reroll cake. Wrap in plastic wrap and refrigerate at least one hour. Sprinkle with powdered sugar before serving, if desired.

COOKING TIP: be sure to put enough powdered sugar on the towel when rolling up the cake so it will not stick.

Enjoy!

ORIGINAL APPLE HILL CAKE
(As submitted by Linda Westphal)

2 cups sugar	2 tsp cinnamon
1/2 cup oil	1 tsp nutmeg
2 eggs	2 tsp soda
2 cups flour	4 cups apples, diced
1 tsp salt	

Combine sugar, oil and eggs, then add diced apples. Sift together the flour, salt, spices and soda, add to apple mixture. Pour into 9×13-inch greased cake pan and bake for one hour in a preheated oven at 350 degrees. Serve hot, warm or cold. Try it plain, frosted or with whipped cream.

APPLE CHRISTMAS CAKE
(Cyndee Johnson)

Use one 8x12 pan or four small loaf pans

2 eggs	2 tsp cinnamon
2 cups sugar	1 tsp salt
1 cup oil	1 tsp vanilla
2 cups flour	1 can apple pie filling
1 tsp soda	

Beat eggs, add all dry ingredients. Mix well. Fold in pie filling.

Bake 1 hour at 350 degrees (for 8x12 pan), or for 40-45 minutes (4 small loaf pans).

PEAR ALMOND CUSTARD PIE (Gemma Juliana)

This only takes 10-15 minutes to prepare and yields 8 servings. Total time: 1 hour 20 min

Pre-heat the oven to 350° and spray a 9-inch pie dish with cooking spray.

Streusel Pie-Filling

½ cup almond flour
¼ cup oats, old-fashioned or quick-cooking
¼ cup brown sugar, packed
¼ tsp ground nutmeg
½ tsp vanilla extract
1 Tbsp butter

Pie-Filling

½ cup almond flour
1/3 cup white sugar
½ cup milk
½ tsp vanilla extract
2 Tbsp butter, softened
2 eggs
3 medium pears, peeled and sliced

Streusel prep first. Stir almond flour, nutmeg and brown sugar together in a bowl. Add soft butter to the mix and blend it in, either with a blender or by hand with a fork. Stop when it is crumbly instead of smooth. Set this aside.

Pie prep next. Stir all the pie ingredients with the exception of the pears with a fork or wire whisk. Pour this mix into the prepared pie dish and arrange the sliced pears evenly over the mixture.

BAKE TIME: 25 minutes for pie-filling only. Then add streusel topping (sprinkle) and bake 10-15 more minutes. An inserted knife should come out clean. Cool 30 minutes before serving. Serve warm on its own or with softly whipped cream. Bon appetit!

VARIATIONS & SUBSTITUTES: almond flour can be exchanged for coconut flour, plain flour or Bisquick; margarine can be used instead of butter; almond or rice milk can be used in place of milk. I use organic non-fat milk. Another great variation is to leave off the streusel entirely and just make the pie-filling with oats instead of flour.

PUMPKIN BREAD
(Brenda Novak)

Ingredients

4 eggs (beaten)

3 c. sugar

2 c. pumpkin

2/3 c. water

1 c. vegetable oil

3 ½ c. flour

½ t. baking powder

2 t. baking soda

1 ½ t. salt

3 t. cloves

3 t. nutmeg

3 t. cinnamon

Directions:

1. I just throw it all in a bowl and mix with beaters.
2. Grease and flour pans.
3. Bake at 325 for 1 ¼ – 1 ½ hours.

PUMPKIN MUFFINS
(Madelyn Schwartz)

3/4 cup sugar
3/4 cup packed brown sugar
1 1/2 cups all-purpose flour
1/2 teaspoon baking powder
1 teaspoon baking soda
3/4 teaspoon salt
1/2 teaspoon nutmeg

1/2 teaspoon cinnamon
2 large eggs
1 cup pumpkin puree
1/2 vegetable oil
1/3 cup water
1 teaspoon vanilla

Preheat oven to 350 degrees. Grease muffin cups with shortening or spray oil or line with paper baking cups.

Combine dry ingredients into a large mixing bowl.

In medium bowl, whisk eggs with fork, stir in pumpkin, oil and vanilla until blended.

Add liquid ingredients to dry and stir until blended. Do not over mix or muffins will be tough rather than tender.

Spoon batter into 12 prepared muffin cups filling 2/3 full. Bake until a toothpick inserted in the center comes out clean, 20 to 25 minutes.

Tip pan to release muffins. Cool muffins on racks completely before frosting or package for storage.

Cream Cheese Frosting
Have cream cheese cold and butter at room temperature for the best texture. Do not overbeat or the cream cheese breaks down.

8 ounces cream cheese
4 tablespoons butter
2 teaspoons vanilla
2 to 2 1/2 cups powdered sugar sifted after measuring

Beat cream cheese, butter and vanilla in a medium bowl until just blended. Add 1/3 of the sugar and beat until smooth. Repeat to incorporate all sugar.

MAN CATCHER BROWNIES
(Kathy Sweeney)

These are to die for......
30 caramels, unwrapped
2/3 c evaporated milk
1 box cake mix, German chocolate
1/2 c butter, melted
3/4 c semisweet chocolate chips
1/2 c chopped pecans or walnuts

Directions
Heat oven to 350 and line the bottom of a 9×13 inch baking pan with parchment paper.

Melt caramels with 1/3 cup of the evaporated milk in a small saucepan, stirring mixture occasionally. Set aside.

Stir together cake mix, melted butter and remaining 1/3 cup evaporated milk to form a dough. Press 1 1/3 cups of the dough into the pan in an even layer. Bake until puffed but not cooked through, about 7 minutes.

Remove from oven and pour caramel sauce evenly over the top. Sprinkle chocolate chips over the caramel in an even layer.

Top with remaining dough, crumbled into bits and scattered across caramel/chocolate chip layer. Sprinkle with nuts and return to the oven.

Bake until brownies are puffy and set, 10-11 minutes more. Cool and cut into squares.

APPLE FRITTER CAKE
(Sandy Haeger)

This is truly the best fall dessert I have made to date. If you like apple fritters you will love this!

For the filling
2 heaping cups of sliced apples (Gala apples from Apple Hill!)
1/3 cup sugar
1/4 teaspoon cinnamon
Small pinch nutmeg
2 Tablespoons cornstarch
2 teaspoons water

Plus
1/2 cup brown sugar
1/2 teaspoon cinnamon

For the cake
1/3 cup butter
3/4 cup sugar
1/2 cup applesauce
1 teaspoon vanilla
2 eggs
2 and 1/4 cups flour
1 teaspoon baking powder
1 teaspoon baking soda
1 teaspoon salt
1 teaspoon cinnamon
1 cup sour cream

For the glaze
2 cups powdered sugar
1 teaspoon vanilla
6 Tablespoons milk

For the filling
Combine apples, water, sugar, cinnamon, and corn starch in a small sauce pan. Cook on low for 5-7 minutes stirring constantly until the apples are soft. Set aside to cool. While the filling is cooling, get a small bowl and combine the "plus ingredients" brown sugar and cinnamon

For the cake
Preheat the oven to 350 degrees. Grease and flour a 9x13 baking dish.
Set aside.

Beat cream, softened butter and sugar until light and fluffy. Add applesauce and vanilla then the eggs one at a time. Add the dry ingredients slowly: flour, baking powder, baking soda, salt, cinnamon and sour cream. Beat together until just combined.

Pour half the batter evenly onto the bottom of the greased and floured 9x13 baking dish. Then carefully spoon the cooled filling on top of the batter. Now sprinkle 2/3 of the brown sugar/cinnamon mixture on top of the filling. Cover with the remaining half of the batter.

Sprinkle the top with the rest of the brown sugar/cinnamon mixture.

Bake for 45-55 minutes. Your kitchen should start to smell amazing and you will probably start drooling. While your cake is baking, make the glaze.

For the glaze
Mix the powdered sugar, vanilla and milk together. When the cake comes out, pour the glaze mixture over the warm cake. Spread evenly and allow to harden on top of the cake as it cools.

Enjoy!

ACKNOWLEDGEMENTS

Many thanks and hugs to the awesome friends who willingly read my early drafts: Cathy Allyn, Dee Brice, Jonathan Corbett, Lisa Dane, and Jana Rossi. As always, my critique group was there to answer my countless emails and what if scenarios: Kathy Asay, Pat Foulk, Rae James, and Terri Judd. Four of my favorite mystery authors, Heather Haven, Liz Jasper, Linda Lovely, and Mary Beth Magee chimed in with wonderful suggestions. And I have to mention Doretta Doyle, my excellent hair stylist, who spends many hours plotting with me.

A special thanks to Larry DeMates, Private Investigator, for letting me bombard him with questions.

A big thanks to High Hill Ranch for letting me take a tour of their kitchen. We sure love your donuts!

The support and encouragement I receive from my fellow Sisters in Crime (Sacramento and Northern California) and the authors who belong to Sacramento Valley Rose, California Writer's Club and NCPA keeps me motivated when my spirits flag.

Thanks to my editor, Baird Nuckolls, and my amazing cover artist, Karen Phillips. I am extremely grateful for the generosity of Rose Margolis who contributed to the Women's Center. I hope you enjoyed your character.

Thanks also to the people who contributed their tantalizing dessert recipes.

I'm lucky to live in such a beautiful part of the world. If you've never visited Apple Hill in the fall then you need to plan a trip. And while you're at it, check out some of the local restaurants featured in this book.

A special thanks to those fans from around the world whose emails make this journey so much fun. Your words bring a smile to my face and magic to my fingertips. It's not easy to wake up each morning and create an entirely new world. Your words of encouragement make it the best job in the world!

ABOUT THE AUTHOR

Cindy Sample is a former mortgage banking CEO who decided plotting murder was more entertaining than plodding through paperwork. She retired to follow her lifelong dream of becoming a mystery author.

Her experiences with online dating sites fueled the concept for *Dying for a Date,* the first in her national bestselling Laurel McKay mysteries. The sequel, *Dying for a Dance,* winner of the 2011 NCPA Fiction Award, is based on her adventures in the glamorous world of ballroom dancing. Cindy thought her protagonist, Laurel McKay, needed a vacation in Hawaii, which resulted in *Dying for a Daiquiri,* a finalist for the 2014 Silver Falchion Award for Best Traditional Mystery

Laurel returned to Placerville for her wildest ride yet in *Dying for a Dude.* The West will never be the same. *Dying for a Dude* was also a 2014 Next Generation Indie Award Finalist in both mystery and humor. Then on to *Dying for a Donut,* the most lip-smacking mystery of them all.

Cindy is a three-time finalist for the LEFTY Award for best humorous mystery and a past president of the Sacramento chapter of Sisters in Crime. She has served on the boards of the Sacramento Opera and YWCA. She is a member of Mystery Writers of America and Romance Writers of America. Cindy has two wonderful adult children who live too far away. She loves chatting with readers so feel free to contact her on any forum.

Sign up for her newsletter to find out about upcoming events and contests. http://cindysamplebooks.com/contact/

Check out www.cindysamplebooks.com for contests and other events.

Connect with Cindy on Facebook and Twitter
http://facebook.com/cindysampleauthor
http://twitter.com/cindysample1
Email Cindy at cindy@cindysamplebooks.com